UNDER FIRE

Holliday sensed it before he heard it, and heard it before he saw it. He squinted, looking for something he wasn't quite sure was there, and then he saw it: a phantom in the mist above the trees, the first flash of sunlight reflecting off the windscreen of a low-flying aircraft. A small plane, maybe a Cessna Caravan, tricked out with floats and painted dark green to blend in with the jungle treetops.

A split second later he spotted a bright double flash from under the wings, followed by a strangely clipped, hollow *whoosh*, like the abruptly terminated sound of a bullet striking water at high speed. The sound was horribly familiar: a pair of underwing Hellfire air-to-ground missles being fired—forty pounds of fire-and-forget high explosive coming at them at roughly a thousand miles an hour.

"Incoming!" Holliday bellowed. And almost before the warning was out of his mouth the Hellfires struck.

Also by Paul Christopher

Michelangelo's Notebook

The Lucifer Gospel

Rembrandt's Ghost

The Aztec Heresy

The Sword of the Templars

The Templar Cross

The Templar Throne

The Templar Conspiracy

THE TEMPLAR LEGION

PAUL CHRISTOPHER

A SIGNET BOOK

SIGNET

Published by New American Library, a division of
Penguin Group (USA) Inc., 375 Hudson Street,
New York, New York 10014, USA
Penguin Group (Canada), 90 Eglinton Avenue East, Suite 700, Toronto,
Ontario M4P 2Y3, Canada (a division of Pearson Penguin Canada Inc.)
Penguin Books Ltd., 80 Strand, London WC2R 0RL, England
Penguin Ireland, 25 St. Stephen's Green, Dublin 2,
Ireland (a division of Penguin Books Ltd.)
Penguin Group (Australia), 250 Camberwell Road, Camberwell, Victoria 3124,
Australia (a division of Pearson Australia Group Pty. Ltd.)
Penguin Books India Pvt. Ltd., 11 Community Centre, Panchsheel Park,
New Delhi - 110 017, India
Penguin Group (NZ), 67 Apollo Drive, Rosedale, Auckland 0632,
New Zealand (a division of Pearson New Zealand Ltd.)
Penguin Books (South Africa) (Pty.) Ltd., 24 Sturdee Avenue,
Rosebank, Johannesburg 2196, South Africa

Penguin Books Ltd., Registered Offices:
80 Strand, London WC2R 0RL, England

First published by Signet, an imprint of New American Library,
a division of Penguin Group (USA) Inc.

First Printing, June 2011
10 9 8 7 6 5 4 3 2 1

"Who will help me grind the corn?" said the Little Red Hen.

—English Traditional

Never think that war, no matter how necessary, nor how justified, is not a crime.

—Ernest Hemingway

Frankly, I'd like to see the government get out of war altogether and leave the whole field to private industry.

—Joseph Heller, *Catch-22*

Be careful what you wish for; you might just get it.

—H. L. Mencken

THE
TEMPLAR
LEGION

PROLOGUE

A.D. 1039
The Nile River at Karnak
One hundred leagues from Alexandria

His name was Ragnar Skull Splitter and his ship was the *Kraka*, named for the daughter of a Valkyrie and a Viking chief. *Kraka*'s carved wooden image, eyes closed in dreaming sleep, long hair covering her naked body, graced the bow of his warship. It was said that Kraka, like her mother before her, had the power to interpret dreams and see the future. Ragnar fervently prayed that it was so and that she would guide him home once more with her prophecies, because for the last ten days he had traveled a river that seemingly had no end and for five of those days had traveled through what he now knew, despite the blistering heat from the relentless sun, was nothing less than Niflheim, the dark and eternally frozen land of the dead.

1

Ragnar was the cousin of Harald Sigurdsson, the head of the Varangian Emperors Guard in Miklagard, the Great Walled City, or Constantinople, as the local people called it. Ragnar was Harald's greatest warrior, and before setting out from that wondrous city at the neck of the world he had vowed to his cousin that he would not return until he had found the secret mines of the ancient king and taken their vast riches in Harald's name.

If he failed it would not be for the lack of a good ship and good men to sail her. From his position on the steering platform at the high end of the stern he proudly looked down *Kraka*'s length.

She was eighty feet from the carved effigy of her namesake in the bow to the high, elegantly curved line of her sternpost. She was eighteen feet wide and barely six feet deep from the gunwales to the keelson that ran the length of the ship. She was made of solid oak from the shallow slopes of Flensburg Fjord, her clinker-built hull created by overlapping planks attached to the heavy ribs with more than five thousand iron rivets, roved between each plank with tarred rope. The planks became progressively thinner as they rose toward the gunwales, making the boat light, strong and flexible. She drew less than three feet and could be rowed right up on the shallowest beachhead.

At sea with her big sail set, *Kraka* could make an easy

ten knots and could travel more than fifty leagues in a single day. Here, on a river as black as night, its waters populated by swimming monsters of dizzying variety, she could barely do two knots and travel six or seven leagues before her thirty-two rowers could no longer lift the ponderous eighteen-foot oars.

Ragnar looked fondly down at his men from the steering platform. Like Ragnar, they were stripped to the waist, the muscles of their backs and shoulders gleaming with sweat as they pulled the ship through the ominous waters. Also like Ragnar, each of them wore the linen head coverings bound with strips of cloth the local people called *nemes*.

In the bow, on a smaller version of the steering platform, stood the strange, high-ranking *negeren* court slave pressed on him by Harald, and the slave's even stranger companion, a gigantic eunuch named Barakah who took care of the *negeren*'s personal needs as well as recording their whereabouts with fantastically detailed maps, sketches and drawings, made at his master's order. The black man's name was Abdul al-Rahman and it was he who suggested that Ragnar and his men adopt the *nemes* after two of the warriors collapsed over their oars, stunned and terribly sick with the sun.

Just below the steering platform, Aki, the last oarsman on the starboard side, called out the cadence with an old kenning chant:

Most men know that
Gunnbjorn the captain
lies long buried in this mound;
never was there
a more valiant traveler
of the wondrous-wide ground of Endil
his tale told proudly and with honor
in the skalds
till Njörðr, god of oceans,
Drowns the land.

Ragnar turned to his steersman, a gruff, powerful man named Hurlu who'd been steersman on *Kraka* for years before Ragnar became her captain. "How long have the men been rowing?"

"Since the morning daymark." Hurlu squinted up at the sun, which was almost directly overhead. "Six hours at least. Too long."

Ragnar nodded. He'd done his time at the oars often enough and knew the weight of the heavy blade digging through the water. His shoulders ached at the memory. "We should pull into shore," said Ragnar. "Let the men rest."

"I agree." Hurlu nodded.

Ragnar let it pass. In a younger man it would have been an insubordinate response, but Hurlu was as old as the planks in *Kraka*'s bilge and he'd been piloting ships since Ragnar had played with balls of yarn in his mother's lap.

"We'll need shade," said Ragnar. He looked out at the bleak, arid land on either side of the river. There was nothing to see but bare rock and high ridges of sandstone baking in the relentless sun.

Hurlu made a brief sound of disgust and spit over the sternpost. He nodded toward the bow. "Ask your pet monkey up there; maybe he'll know where we can find some." Hurlu had a superstitious mistrust of the black man and made no bones about it to anyone, including Ragnar.

Ragnar whistled shrilly, and when al-Rahman looked back he gestured for the black man to join him in the stern. Al-Rahman said something briefly to Barakah, who nodded, then stepped off the little platform down onto the narrow plank gangway that ran the length of the ship. As he moved, his long white robes swirled elegantly around his ankles.

Al-Rahman had the grace of a dancing girl but he was no simpering *rassragr*; Ragnar had seen evidence enough of that when they were loading stores in Alexandria. That same dancer's grace had turned to a warrior's brutally agile fury when a gang of cutpurses had confronted him in an alley and demanded payment for passage through to the street beyond, making it clear that he would suffer the consequences if he refused. Al-Rahman had sliced all four ragged men to ribbons in a few short seconds, a short, curve-bladed Saif appearing magically in his right hand from beneath those same swirling robes.

5

"*Aasalaamu Aleikum*, Ragnar; you wished to speak with me?"

"*Wa-Aleikum Aassalaam, Abdul,*" said Ragnar, using the response he'd been taught by al-Rahman. Beside him, Hurlu scowled and spit over the side again, just as Ragnar knew he would. Ragnar grinned; he enjoyed getting the older man's goat whenever the opportunity presented itself. Al-Rahman's ornately tattooed face broke into a smile as well; he knew just what the tall, blond Dane was thinking. They were a strange pair: Ragnar as broad as an oak, al-Rahman as slim as a willow, but both equally strong, each in his own way. They were too different ever to become real friends but over their time together they'd developed a mutual trust and respect.

"We need shade and freshwater, and soon; my men are wilting like flowers, Abdul. How likely are we to find it in this oven of a place?"

"Flowers," grunted Hurlu. "Huh."

Al-Rahman turned and pointed. "We will pass this ridge and the Great Snake will make a sudden turn. In its coils you will find a *waha* the old Greeks called Chenoboskion."

"*Waha?*" Ragnar asked.

"A watering place in the desert, a sanctuary," explained al-Rahman.

"How long?"

"At this rate?" Al-Rahman shrugged. "An hour perhaps."

Ragnar turned to Hurlu. "You hear that, steersman? It seems we're not dead yet."

"No," said Hurlu, "just dried-out old corpses like they use for their cooking fires in that pigsty of a city back there." He nodded his head downriver.

"Al-Qahira," said Ragnar, remembering the name of the squalid place and its ironic meaning: "the victorious."

"That'd be the one," said Hurlu. "Using the corpses of their forefathers for kindling, pah!"

"Well, Hurlu, can our wilting flowers do it?"

The grizzled older man spit over the side again. "Can they do it?" He turned and called down to the stroke oarsman seated on the bench below him. "Aki! A war song for our lord and master here! Battle speed!" *Kraka* leaped forward.

In less than half the time al-Rahman had predicted, they came within sight of their goal, the dark river churning white under *Kraka*'s stern as the oars bit smoothly into the water. The *waha*, as al-Rahman had called it, was a few rudely built huts of mud and daub huddled under the protection of a gathering of date palms, their high, broad leaves bright green in the dazzling sun. The dark windows of the huts had the blank, sightless look that marked long abandonment.

Ragnar shaded his eyes and looked toward the shore. Perhaps a few fishermen had lived here once, but like everything else in this forsaken country, that was long past. The huts would be home only to scorpions and spiders now, seeking shade, just like Kraka's crew. Ragnar could also see a small stream tumbling down the shallow bank of the river, coming from some spring hidden within the stand of trees. Back home, on the shores of Flensburg Fjord, the stream, barely a trickle, would have been ignored; here it was a life-giving torrent.

The men scarcely needed the order to pull toward the shore. Grunting a little with the effort, Hurlu turned the long steering oar against the current. According to al-Rahman this was the time of full flood for the river, and the water was high. A few moments later *Kraka* ran easily up onto the muddy bank. The two forward oarsmen hauled up the stone-heavy wooden anchor and heaved it over the side to hold *Kraka* against the flow. The landing was done silently and with ease; these men had beached their ship a thousand times on a thousand different shores, and the operation went with almost mechanical smoothness, but even so the men sat with rigid discipline until Hurlu called out the order; their throats were parched and their lips cracked with thirst but, as always, the ship came first.

"Ship oars!" Hurlu bellowed. The oars rattled through their leather-slung tholes as the men pulled them inboard until all thirty-two stood like a forest above the gunwales.

"Rack oars!" Moving from bow to stern the men swung their oars inboard and dropped them into the forward and aft cradles that already held the stepped mast, furled sails and boom as well as an entire set of replacement oars. In bad weather the filled racks sometimes acted as ridgepole for a tentlike space above the stores to keep dry under.

"Out you go, lads!"

With weak, croaking shouts of approval the men went forward to the bow and jumped down onto the mud- and pebble-strewn beach. Usually, if the water was shallow enough, the men would simply jump over the side where they rowed, but not here.

They'd all seen the gigantic, long-jawed, scaly creatures that lived in the shadowed waters of the Great Snake, and watched in horror as a pair of them took down a bullock calf quietly drinking at the shore just outside the town al-Rahman called Al-Qahira. The two creatures, acting in concert, had nearly bitten the bullock in half before they hauled it into deeper water, still bleating piteously until its cries were swallowed up and drowned.

With *Kraka* empty, the men staggering into the trees to find the hidden spring, Hurlu turned to Ragnar.

"Good enough?"

"Good enough." Ragnar nodded.

Hurlu jumped down from the raised platform, stomped down the long gangplank and heaved himself over the side. Finally Ragnar and al-Rahman went ashore themselves, followed by Barakah, the silent eunuch.

The source of the tiny trickling stream turned out to be a large pool of almost unbelievably cool freshwater sparkling beneath the little forest of palms. Some of the men dropped down on their bellies and stuck their heads into the water; others simply stripped off their tunics and boots, then flung themselves naked into the pool.

Ragnar and al-Rahman slaked their thirsts with a little more decorum, then watched the men.

"Man needs; Odin provides." Ragnar laughed, quoting an old saying his mother had taught him at her knee.

Al-Rahman smiled. "Not Odin or any other god," he said. "This pool is the gift of time."

"I thought you believed in your own god, Allah," said Ragnar.

"I believe in the teachings of his great prophet Muhammad, may he be blessed, but Allah is not for man to know or pretend he understands. The Hebrews will not even speak their own god's name for the same reason."

"And *kuffār*, like us. Infidels?" Ragnar smiled, remembering the word al-Rahman had taught him.

Al-Rahman smiled back at the burly Dane. "Muhammad commands us to pity you and teach you the True Way."

The two men left the pool and strolled through the stand of palms. The grass grew long here, and where rotted dates had fallen more sprigs of greenery grew. Ragnar realized that it was the first time he had relaxed in days. On the edge of the little grove of trees, with nothing but the open desert sands before them, they discovered a great slab of rock jutting from the soil. It was black and smooth as glass except where it had been deeply etched with lines and figures. Some of the figures were clearly meant to be men but others were pictures of strange, fantastic animals: huge horned bulls, some sort of gazelle with a neck so long it looked over all the other figures and additional, smaller creatures: a cat with enormous fangs, and something with gigantic ears and legs like tree stumps, two horns jutting from between its lips. Smaller lines had been scratched to indicate fields of grass and below everything was a thick black snake that could only be the great river behind them.

"Some man's fever dream from long ago?" Ragnar said, letting his fingers trail over the lines.

"Or a memory," said al-Rahman. "Perhaps this place was once a paradise of green grass and trees and hunters' game. Perhaps the pool your men are bathing in is nothing more than rain that fell ten thousand years ago and now springs up here and there to remind us of the past."

"How can paradise become a desert?" Ragnar asked.

"How can the civilization that built the great pyramids and the ancient temples we passed have vanished?"

al-Rahman responded. "Nothing is impossible; everything fades away."

Ragnar turned back and stared through the stands of trees at the river.

"Is our quest possible? Will we really find the Mines of Solomon?"

"The Romans thought it was real enough." Al-Rahman shrugged. "There are other stories." The black man paused. "There was once a great king named Sogolon Djata who could have been mistaken for Harald's Solomon. His children grew very rich and it is said their very houses were made of gold. There are also tales of their great city in the desert, called Timbuktu, a place of vast wealth and a storehouse of even greater knowledge."

"Could such a place really exist?" Ragnar said.

Al-Rahman laughed loudly, then clapped Ragnar on the shoulder. "I think we shall find out, Ragnar Skull Splitter, the two of us, and perhaps even return to tell the tale."

1

"Except for that one unfortunate trip we made into Libya to rescue cousin Peggy, Africa isn't really my thing," said Colonel John "Doc" Holliday. "I'm more of a knights-in-shining-armor or Roman Empire kind of guy."

"This is different," said Rafi Wanounou. They were sitting in the living room of the archaeologist's bright, spacious apartment on Ramban Street in the Rehavia district of Jerusalem. From the kitchen Holliday could smell the aroma of almond mushroom chicken, beef kung pao and soya duck as Peggy plated their take-out dinner of kosher Chinese food. According to Peggy the art of knowing which restaurant to order from was even more important than knowing how to cook, a philosophy she'd practiced since high school.

"All right," said Doc. "I'll bite. Why should I give up six months of my life to run around Ethiopia, the deserts of Sudan and the jungles of the Congo with you and Peggy when I've got a perfectly good job offer from the Alabama Military Academy and a chance to write my book on the Civil War?"

"Because Mobile is a sauna in the summer," called Peggy from the kitchen.

"And the last thing the world needs is another book on the Civil War." Rafi grinned.

"Okay, what do you have to offer besides malaria, fifty kinds of poisonous snakes and blood-crazed rebel hordes?"

"His name was Julian de la Roche-Guillaume," said Rafi. "He was a Cistercian monk, and he was a Templar."

"Never heard of him," said Holliday.

"I'm not surprised; he was pretty obscure," said Rafi, popping a dumpling into his mouth. He chewed thoughtfully for a moment. "He's usually referred to as the Lost Templar if he's referred to at all. He's basically been forgotten by history, and if he is referenced in some obscure footnote he's remembered as a coward who deserted his holy brothers."

"Sounds like Indiana Jones material, doesn't it?" Peggy said.

"What is this *thing* you have for Indiana Jones?" Rafi said. "He certainly doesn't use the appropriate field technique for a proper archaeologist."

"You don't get it." Peggy grinned. "It's not Indiana Jones I have a *thing* for; it's Harrison Ford."

"Tell me more about this Lost Templar of yours," said Holliday.

"He was always more of a scholar than a real Templar Knight," said Rafi. "When Saladin entrusted the scrolls from Alexandria and the other libraries to the Templars when Jerusalem fell, Roche-Guillaume was one of the men brought in to evaluate them. He was apparently brilliant and could speak and write more than a dozen languages."

"Sounds like an interesting guy," said Holliday. "What does this have to do with Ethiopia?"

"I found him there," said Rafi. "I discovered his tomb while I was excavating at Lake Tana last year when you and my dear wife were gallivanting around Washington getting yourselves into all kinds of trouble."

"We weren't gallivanting," said Peggy, bringing in the plates and setting them down on the table at the far end of the room. "We were running for our lives; it's an entirely different thing." She looked at her watch, then turned and used a wooden match to light the twin Shabbat candles on the old Victorian buffet. When they were lit she gently waved her hands over the flames, covered her eyes and said the blessing:

"Barukh ata Adonai Eloheinu Melekh ha-olam, asher kid'shanu b'mitzvotav v'tzivanu l'hadlik ner shel Shabbat."

"Listen to that, would you?" Rafi said proudly as he and Holliday got up and went to the table. "She's a bet-

15

ter Jew than I am. She does the *licht tsinden* and the blessing like a pro."

"And Granddaddy was a Baptist preacher," said Peggy, sitting down. "Who would have thunk it?"

"Thirteen twenty-four is more than a decade after the Templar purge by King Philip," said Holliday. "How did he manage to get away?"

"He never went back to France," explained Rafi. "Roche-Guillaume was no fool. He was in Cyprus after Jerusalem fell again and he could see the handwriting on the wall. The Templars had too much money, too much power and they flaunted it to the king of France and to the pope. Not healthy or smart. They were politically doomed. Rather than go down with the ship, so to speak, Roche-Guillaume fled overland to Egypt. Alexandria, to be exact. He became a tutor to the sons of the Mamluk sultans."

"Alexandria is a long way from Ethiopia," said Holliday.

"You don't have a romantic bone in your body, do you, Doc?" Peggy chided, spearing a piece of duck. "It's a *story*."

"Sorry," said Holliday.

"Roche-Guillaume was a historian, just like you, Doc, and a bit of an archaeologist to boot—you could even say he was a little like Peggy, because he documented all his work with sketches. Hundreds of them, mostly on parchment. Among other things Roche-

Guillaume *was* a romantic. He'd become convinced over time that the queen of Sheba really did have a relationship with Solomon, and it was the queen of Sheba who showed Solomon the location of the real King Solomon's Mines. He was also of the somewhat unpopular opinion that the queen of Sheba was black. Coal black, in fact."

"You've got to be kidding me." Holliday laughed. "*King Solomon's Mines* is a fiction. A story by Rider Haggard from the nineteenth century. The mines are a myth."

"Solomon existed; that's historical fact and so is Sheba. Some people think Sheba was a part of Arabia, perhaps Yemen. Given what I've uncovered I'd be willing to bet it was Ethiopia. Or at least it began there."

"What makes you say that?" Holliday asked, picking at his food.

"Because of Mark Antony."

"The 'I come to bury Caesar, not to praise him' Mark Antony? Cleopatra and Mark Antony, that one?"

"That one." Rafi nodded.

"He's involved?"

"Instrumental. It's thirty-seven B.C. and Mark's running out of cash. Cleopatra's paid for his wars so far but the cupboard is dry and his enemies are closing in."

"Marcus Vipsanius Agrippa and his pals. I know the history, Rafi. I taught it at West Point for years."

"Mark Antony's broke. He's got an army to feed, but

17

like I said, the cupboard is bare and his mistress is nagging him. So what does he do?"

"Don't keep me in suspense," said Holliday.

"He sends a legion up the Nile to look for the treasure of the land of Sheba and King Solomon's Mines."

"What legion are we talking about here?"

"Legio nona Hispana," said Rafi. He rolled a piece of steamed bok choy around his fork and ate it. "The Ninth."

"The lost legion?" Holliday laughed. This was getting more Byzantine by the second. "They disappeared up by Hadrian's Wall. They were wiped out."

"That's one theory," said Rafi. "The other is that they suffered heavy losses and changed their name when they were sent to Africa under Mark Antony. They became the Eighteenth Legion *Lybica* under Mark Antony and a questionable general named Lucius Gellius Publicola, who was inclined to betray you depending on which way the wind blew."

"Says what historical source?"

"Julian de la Roche-Guillaume, the Templar turned rich kids' tutor," responded Rafi. "While he was in Alexandria he found the legion's records detailing their orders, equipment, stores, all kinds of things. The Imperial Romans were like Germans, meticulous about their records, but there's no record anywhere of their return. They simply vanished up the Nile."

"Looking for King Solomon's Mines."

"Apparently."

"That's quite a rabbit hole you've got there, Alice," said Holliday. He dipped a spring roll in a small dish of soy sauce and took a bite. "What's next, the Mad Hatter?"

"Better," said Peggy, grinning. Outside a light breeze gently ruffled the leaves on the olive trees in the court-yard. In the distance they could hear the arthritic creaking of the old stone windmill that had once generated electricity for the neighborhood.

"Better?" Holliday said.

"Harald Sigurdsson," said Rafi.

"A Viking? The one who became Harald Hardrada, Harald the Hard Man? This is starting to get silly, guys."

"Harald Sigurdsson was, among other things, the head of the eastern emperor's Varangian Guard in Constantinople. He also led the Varangians into battle in North Africa, Syria, Palestine and Sicily gathering booty. While he was in Alexandria raping and pillaging he heard rumors about the lost legion and sent one of his best men, Ragnar Skull Splitter, to lead a crew up the Nile looking for them."

"When was this?"

"A.D. ten thirty-nine. About three hundred years before Roche-Guillaume."

"So what happened to Ragnar Skull Splitter, or should I ask?"

"He disappeared, just like the lost legion."

"So where is this going exactly?"

"Ragnar Skull Splitter took a scholar much like Roche-Guillaume with him to record the story of the journey. His name was Abdul al-Rahman, a high-ranking slave from Constantinople with a yen for travel and adventure. He was also useful as an interpreter. He also had his own artist to record what he saw, a court eunuch named Barakah. An eleventh-century version of Peg here."

Peggy gave her husband a solid swat on the arm. "I ain't no eunuch, sweet lips."

"And they went looking for King Solomon's Mines, right?" Holliday asked.

"Not only did they look for them; they found them. Ragnar died of blackwater fever on the journey home but Abdul al-Rahman survived and made it as far as Ethiopia. While Roche-Guillaume was at Lake Tana he found al-Rahman's chronicle of the journey at an obscure island on the lake. He copied the parchments, which were buried with him."

Holliday shrugged. "Who's to say Roche-Guillaume didn't make it all up, a pleasant fiction? A Homeric epic. Where's the proof?"

Rafi got up from the table and went to the old Victorian buffet where the Shabbat candles burned. He took out an old, deeply carved wooden box and set it gently down in the center of the table. The carvings appeared to be Viking runes.

"Open it," said Rafi.

Holliday lifted the simple lid of the dark wood box. Nestled inside was a piece of quartz about the size of a roughly heart-shaped golf ball. Threaded around one end of the stone was a thick, buttery vein of what appeared to be gold.

"That was in Roche-Guillaume's tomb," said Rafi. "If the thugs at the Central Revolutionary Investigation Department in Addis Ababa knew I'd smuggled it out they'd probably arrest me."

"For a bit of gold in a quartz matrix?" Holliday said.

"It's not quartz," replied Rafi. "It's a six-hundred-and-sixty-four-carat flawless diamond. VVSI, I think they call it. I asked a friend who knows about such things. According to him it's the tenth-largest diamond in the world. Fair market value is about twenty million dollars. The historical value is incalculable."

"And this supposedly came from King Solomon's Mines?" Holliday said, staring at the immense stone.

"According to al-Rahman's chronicle that Roche-Guillaume copied there's a mountain of stones just like it. Tons."

"Where exactly?"

"That's the problem," said Rafi. "As far as I can figure out the mines are located in what is now the Kukuanaland district of the Central African Republic."

"Oh, dear," said Holliday. "General Solomon Kolingba."

"Kolingba the cannibal," added Peggy, eating the last piece of lemon chicken. "The only African dictator with his own set of Ginsu knives for chopping up his enemies."

2

Dr. Oliver Gash drove the black-and-yellow-striped Land Rover down the dusty dirt road from Bangui at seventy miles an hour, the air-conditioning going full blast and Little Richard screaming out "Rip It Up" on the eight-speaker Bose. Since crossing the border into what had once been known as the Kukuanaland district of the Central African Republic and which was now known as the Independent Democratic Republic of Kukuanaland, Dr. Gash hadn't seen another vehicle on the road. Every village he drove through seemed deserted, every roadside stall shuttered and dark.

The young black man behind the wheel wasn't surprised. In fact, the apparent emptiness made him smile. It was a demonstration of fear, and fear, as he well knew, was power. The bumblebee-striped Land Rover had the Kolingba royal crest on the doors, and news traveled fast in the new Kukuanaland about anything and anyone to do with General Solomon Bokassa Sesesse Kolingba.

Dr. Gash was the minister of the interior in the Independent Democratic Republic of Kukuanaland, as well as the young country's minister of revenue and secretary of state and director of foreign affairs. Oliver Gash was not the name the man behind the wheel had been born with; nor was he a doctor of any kind. Gash had once been Olivier Hakizimana Gashabi of Rwanda and had left that country with his older sister, Eliane, during the genocide of 1994, traveling across the Democratic Republic of Congo to eventually settle in Bangui, the capital of the Central African Republic.

Three years after their arrival in Bangui, Olivier's sister had been chosen from an online catalog as a contract e-mail bride by an American named Arthur Andrew Hartman, who lived in Baltimore. Nineteen-year-old Eliane had agreed to the marriage only on the condition that Hartman formally adopt her eleven-year-old brother.

Hartman was in no position to refuse Eliane's proposition. As an acne-scarred, introverted, sexually problematic, onetime Section 8 discharge from the United States Army for an unspecified "condition," and an ex–postal worker now on psychiatric disability, Arthur Andrew Hartman had little or no opportunity for meaningful contact with members of the opposite sex and was far too paranoid about contracting a sexually transmitted disease to purchase relief from his lonely predicament.

Three years later Arthur Andrew Hartman was found with his pants around his ankles, his genitals mutilated and his throat slit in an alley behind a shopping center in the Gardenville district of Baltimore. For a brief period Hartman's fifteen-year-old adopted son was suspected in the killing of his "father" but there wasn't enough evidence to prove the case, and the Baltimore state prosecutor's office declined to go forward. The successful murder of his despised and adopted father was Olivier Gashabi's first foray into the world of crime. It was not his last.

Eliane used her share of Hartman's postal life insurance policy and the money from the quick sale of his house on Asbury Avenue to purchase half interest in a mani-pedi salon. Olivier Gashabi, his name now legally changed to Oliver Gash, invested the fee paid by his sister for murdering Hartman into two kilograms of cocaine. That was in 2001. Ten years later Eliane Gashabi owned four mani-pedi salons outright and her brother had increased his original investment a hundredfold. He had also developed a number of serious enemies within the state prosecutor's office, the Baltimore Police Department and the extensive criminal network that ran between Washington, D.C., Baltimore and New York City. The twenty-five-year-old criminal entrepreneur was suddenly consumed by a passion to seek out his roots, and, traveling on his perfectly valid United States passport, he returned to the Central African Republic.

Criminal enterprise in Bangui was already controlled by a number of tribally centered gangs that enforced their rule with machetes, so Gashabi-Gash decided to travel into his own heart of darkness and went up-country by steamer on the Kottu River to the Kukuana-land town of Fourandao.

Fourandao had once been a French colonial town best known for its cocoa and tobacco plantations, both crops controlled by the old Portuguese family that had given the town its name. The town, a collection of one- and two-story mud-brick buildings with corrugated iron roofs, sprawled untidily along the banks of the Kottu for half a mile or so, and straggled into the sur-rounding jungle toward the distant Bakouma hills that marked the border with Sudan and Chad.

Oliver Gash arrived at the Fourandao docks early one morning to find the small city in the midst of a revolu-tion. By the early afternoon, seeing which way the wind was blowing, he had allied himself with the forces of the KNRA, the Kukuanaland National Revolutionary Alli-ance, led by an upstart lieutenant in FACA, the Forces Armées Centrafricaines, named Solomon Kolingba. The actual governor of the territory, a doctor named Amobe Limbani, a member of the Yakima minority, fled into the jungle, never to be heard from again.

By late evening Oliver Gash had been made a full colonel by the newly minted General Kolingba, and by midnight Gash and Kolingba were celebrating the birth of the Kukuanaland nation with a bottle of Veuve Clicquot champagne liberated from the bar of the Hotel Trianon in the town's central square, now grandly renamed the Plaza de Revolution de Generale Kolingba.

The following day Gash and Kolingba got down to business. Due to various and sundry wars, political upheavals and criminal restructurings around the world, the normal trade routes for heroin at various levels of refinement were no longer available. Using his contacts within the United States, Oliver Gash suggested to Kolingba that Kukuanaland become the new Marseilles, acting as a refinement and distribution center for high-grade narcotics, then branching out into the small-arms trade, contract terrorism, blood-diamond marketing, large-scale money laundering and an assortment of other disagreeable but profitable occupations that would make the open city of Fourandao into the new home of Gangster, Incorporated. A 1930s Chicago for the twenty-first century. The American dream in the middle of an equatorial African jungle.

It worked beyond Olivier Gashabi's wildest expectations. Fourandao and the surrounding area had flourished. The airport had been refurbished with extended runways for private jets, and the ragtag army had been issued brand-new uniforms and new weapons, all donated by the General Armament Department of the Chinese government. The Chinese were also putting in a proper filtration plant for Fourandao and paving the surrounding roads. Oliver Gash had discovered a surprising talent for politics and diplomacy; as it turned out they had a lot in common with crime. In Africa, as anywhere else, corruption and greed in the realm of politics was a way of life; the only difference was that in Africa it was expected and accepted.

Eventually the bumblebee-painted Rover reached the tumbledown docks of the town. A few barges were being loaded with fruit and bales of rubber for the long trip downriver but they were really no more than protective cover for the loads of drugs, weapons and other illicit goods distributed out of the harsh jungle country. Docked ahead of the barges was the single boat in Kukuanaland's navy—a donated thirty-five-foot river patrol boat from the Djibouti navy equipped with a fifty-horsepower Evinrude and a leaky cabin. Its only armament was a single Kord heavy machine gun left over from a Russian delegation that managed to offload it to Kolingba in the early days of his regime. When the general was in a particularly sporty mood he and Gash and a quartet of bodyguards would go fishing in the boat and hunt crocodiles with the machine gun.

The only thing worrying Gash as he drove along the waterfront was a recent meeting he'd had in Bangui with one of the more corrupt bankers in the city. The man had asked Gash what he thought about his future if Kolingba was no longer a factor. The man's meaning was clear—if Kolingba was removed, would Gash be willing to take his place? At the meeting Gash had been noncommittal—the banker could easily have been a trap set by Kolingba himself—but on another level the question had nagged. Gash hadn't survived this long by being stupid; he knew perfectly well that African dictators had the life spans of fruit flies, so perhaps now was the time to start considering an escape route if worse came to worst. He bribed everyone worth bribing and continued to do so, giving him an intricate web of ears to the ground within Kolingba's inner circle, but maybe he should be doing something more.

Gash turned the truck up the road to the center of town, passing tin-roofed shacks and open-fronted stores selling everything from bicycles to knockoff handbags and long Chicago Bulls T-shirts.

He finally reached the square and turned toward the compound that had once been home to the Fourandao family and was now the presidential compound. Kolingba had wanted to call it the Royal Compound, but Gash convinced him that although he was king, he was also the president, and calling himself that to the outside world would result in his being taken more seriously.

Essentially the compound was a high-walled fort, cement and straw under a layer of yellowing stucco with a wooden parapet and a pair of heavy oak doors. Inside the compound there was the presidential residence along one side, a barracks along the other and a mess hall, armory and jail cells along the back wall. Two guards who stood outside the gate carried stubby little Chang Feng submachine guns. Gash knew that the magazines in the weapons were empty, as were the weapons within the compound—all except those belonging to Kolingba and his two personal bodyguards, both of whom were his younger brothers.

Seeing the Rover come into the square, the two guards snapped to attention and the gates magically opened as he approached. A quick phone call from one of the dockside warehouses would have warned the gate guards of his approach and they would have been ready and waiting. A guard who had failed to open the gate quickly enough had been placed in the wooden strangling scaffold that had replaced the bronze statue of Ambrosio Fourandao in the center of the square, while the rest of the townspeople were forced to watch. A rope was threaded through holes in the neck piece of the scaffold, then twisted around a metal pole at the back, slowly and very painfully choking the life out of the man.

Kolingba had watched from the parapet of the compound as the executioner drew out the process over more than an hour, choking and releasing until a nod from Kolingba finally put the man out of his misery. It was the kind of thing that gave Oliver Gash the creeps but the money was too good to complain. Another year and he'd have enough to slip out of the madman's clutches and disappear forever. Like it or not, the king of Kukuanaland was as crazy as a box of crackers and, like any wild beast, he was capable of turning on you at any time. Dealing with the man was like walking a high wire over Niagara Falls. But the money just was so damned good.

Gash parked the Land Rover in front of the presidential residence, then went up the three wide steps to the covered veranda. There was a distinct colonial flavor to the porch, complete with wicker armchairs for the plantation owners to sit on in the cool of the evening with their tall gin drinks as they complained about the heat and the lack of civilized pursuits.

The two guards at the front doors snapped to attention as Gash went by, their eyes wide with terror. Gash went up the stairs to the second floor of the building and found his way to Kolingba's study, which overlooked the compound.

As usual Kolingba was at his immense desk, brooding over some document under his immense hand. He was wearing his full uniform: dark blue jodhpurs with a red stripe down the outer seam, a light blue shirt with black and gold shoulder boards, and a chestful of medals. A huge, steel-bound copy of the Old Testament stood between two wrought-iron lion's-head bookends at the front of the desk. A chrome-plated World War Two–era tank commander's helmet rested on one corner of his desk and an ornately scrolled silver-plated presentation

Colt .45 automatic pistol lay close to his right hand. Gash knew that its mate was in the holster at Kolingba's hip. There was a narrow bookcase against one wall, mostly filled with books about General George S. Patton. There was even a photograph of the actor George C. Scott on the wall, dressed for his role as the famous general. Kolingba's big head lifted as Gash entered the room. His eyes narrowed.

"'Now the weight of gold that came to Solomon in one year was six hundred and threescore and six talents of gold—beside that which chapmen and merchants brought. And all the kings of Arabia and governors of the country brought gold and silver to Solomon.'"

"Truer words were never said, Your Majesty," murmured Gash. He didn't have the faintest idea what the big man was talking about, but he presumed Kolingba was quoting from the Bible.

"The Bible speaks of my ancestor with great reverence," rumbled Kolingba, the sound of his voice like the throaty growl of some immense beast, barely contained.

"Of course they do, Your Majesty." Gash nodded.

"We must act quickly, Gash, before it is too late."

"Of course, Your Majesty."

There was no doubt about it; Solomon Kolingba was right out of his mind.

3

"Herodotus said that Egypt was an acquired country; it was the Nile's gift," Holliday said, staring out at the arid landscape of the Ethiopian Plateau from the backseat of the battered old Toyota Land Cruiser.

"Herodo-who?" Peggy said, sitting beside Rafi, who was behind the wheel.

"How could a nice Jewish archaeologist marry a Philistine like her?" said Holliday, giving his cousin a playful swat on the back of the head.

"She's your relation." Rafi laughed.

"She's your wife," countered Holliday.

"Why doesn't one of you answer my question?" Peggy asked.

"Herodotus was an ancient Greek. He's sometimes called the father of history," answered Holliday. "He traveled all over the ancient world collecting stories about each country he passed through."

"He was also called the father of lies," said Rafi. "He

collected fables and legends as much as he did hard facts."

"Like King Solomon's Mines?" Peggy asked.

"Herodotus was before Solomon's time," said Holliday.

"But he planted the seed," said Rafi. "He had all sorts of stories about the mysterious land of Punt."

"Punt?"

"Like a football," said Holliday. "No one's ever quite figured out where it was."

"And the Russian armored personnel carriers?" Peggy asked, nodding out the window at yet another burned-out BTR-60 rusting away beside the road. The highway had been littered with them all the way from Addis Ababa.

"Remains of the Ethiopian Civil War," said Holliday. "Almost twenty years of murder and mayhem that accomplished absolutely nothing. Two Marxist groups fighting for power while the arms dealers got fat. All that was left when they were done was wholesale corruption and poverty. That was in 1991. Not much has changed since." They went past a road sign: BAHIR DAR 20 KM. They had almost reached it: Lake Tana, the source of the Nile.

Archibald "Archie" Ives wiped the sweat off his face with a T-shirt he was using as a towel and prepared the single stick of high explosive, carefully fitting the detonator wires into the open, puttylike end of the seven-inch tube. A hundred feet down the sloping hill the trickling stream that would eventually become the Kotto River burbled along through the jungle foliage.

Ives had come into Kukuanaland by the back door, flying in on a helicopter from Chad. He'd been in the tiny hellhole of a country for the better part of a week now, looking for likely locations chosen from the file of aerial shots the company had commissioned more than a year ago. Today was his last day; tomorrow he'd be back at the extraction point and twelve hours after that he'd be having a beer at the Café Khartoum in the Burj Al-Fatah Hotel.

He rubbed a hand across his leathery, sun-worn jawline and felt the grimy, gray-blond stubble. At sixty-three he was getting far too old to be running around in the jungle like this. On the other hand retirement didn't come cheap these days, which was why he'd bullied the company into putting a profit-sharing clause into his contract this time. He was sick and tired of making fat cats like Sir James Matheson rich while he worked for peanuts.

Ives dropped the explosive into the hand-drilled shot hole, tamped the claylike soil on top of it, then ran the detonator wires back up to his position on the top of the hill. He sat down on the ground with his legs crossed and attached the wires to a small USB unit, which he then plugged into his laptop. He set the controls, switched on the recorder and took one last look down the hill. Nothing on the ground and no planes in the sky, not that Kukuanaland had much of an air force: a single aging Soviet Mil Mi-24 attack helicopter from the seventies with no one to fly it. Kolingba, the lunatic leader of the country, had an even older Cessna 170 single-engine he sometimes flew himself but apparently he was terrified of being brought down by ground-to-air missiles from one of the adjoining countries, so he rarely took to the air.

With the laptop balanced on his lap Ives hit "enter." There was a split-second pause, a distant muffled crumping sound and then the earth beneath him shook briefly. There was another pause and then the data began forming on the screen.

"Bloody hell," the geologist whispered. He replayed the data to make sure there were no mistakes, then set the recorder aside and stood up. He walked down the hill to the stream and squatted, thinking hard, then splashed water on his face, being careful not to swallow any; he was well aware of the parasites that could be living in the water—everything from schistosomiasis to cholera, typhoid and a dozen other horrors. He wiped off his hands and face with the T-shirt towel, then took out a cigarette and lit it. He coughed once, spit out a wad of phlegm, then took a long, satisfying drag.

At best he'd expected to see a few small circular

patches of the familiar alluvial "pipes" on his computer screen, evidence of some sort of deposit. What he hadn't expected was what he'd seen: so many of the circular blobs that they merged into a single gigantic pipe, indicating that the hill he was on was no hill at all; it was a single, enormous kimberlite deposit bigger than anything he'd ever seen before. It was easily as large as the Venetia strike in 1992 and perhaps even larger. On top of that the kimberlite appeared to be surrounded by a reef of precious metals dense enough to be gold or perhaps even platinum. His eyebrows rose at the next stream of data. This was better than all the others put together, or worse, depending on your point of view.

Ives stood there for a moment having a silent conversation with himself. He could tell his bosses what he'd found, he could keep it to himself or, God help him, he could tell Kolingba, since it was on his land, after all. It was a short conversation. If he told his bosses he might make something out of the find; if he kept it to himself there was no way he could work the deposit without a huge investment; and if he told Kolingba the madman would promise him great riches, then slit his throat as soon as he had the location. He marked the site in his memory, even though the satellites would do a better job of it. Three hills, this one the highest, the river at his back and the sound of the three-fingered Kazaba Falls a mile or so upstream. A thousand years ago this would have been a paradise for the native Yakima tribe, an unparalleled source of food and water. But with no known resources and no obvious reason to be developed, it had languished, empty and unexplored for as far back as anyone could remember, a place of ancient legend and taboo. In creole Sango it was the Guda Kwa Zo, the Land of the Dead.

Ives gave a little sigh, then unclipped the satellite phone from his belt. Any remnants of that distant paradise would be destroyed by the phone call he was about to make. He dialed a private number in London, then listened to the ethereal buzz and hum as the connection was made. The call was answered on the second ring.

"Gardenia quadrant. Primrose seven by magnolia four." The code was the same one the Royal Navy had used for tracking U-boats in World War Two. Ives thought it was James Bond nonsense.

"Yes?"

"Westminster," said Ives. There was a long pause.

"What sort?"

"House of Lords at the very least," said Ives. "The House of Commons as well."

"You're sure?"

"Positive."

"Good Lord."

"Too right," said Ives.

"I shall inform His Majesty."

The phone went dead.

"You bloody well do that," said Ives. He trudged

back up the hill to collect his gear and get the hell out of Kukuanaland. He could almost taste that first beer.

Michael Pierce Harris—formerly deputy director of operations for the CIA before being forced to resign or face a long jail sentence—sat in one of the comfortable leather club chairs in the office of the special projects director of Matheson Resource Industries. He was sipping single-malt Scotch from a heavy crystal glass and smoking an aged Cuban El Rey del Mundo Gran Corona. The tall windows to his right looked across Park Place to the looming brick pile of the St. James's Club directly across the narrow, out-of-the-way street.

Major Allen Faulkener, the Rifles (retired), hung up the phone on the leather-covered top of his seventeenth-century desk. As director of special projects for MRI, it was his job to make sure that the sometimes "socially unpleasant" aspects of the huge mining corporation's affairs were smoothed out long before the first ton of ore was extracted from a site.

MRI was the second-largest mining company in the world, right after the massive Barrick Gold. Like Barrick, MRI was officially headquartered among the bleak, featureless towers on Bay Street in Toronto but did virtually no business there, simply taking advantage of Canada's very liberal and freewheeling laws regarding mining ventures.

The real business of MRI was done in London and the company presently operated in Papua New Guinea, the United States, Canada, the Dominican Republic, Australia, Peru, Chile, Russia, South Africa, Pakistan, Colombia, Argentina and Tanzania. For some time now it had been studying the geological possibilities of embarking on a venture based in the hinterlands of Kukuanaland.

"Well," said Harris, putting his glass down on a silver coaster that sat permanently on the lacquered twenties Chinese end table. "What's going on?"

"Apparently we've been given the green light by His Majesty," said Faulkener, thoughtfully looking up at the rather gruesome watercolor on the wall of his office. It was called *The Last Stand at Islandhula* and showed a regiment of red-coated, mounted British soldiers being slaughtered by an enraged group of Zulu warriors.

Africa was never Faulkener's battlefield of choice, but these days that was where the goodies were. "Time to show us your mettle, Harris. This is the sort of thing you and your CIA brothers were so good at."

"Do tell."

"I'm afraid it's Africa this time. A wretched little place called Kukuanaland."

"Solomon Kolingba." Harris nodded. "A true-blue nut bar."

"He has something we want," said Faulkener. "We need to figure out how to get it."

"I'll drink to that," said Harris, lifting his heavy glass.

"You'll drink to anything," said Faulkener. He stood, went to the sideboard and poured himself a glass of the same single-malt Harris was drinking. He stood there for a moment, his gaze turning once again to the watercolor of the Islandhula massacre. "There's one other thing," he muttered. "Nothing more than a loose end, really."

"Oh?" Harris said.

"Have you ever been to Khartoum, Mr. Harris?"

4

The rowboat-sized fishing craft burbled across the immense, glassy expanse of Lake Tana, powered by the oldest and smallest outboard motor Holliday had ever seen. According to Rafi, it was a 1939 Evinrude one-and-a-half-horsepower Mate. Somehow it had found its way to Ethiopia and into the hands of the Halebo family, who had cared for it meticulously ever since. Halebo Iskinder, the current owner and head of the family, had rented the boat and the motor to Rafi only after a rigorous test to prove that he knew how to handle such a delicate and marvelous device. The noise it made was like somebody rattling marbles around in a tin can, but it was remarkably speedy.

"I'm surprised they let you dig here," said Holliday, lifting his voice over the engine's racket. Clouds of blue-white exhaust followed in their wake. "Between Communists, Orthodox Christians and Muslims, I always figured Ethiopia as being pretty anti-Semitic."

"Israel was always the monkey wrench in the gears," said Rafi, sitting at the tiller. "In the eighties the U.S. saw Ethiopia as either going over to the Communists or heading toward radical Islam. Somalia, Eritrea and the Sudan on three sides and Yemen on the other side of the Red Sea. There were 'Cuban observers' everywhere. It was a hot spot that needed cooling down, so we always provided the democratic Christians with arms and anything else they needed. Then we took fifteen thousand Beta Jews off their hands in Operation Solomon. It's like a marriage of convenience—no real love involved but it works for everyone concerned. Anyway, they didn't let me dig here."

"You went in without government approval?" Holliday said. "That's not like you."

"Well, I didn't actually 'dig,'" the archaeologist replied. "It was more like . . . uh, poking around."

"Now, there's a scientific term." Peggy snorted.

As they approached the island Peggy started taking pictures from the bow with her Nikon digital.

"The big island on your right is Tana Kirkos; the little one on the left, which is where we're going, is Daset T'qit, which literally means just that in Amharic: small island." He pointed to the bigger of the two. "Tana Kirkos was supposedly the resting place of the Ark of the Covenant for a time," he added.

"No more arks, please," said Holliday. He'd had more than enough of them with the late Sister Meg and her viperous mother.

"Any poisonous snakes or insects?" Peggy asked.

"Dozens," said Rafi, "which is why you're wearing long trousers tucked into high boots. Everything from spitting cobras to green mambas, scorpions, centipedes and the occasional Nile crocodile. There're a few dangerous plants, so don't eat any berries or anything."

"For the love of Pete, Rafi, why do you always tell me this stuff when it's too late to back out?" Peggy complained.

"So you won't back out," explained Rafi, smiling broadly.

They came up on the small island and Rafi backed off on the throttle. They slowed, slipping through the dark, placid waters. The island was completely covered by dense foliage rising right up from the edge of the water. There were shrubs, vines, trees and just plain jungle. The only sign of civilization was the cut-stone ruins of some sort of dock and what appeared to be a watchtower behind it.

"Looks like the set for an Indiana Jones movie," said Peggy. "I'm expecting to see Harrison Ford waving his hat and cracking his whip any second now."

"Nobody's lived on Daset T'qit in a very long time, if ever," said Rafi as he cut the tiny motor and drifted toward the dock.

"Why did you choose this place?" Holliday said.

"I didn't," said Rafi, using the tiller to guide the old boat between the stone arms of the dock. Holliday could see worn steps carved into the stone that went right down into the water. "I was doing research on the Ethiopian Beta Jews and their original settlements at Tana Kirkos, the bigger island. I just casually asked about Daset T'qit in passing, and one of my translators got really spooked, went white as a sheet. He told me the place was taboo and that its nickname was Maqabr Aswad Muslim—the Tomb of the Black Muslim."

"This gets us back to Ragnar Skull Splitter and his Arab friend, doesn't it?" Holliday asked.

"That's right," said Rafi. "Abdul al-Rahman."

"But I thought you said this was Roche-Guillaume's tomb," said Holliday.

"It is." Rafi grinned. Peggy looped the rope in the bow around a rock peg that looked as though it had been there for a thousand years. She stepped out of the boat onto the steps and trotted up to the top of the dock. Holliday and Rafi followed her up to the narrow stone pier at the head of the stairway.

"It's beautiful!" Peggy said. "It's like one of the paintings by that French guy . . . the customs clerk. . . ."

"Rousseau," said Holliday. She was right; the solid mass of foliage in front of them was as detailed and exotic as one of the famous artist's strange and wonderful jungle scenes. There was every shade of green, from forest shadow to vivid lime, celadon and emerald, pinks and reds and bright yellows. Smooth leaves and serrated, big and small, vines that curled up and around larger trees and huge gnarled roots dragging up from the rich black earth like the groping fingers of buried giants. The only thing missing were the gazing lions and the naked women. He could hear the chittering of monkeys high above them and the shrieking calls of angry birds.

There was something sinister here as well, so real that Holliday found himself wishing he had some sort of weapon with him. From his arrival in Vietnam barely six months after his eighteenth birthday to tours in Afghanistan and Somalia, he'd been in some dangerous places in his life, but this was different. Somehow he knew that stepping into that forest would be like stepping off the edge of the world and that once within it he might never find his way out again. Holliday suddenly remembered a quote from Conrad's *Heart of Darkness* he'd memorized in high school but hadn't understood until now: "And this also has been one of the dark places of the earth."

More than once he'd been in locations where he sensed and somehow almost felt the past and present occupying the same space and time: the Rue de Rivoli in Paris, where you could almost hear the echoing boot heels of the SS troops marching on parade each noon of the occupation. The killing fields of Antietam in Maryland, where you could still hear the screams of the twenty-two thousand men who were struck down there, still taste the cloying grit of gunpowder in the air. Or a quiet little forest in Picardy in the north of France called Belleau Wood whose dark, rich soil was fertilized with the blood of ten thousand U.S. Marines and an uncounted number of their German adversaries.

Holliday felt it here more than he'd ever done before. He knew without a doubt that this place would somehow take them all into a world of madness, into the deep, true heart of darkness, beating like some monstrous drum. He shivered, even though it was stunningly hot. He tried to shake off the feeling, but it still lingered faintly. Every nerve in his body was screaming, *Run*.

"Watch out for the monkeys," warned Rafi. "They tend to hurl their feces at you."

"Lovely," said Peggy. "Poisonous snakes and poop-throwing monkeys."

They stepped into the forest.

Within a few feet it was obvious that they were on some kind of well-worn trail. Vines and boughs had been slashed, and recently by the looks of it. The trail was also littered with half-chewed bits of bark and rotting, partially eaten fruit.

"The monkeys aren't fussy eaters, I see," said Peggy.

"Who's your gardener?" Holliday asked. "This trail's man-made." He was getting unpleasant flashes of the Viet Cong jungle trails around Bu Prang.

"Maybe it's the ghost of the Lost Templar." Peggy laughed.

"Nothing so spooky," said Rafi, who was leading the way. "Halebo Iskinder comes out every few weeks and keeps it clear."

"I thought it was haunted," Peggy said.

"The money I pay Iskinder isn't," Rafi said. "Besides, Iskinder likes having a secret from the other ferrymen on the lake."

"What secret?" Peggy asked.

"That," said Rafi as they stepped out into a small natural clearing.

Under the protective overhanging branches of a single baobab tree there was a windowless stone building that looked very much like a small chapel or a large mausoleum. The structure was built of the same brown basalt as the Coptic monasteries and churches scattered along the shores of Lake Tana. The arched door was made of dark wood with broad strap hinges. Above the door, worn with time but still clearly visible, was a heraldic crest: a lion, rampant, looking right on a field of seven stripes.

Peggy lifted her camera immediately and took a half dozen shots. "Indiana Jones and the Tomb of the Lost Templar."

"Doesn't it ever start to bug you?" Holliday asked, raising an eyebrow. "All the Indiana Jones stuff?"

"I'm used to it," said Rafi. "Water off a duck's back by now. At least she doesn't ask me to wear a fedora and carry a bullwhip. It's just Peggy being Peggy."

They approached the building.

"When I arrived the door was sealed with pitch," explained Rafi, pointing to the thick, black, tarry substance that still could be seen around the edges of the arched doorway.

"It was sealed?" Holliday asked, running his hands over the wood surface. It was ironwood of some kind, extremely hard and very old.

"Hermetically," answered Rafi.

"How's that possible?" Holliday asked. "The door's solid but there had to be some air exchange through the stones or the floor."

"Let me show you," said Rafi. He leaned hard against the door and pushed. It didn't budge. Holliday put his shoulder to it as well and the door grudgingly opened, a long lance of sunlight spearing dramatically into the room and illuminating the object in the middle of the floor.

It was a stone sarcophagus, eight feet long and four feet wide and made of huge slabs of polished black basalt. The sides of the sarcophagus were carved with extraordinary scenes: what was surely a Viking ship being attacked by crocodiles, men in Roman tunics marching, their standard held high, and laboring slaves, backs bent with the weight of heavy baskets, their legs shackled to one another. The top of the sarcophagus was slightly more conventional, showing the stone effigy of a knight in chain mail, gripping his sword in both hands. The sword's blade was entwined with a snake and at the knight's feet a baboon slept, curled into the fetal position. On the knight's free arm was a stone shield carved with the familiar Templar cross inlaid in a darker basalt. The sarcophagus was resting on the backs of six crouching lions made of the same black stone as the cross.

"The tomb of Julian de la Roche-Guillaume, I presume," said Holliday, his voice suddenly a bit breathless. He went to the sarcophagus and let his fingers trail the length of the old warrior's sword, a sword in stone not much different from the one in Damascus steel he'd found hidden in his uncle's home in Fredonia, New York, and which had started him on his long Templar adventure—a world within a world and plots within plots, stretching up through the centuries until today.

"More than that," said Rafi. He turned away from the huge stone coffin and went to the far wall. For the first time Holliday noticed that the walls had been covered with tarpaulins that hung on lines and rings like shower curtains. With no pause for dramatic effect Rafi pulled the dull green cloth aside.

Peggy's eyes went wide.

"Holy crap," she whispered, awestruck.

5

It was a vision of paradise.

"The Garden of Eden," said Peggy, her camera forgotten.

As Rafi pulled the curtains back from all four walls he revealed an enormous panorama, the sarcophagus in its center. The artist had painted it from some high vantage point, capturing the jungle, the enormous cascades of the waterfall and the nearby hills in perfect detail. Every tree, every branch, every leaf, every rocky crag and outcropping was captured in glowing greens and ochres, blues and whites and brilliant yellows, the magnificent arc of the rainbow as the water dropped into the foaming gorge as perfect as a photograph.

Looking closer, Holliday could see that the jungle was alive, populated with birds, beasts and reptiles, snakes hanging from trees, a jaguar half-hidden by dappled shadows and perfectly in proportion, a line of tiny black human figures winding along the middle hill, wicker baskets balanced on their heads and shoulders as they walked down the hill and delivered their load onto strangely shaped dugouts waiting on the river. It was a masterpiece and a perfect dreamscape for the sleeping knight in the center of the tomb, beautiful enough to last him for eternity.

"It's magnificent," said Holliday. "Who painted it, I wonder?"

"It was almost certainly Roche-Guillaume himself," said Rafi. "The painting is in much the same style as the sketches he made of his other travels."

"He painted the inside of his own mausoleum?" Peggy said, frowning. "That's a bit icky, don't you think?"

"From what I can tell he probably lived here," said Rafi. "The mausoleum is in the same style as the Coptic monasteries around the lake, so presumably he paid local builders and quarrymen to put it up, building it to his design. The same holds true for the sarcophagus; it's a European tradition reserved for emperors. Most burials here are much simpler affairs—a mummified body is stacked with dozens or hundreds in a church crypt or a cave. Roche-Guillaume clearly designed the sarcophagus and may even have overseen its construction."

"And the interment?" Holliday asked.

"Bought and paid for. Most likely a hired priest from the monastery at Tana Kirkos, the big island I pointed out to you on the way here."

"Once again, ick," said Peggy. "Paying that much attention to your own death. It's just a little bit obsessive-compulsive, don't you think?"

"I don't know," said Holliday, looking at the mural. "He visualized paradise and made sure he'd spend eternity right in the middle of it."

"The mural's no vision," said Rafi. "It's a real place. Ten degrees, twenty-eight minutes, thirty-six seconds north by twenty-three degrees, seventeen minutes, forty-eight seconds east, to be precise. The exact location of King Solomon's Mines."

"You've been there?" Holliday asked skeptically. "Maybe Roche-Guillaume went looking, but this isn't done from life," he said. "It's a dream, Rafi. He smoked too much local weed, which I understand Ethiopia is famous for. It's like Coleridge and the Ancient Mariner—a drugged-out fantasy."

"How do you explain the diamond?"

"He bought it from someone who thought it was worthless. It was a souvenir, like one of those pennants that says, 'Come to Cleveland,' on it."

"Look," said Rafi, gesturing to Holliday, then stepping over to the wall. He dug into his pocket, took out his Swiss army knife and pulled out the large blade. He began digging into the plaster at a point where the side and front walls of the little mausoleum joined. The plaster was at least half an inch thick and it took a little time but eventually he removed a two-by-two-inch square.

He stepped aside and let the weak sunlight play on the exposed surface.

It glittered.

"What the hell?" Holliday said, stepping closer. Instead of the brown basalt stone he'd expected, the little patch was a rich, buttery yellow. He reached out and touched it with the pad of his index finger. "That's crazy," he whispered.

"No," replied Rafi. "That's gold. Ninety-nine nine pure. I had a few slivers assayed in Jerusalem. All four walls, the ceiling and the floor. This whole place is lined with solid gold almost an inch thick."

"Where on earth was it smelted?" Holliday asked. "He didn't bring sheets of it out of the jungle."

"It's in two-by-eight panels, heated and welded together. I found a slab of basalt that was used as the form for pouring the sheets buried in the jungle just beyond the clearing."

"And he kept all this secret?"

"Apparently."

"This is an incredible find, Rafi. Why haven't you said anything or published?"

"The country has been on the verge of another civil war for years. Unstable isn't the word. The Ethiopian government isn't big on protecting its cultural heritage and it's as corrupt as most bureaucracies. If word of this got out the place would be overrun and gutted within days if not hours. At the very least it would be turned into a tourist trap. As a site for serious archaeological work it would be ruined. I can't say anything, not yet anyway." He paused. "And there's more."

"More?" Holliday said, dumbfounded.

"How's your Latin?"

"Still passable," answered Holliday.

"Read the inscription on the sarcophagus."

"What inscription?"

"Just under the overhang of the lid," said Rafi. For the first time Holliday saw the stone-carved ribbon of writing that ran around the immense stone coffin. He translated as he went along.

"'My past is my shield, my' . . . uh, *cruces*, 'cross is my future. Here lies, in the site of their gods, all that remains of the knight Guillaume and the' . . . *servus*, what the hell is *servus*?"

"Slave, I think," said Rafi.

"'Slave and Great Discoverer, Abdul al-Rahman. *Requiescant in pace in aeterno*. May they rest in peace for all eternity."

"Al-Rahman's bones are buried in the same coffin?"

"Either that or the mausoleum was built on the previous site of al-Rahman's grave."

"'My past is my shield, my cross is my future. . . .' What's that supposed to mean?" Holliday asked.

"I didn't get it at first either," said Rafi.

"Get what?" Holliday said.

"Press down hard on the cross on his shield," instructed Rafi.

Holliday leaned over the stone effigy of the knight and pressed down on the center of the black basalt–inlaid cross in the center of his shield. Nothing happened.

"A little harder," said Rafi.

Holliday did as he was told. There was a grating sound, and then Rafi pulled out a tongue of stone that had eased out from the side of the sarcophagus. It was a stone drawer, released by some mechanism within the massive coffin. Inside the drawer was what appeared to be a book bound in leather. With the delicate touch of an archaeologist, Rafi lifted the volume up and laid it on the stone effigy. Slowly and with extreme care, he slipped a leather thong through the cover, which turned out to be a strap keeping the volume tightly shut.

He carefully unfolded a series of thick papyrus pages like an accordion, spreading them out over the top of the sarcophagus. Holliday leaned over it. The pages were covered with line after line of text, the letters so small they were barely readable. Interspersed with the text were simple black-and-white ink drawings.

"It's Latin and French, side by side," he said. "What is it?"

"I call it the Templar Codex," said Rafi. "From what I can tell Roche-Guillaume translated al-Rahman's description of finding the mines and the eventual trip back to civilization." The archaeologist pointed to a tiny illustration. As small as it was it was instantly recognizable—a Viking ship in flames, empty except for a funeral pyre and a body. "At a guess I'd say this relates to the death of our friend Ragnar Skull Splitter." Rafi paused, clearly moved as he stared down at the seven-hundred-year old manuscript. "As I said, Roche-Guillaume was a historian. He wanted his own and al-Rahman's stories to survive; and they did."

"People would pay millions for this, wouldn't they?" Peggy said.

"Easily." Rafi nodded. "The manuscript is priceless, let alone what it reveals."

Holliday looked up from the pages and shook his head. "No, much more than just that. People would kill for this book."

"It belongs in a museum; the question is, How do I get it there?" Rafi said.

"What's the border situation?"

"It varies. Kenya, the guards are all stoned on Khat and it could go either way; Eritrea is men with guns. Sudan, sometimes it's a bunch of goats; sometimes it's a full-scale military crossing. Somalia—don't even think about it."

"Too risky to smuggle it out, then."

"So what do we do?" Peggy asked.

"I want to at least get a photographic record of it," said Rafi.

"That's easy enough," said Peggy, lifting the big Nikon. "But what do we do after that?"

"Put it back where we found it for the time being," said Rafi. "Show the pictures to some museums, see if I can get one of them to back a proper expedition."

"Where's the nearest border crossing into the Sudan?"

"Metemma," said Rafi. "Then Al Qadarif and Khartoum."

"Then that's how we go," said Holliday. "Photograph the codex and everything else, put it all onto a memory stick and change the chip in your camera. If some nosey parker wants to see your vacation snaps, we'll show him a lot of goats and smiling kids. I'll carry the memory stick and the chip, Peggy plays photographer and we keep Rafi innocent as a lamb."

"That'll be the day." Peggy snorted. "Considering who got us into this mess."

"Sorry," said Rafi. "I didn't really think; I just wanted both of you to see this place and the codex."

"Spilt milk and all that," said Holliday briskly. "Let's get the pictures taken and then let's get the hell out of here."

Out of the corner of his eye Holliday thought he saw a movement in the jungle at the edge of the clearing. He turned quickly and stared out the open doorway of the mausoleum. He kept his eyes fixed on the edge of the clearing and waited. Nothing moved.

"What's that all about?" Peggy asked, looking at her cousin carefully. She knew that look. He was on high alert.

"Nothing," said Holliday slowly. "Just a little spooked, I guess."

6

Archibald "Archie" Ives had been an old Africa hand for most of his adult life. The son of a Welsh coal miner, with a second-rate degree in geology from a third-rate college, Ives paid his dues as a prospector and assayer in British Columbia and Nevada, but his first job in Sierra Leone for a Canadian fly-by-night diamond exploration company was a perfect fit. He didn't find any diamonds but it felt like coming home.

For the next thirty-five years he'd roamed around Africa, sometimes working for himself and sometimes working for corporate interests, big and small. He'd gone from rags to relative riches a half dozen times, but what he really liked doing was tramping around in the desert or the jungle, looking for the next big strike and not really caring much whether he found it or not. He lived for the hunt. He hadn't been back to England in a dozen years, and he had no intention of doing so. His recent job for Matheson had come through their office in Bamako, Mali.

Ives had never worked for Matheson before, but he'd heard stories about the company's questionable business tactics. Still, stories were just stories, and the money they were offering was real. In fact, it was *too* real, and it was *too much*, which raised all sorts of alarms in Ives's head. All of which he ignored. Beggars couldn't be choosers and there was no question of his beggarly status at the time the offer was made; in fact, he had less than a hundred Mali francs in his pocket and a long-overdue hotel and bar bill at the Kempinski El Farouk. He'd taken the money and he'd done the job and, according to Major Allen Faulkener, the Rifles (retired), he had also earned a bonus that would put him on easy street for the rest of his life. He was supposed to meet with Faulkener in Khartoum, sign a nondisclosure, hand over his paperwork and get his bonus. Easy as pie.

Except Archie Ives didn't believe a word of it.

He drove the Land Rover along the flat, featureless Al Qadarif–Khartoum highway, the air-conditioning on full blast. There was nothing but desert on either side of him, and the black road ahead. He hadn't seen another vehicle for two hours. The sun beat down on everything like a great hot hammer. Nothing moved except the Land Rover. Anything in the desert in this heat was well on its way to being dead.

Ives lit a cigarette. The site he'd discovered in the jungle outback of Kukuanaland was worth billions. The fact that the site even existed was itself a priceless piece

of information, of course, and at the same time dangerous. Was Faulkener simply going to give him his bonus
and then let him walk away? It was doubtful. According
to the scuttlebutt, Faulkener was no more a member of
the Rifles than Archie was. The SAS was more likely, or
maybe even MI6. In the rarefied atmosphere where
people like that did their business, the Archie Iveses of
the world were nothing but loose ends, a note in a file
folder with the word "terminated" stamped across his
photograph. Like a spot of gravy on a club tie, Archie
was something to be wiped away and forgotten.

The smart money said he should drive on past Khartoum and follow the Pan African all the way to Cairo.
But that wasn't really smart at all. He was a prospector,
and prospecting was all he knew. Bloody Africa was all
he knew. He could hide out for a while, but eventually
his money would run out and he'd have to look for
work. Bells would ring when he showed up in a mining
office anywhere on the continent, and Faulkener and his
people would be on him like dingleberries on a camel's
arse.

Ives dragged on the cigarette. He was boxed in and
he knew it. He needed Faulkener's bonus and getting it
would probably be his death warrant. He crushed out
the cigarette in the ashtray and blew a cloud of smoke
at the windshield. A sign ticked by. Two hundred kilometers to Khartoum. He still had time to figure something out. Something to save his life.

*　　*　　*

The border crossing at Gallabat was of the herd-of-goats variety. Holliday watched as a bored Sudanese customs official in a round hut with a thatched roof checked their papers, held out his hand for a bribe as though it were the most normal thing in the world and looked longingly at Rafi's Rolex. Rafi studiously avoided the look and gave the man a hundred Ethiopian birr—a little over ten dollars—which seemed to do the trick. The customs man was armed with a Type 56 assault rifle, the Chinese knockoff of the Russian AK-47. Holliday thought that kind of hardware was a little extreme for a border crossing populated by more goats than people, but then again, for a country that had been at war in some form or another since Muhammad Ahmad bin Abd Allah came out of the desert in 1881 claiming to be the Mahdi, the Second Coming, carrying weapons in the Sudan was probably second nature.

The customs official followed them out of the little hut, weapon across his chest, still staring at the Rolex. Holliday didn't take his eye off the man's trigger finger until they were well on their way.

"That was fun," said Rafi.

"Serves you right for wearing that thing in public," said Peggy. "I wasn't sure if he was going to propose marriage or shoot you."

They went west for another hour, eventually finding

their way along rutted dirt roads to the two-lane black-top of the Pan African Highway. There was nothing to see but the desert, scorched by the blinding sun.

They thumped onto the highway and turned north.

"I'm beginning to wonder if this whole thing is a such good idea," said Holliday.

"What do you mean?" Rafi asked.

"We're already keeping things from the Ethiopian government, not the most stable bunch in the world, and to get in through Kolingba's back door we're going to have to go through Sudan or Chad—once again, not models of stability."

"It's not like I'm trying to steal anything," argued Rafi. "This is about knowledge; it's not a treasure hunt."

"Tell that to Kolingba," answered Holliday with a grimace. "As I recall his big rant has something to do with white colonials and Jews raping the entire African continent, and his backyard in particular. It's the same party line Amin used in Uganda, and we all know how that ended up."

"So we just give it up? The biggest archaeological find since King Tut, and we just give it up?" Rafi asked bitterly.

"We think about it," said Holliday. "We think about what's at stake."

They drove on in silence, each of them lost in their own thoughts.

"Sometimes I wonder why countries like this exist," Peggy said finally, staring out the windows. Holliday looked ahead. There was traffic in the distance now, a sure sign they were getting close to Khartoum.

"It wasn't always like this," said Rafi. "This whole area was once like Kansas, or the veldt country of Kenya. Enough rain for crops and grazing for animals as large as elephants; there were even forest areas."

"Hard to believe," said Holliday. They were pulling up on a battered tan Land Rover that looked like it belonged in a World War Two movie.

"Some geologists see the Sahara as a living thing, moving slowly from west to east and north to south. There's a whole school of thought that says the Sahara is on a cyclical schedule, growing and shrinking, growing and shrinking over millions of years."

A hundred yards ahead of them the Land Rover suddenly lurched and then swerved, striking the low railing of a bridge spanning a dry waterbed far below.

"Holy crap!" Peggy said.

The Land Rover climbed the rail, swung sideways and then toppled off the bridge. Rafi quickly checked the rearview, then braked. They were a few yards onto the bridge.

"Flat tire?" Rafi said.

"Maybe," answered Holliday. He looked around. The only feature on the trackless desert was a low, stony ridge away to their right.

"What do we do?" Peggy said.

"We see if anyone survived," Holliday said. He pushed open the door and stepped out onto the road. The heat hit him like a slap in the face. "Bring some rope," he said over his shoulder to Rafi. He slammed the door and sprinted across the deserted highway to the bridge abutment.

Holliday stared down into the shallow gorge. The old Land Rover was on its back like a turtle, smoke and steam wafting up from the rear of the vehicle. Quickly, Holliday estimated the distance from the bridge to the hard-packed bottom of the ancient watercourse; the Land Rover had fallen at least thirty or forty feet. In this part of the world, the chance that it was equipped with seat belts was nonexistent, which meant that the driver and whatever passengers were accompanying him would have been thrown around like dice in a craps cup. The odds of anyone surviving the fall were slim.

Rafi appeared with a skein of rope.

"How much is there here?" Holliday asked.

"Twenty-five meters." Eighty feet.

"Should be enough."

Holliday looped a quick double-figure-eight knot around one of the bridge rail pipes, pulled it taut, then eased himself over the edge. The side of the shallow gorge was a mixture of rock, baked mud and crumbling sand. Without the rope, getting down to the overturned

Rover would have been impossible. He reached the bottom and stepped back, looking upward.

Rafi was already on the rope, the first-aid kit from the Land Cruiser dangling from his shoulder on its strap. Holliday didn't wait. He crossed the cracked-mud surface of the bottom of the gorge and approached the overturned Rover. The driver's-side door hung open, twisted and bent. Smoke and steam were coming up out of the crumpled engine compartment.

He reached the door and squatted down. The windshield was shattered, covering the driver in a glittering shroud. The man's eyes were closed and there was blood coming out of his mouth and nose. There was also a large bloodstain on the front of the man's tan shirt. The stain went from the left center of the man's chest and spread down his shirt to the belt of his shorts.

The man was still breathing, but only barely. Holliday gently eased him out of the vehicle and onto the sand. It was at that point that Holliday saw the ragged hole in the back of the seat and the matching entry wound in the man's back.

"We've got trouble," he said as Rafi joined him. "He's been shot, whoever he is. Large-caliber through the back of the seat and into his lungs."

"Bandits?" Rafi asked. He paled and looked back up to the top of the gorge. "Peggy!"

"Not bandits," said Holliday. "Bandits aren't that accurate. This was an assassination. There's a pro out there somewhere."

"We've got to get him to some kind of hospital."

"Move him and he's dead," said Holliday. There was a cold distance in his voice. He'd seen this kind of thing too often to disguise it with platitudes. The bullet had probably chewed up the man's insides like a Weedwacker.

"Why this guy?" Rafi asked, stunned. He stared at the man, listening to the bubbling, ragged breath.

"Get his wallet; find out who he is."

Holliday ducked back into the overturned truck; he'd seen two things of interest when he dragged the body out: an old, well-worn leather dispatch case and the familiar shape of a canvas rifle case. He tossed the dispatch case out through the open doorway, then clambered farther into the interior of the truck and grabbed the rifle case. He wriggled backward, hanging on to the gun case, and ducked out into the open. Rafi was leaning over the wounded man, listening intently. As Holliday opened the back flap of the gun case he heard a shouting voice echoing from above.

"What's going on down there?"

Holliday looked up to see Peggy, camera slung around her neck, peering over the bridge rail.

"Get down!" Holliday yelled.

"Peggy!" Rafi yelled, still crouched over the dying man.

There was a clanging sound and the whine of a bullet ricocheting off one of the bridge stanchions less than a foot from where she was standing. A split second later echoed the cracking sound of the gunshot. Peggy screamed and jerked back.

"Get behind the truck!" Holliday yelled. Peggy didn't need to be told twice. She dropped out of sight. Holliday pulled the gun out of its case. The weapon was an old-fashioned Winchester 76 complete with a modern Swift 687M telescopic sight and a canvas sling. Holliday rummaged around in the case and came up with a fistful of rounds. The original caliber had been 45.40 but these shells looked like .357 magnums. He took a long, desperate minute to slide the rounds into the loading port.

"He's dead," said Rafi, staring down at the body of the man from the Rover.

Holliday slung the loaded rifle over his shoulder. "We're not." He headed for the rope and then began to climb.

"Son of a bitch!" Mike Harris stared through the big Steiner binoculars at the road below. He was flat on his belly at the top of the ridge above the bridge. Seeing Holliday getting out of the Land Cruiser was like a nightmare come to life.

"What's the matter?" said the man with the rifle, lying beside him. His name was Pieter Jonker, an ex–Project Barnacle assassin provided by Faulkener. "I got the *krimpie*, didn't I?"

"You missed the woman, you idiot!"

"I wasn't hired to shoot the *dom doos* woman, was I, mate?" Jonker said. "I can't help it if a Good Samaritan comes along."

Harris kept his eyes glued to the binoculars. He saw Holliday crawl up over the top of the gorge, something slung over his back.

"You want him dead, too?" Jonker asked, his eye up to the rifle scope.

"Shoot!" Harris bellowed.

Jonker squeezed the trigger of the Truvelo CMS rifle. A puff of sand erupted inches from Holliday's head.

"Mutterficker!" Jonker snarled.

The sound of the rifle hammered painfully in Harris's ear. He winced. When his eyes opened again Holliday was gone.

"God damn it! You missed again!" Harris yelled.

"Loop naai, pommie," said Jonker, curling his lip.

Suddenly the top of the sandy ridge exploded an inch away from Harris and his companion. A rock chip tore a gash in Harris's cheek. A split second later the sound of four or five rapidly fired rounds reached them. In an instant Jonker was wriggling backward down the back slope of the ridge.

"Get back here!"

"I signed on to shoot, not to get shot at," said Jonker, scuttling backward, leaving the heavy weapon behind. "I did my job. The *krimpie*'s dead."

"I need his briefcase!"

"Not my problem."

The binoculars shattered into splinters of glass and hard plastic as a shot from below found its mark. A razor-edged piece of glass almost took out Harris's eye. He followed Jonker down the slope.

Holliday drove, Rafi on the seat beside him with the dead man's briefcase on his lap. Peggy kept an eye on the road behind them. They'd waited for almost an hour, until Holliday was certain that the shooter had gone. Ten minutes after the first shots, they heard the sound of an engine in the distance, then only silence. Before leaving the bridge Holliday picked up his brass and wiped down the rifle. That done, he'd tossed the weapon back into the gorge. The last thing he needed was to be found with an unlicensed weapon by a roving Sudanese army patrol.

"According to his driver's permit his name was Archibald Arthur Ives," said Rafi, going through the dead man's wallet. "From the papers in his briefcase it would appear that he's a freelance geologist working for a company called Matheson Resource Industries. There are some maps but I'll have to give them a closer look when we get to Khartoum."

"Anything else?"

"A satellite phone."

"We can check the call list, I guess," said Holliday.

"You don't sound too eager, Doc. Aren't we going to report this?" Peggy asked, still watching the highway behind her.

"I don't think we can," answered Holliday. "Not without getting ourselves seriously in the glue." He shrugged. "What would be the point? We were just in the wrong place at the wrong time. Somebody wanted this guy Ives dead and I for one don't have the foggiest idea why."

"He said something before he died," said Rafi. "I don't know what it means."

"What did he say?" Holliday asked.

"'Limbani,'" said Rafi. "'Tell Amobe Limbani.'"

7

"So who is he exactly?" Holliday asked.

Peggy looked up from the laptop. She'd been surfing the Net for most of the afternoon, using the Wi-Fi hookup in their apartment suite at the Grand Holiday Villa Hotel & Suites in Khartoum. For a hotel built in 1880, it was remarkably up-to-date. It was also remarkably expensive.

"Dr. Amobe Barthélemy Limbani, sixty-three years old when the coup took place. Medical degree from the Université de Paris, specializing in tropical and infectious diseases. His father was also a doctor and also governor of the Vakaga prefecture, of what had originally been part of French Equatorial Africa. Limbani was part of the Yakima minority. When his father died under mysterious circumstances he ran for the governor's job and got in."

"Who are the majority?" Rafi asked.

"Baya and Banda. They're sixty-five percent of the

population. In Vakaga it's more like eighty-five percent. The Yakima are less than ten percent."

"If they're in the majority how did Limbani get the votes to become governor?" Rafi asked.

"The Banda and the Baya are rural tribal villagers without much use for or knowledge of the outside world. The literacy rate is much higher among the Yakima, who are mostly shopkeepers and merchants, or at least they were."

"Presumably Kolingba's a Banda or a Baya," said Holliday.

"Banda. One of the 'lucky' ones who got sent to a missionary school. He ran away, joined the army and the rest is history. There's a story that after the coup one of the first things he did was go back to the missionary school and hack the nuns into pieces."

"What about Limbani?" Rafi asked.

"Either he died in prison outside Fourandao or he escaped and went into the jungle. There are all sorts of stories about Limbani organizing a rebel army in the jungle à la Castro, but there's no real evidence of any rebellion. In fact if anything things have gone from bad to worse. In the past two years Kolingba's power has spread to Bamingui-Bangoran and Haute-Kotto, the two neighboring prefectures to Vakaga. That's almost a third of the Central African Republic. The borders with Sudan and Chad are wide-open. It's Wild West time for crooks of all kinds, arms dealers, druggies, terrorists, slavers, conflict minerals, you name it."

"What about the maps?" Holliday asked, turning to Rafi. The archaeologist had the contents of Ives's dispatch case spread out on the coffee table in the living room of their suite. Outside the picture window, the White Nile stretched toward the junction with its small sister, the Blue Nile.

"The Kotto River flows out of the Sudan massif. He drew these maps himself. I can't make heads or tails of the grid references, but it matches exactly with the Google Earth images I took from the geography of the image in the tomb. Three hills and a triple-forked cataract. According to Ives's maps, he found what he was looking for on the largest of the three hills."

"Don't tell me," said Peggy. "Gold and diamonds. King Solomon's Mines."

"He found gold and diamonds, all right," said Rafi, "but according to this that's not what he was looking for."

"Spill it," said Peggy.

"He was looking for, and found, a gigantic deposit of something called neodymium at a concentration of almost seven thousand parts per million, and the same for something called tantalum."

"What on earth does that mean?" Peggy asked, bewildered.

"It means that Kolingba's sitting on something far

more valuable than a gold mine, or even a diamond mine," answered Holliday.

"I guess I've been out of the loop too long," said Peggy. "I don't get it."

"I do," said Rafi. "Most tantalum is mined in Australia, but it's a lot cheaper to buy it from the warlords in the Congo. Neodymium is mined only in China and they've steadily been shutting down the market over the past few years."

"So what?" Peggy shrugged.

"You can't make cell phones, computer hard drives, nuclear reactors and most electronic gadgets without them. Tantalum is used in the guts of jet engines. If Kolingba found out he was sitting on a pile of the stuff, Kukuanaland would become the most strategically important nation in the world."

"The fairy dust of the twenty-first century," Peggy said.

"Steve Jobs probably thinks so. Bill Gates, too," Holliday added.

"What if Limbani found out about it first?" Rafi said slowly.

"The odds are Kolingba had him killed years ago," said Peggy, nodding toward the laptop. "That's what most people seem to believe."

"Not Ives," said Rafi.

"Rafi's right," said Holliday. "Somebody breathing his last doesn't mention a fantasy. He was obviously out there in the jungle. Maybe he *knew* Limbani was still alive. Maybe he met up with him, or someone who'd seen him."

"And we're supposed to warn him?" Peggy said.

"Something like that." Rafi nodded. "If Kolingba finds out about the deposits there's going to be hell to pay all over the world. If Limbani was the man to control it instead . . ."

"So who killed him?" Holliday said after a moment. "It wasn't Sudanese bandits armed with flintlocks. Whoever killed Ives was potshotting at us with a high-powered sniper rifle with a scope. We're lucky not to be vulture food right now."

"Matheson Resource Industries has to be behind it somewhere," said Peggy. "That's who he was working for, and according to what Google's giving me that kind of thing isn't exactly out of line with Matheson's background. In the seventies he bought a couple of old World War Two bombers and napalmed the local Yavaro Indians so they'd get off an oil patch he was developing in Brazil, all in the name of progress. There've been a few weird things between him and the Russians, too."

Holliday stared out the window at the majestic river flowing past. Did Vikings really make it this far, and farther, a thousand years ago? Did a Templar Knight follow in their footsteps, just as they were following in his? For a moment he had that strange sensation of the past and the future sliding together, just like the White

Nile and the Blue Nile joined together a mile or so downstream. He'd had the same feeling back on that little island on Lake Tana. Like being on a ship in rough seas and having someone walking over your grave at the same time. Once again he tried to shake the feeling off.

"Too much coincidence," he said finally. For the first time in a long while he wished he were still smoking. "I'll buy that we were on the same highway in the Sudan—we were both looking for the same thing—but what was Ives doing in that particular piece of jungle in the first place? Kukuanaland isn't what you'd call a tourist destination. It can't be just coincidence that Rafi finds that tomb and Matheson sends in a geologist to the same territory. There has to be some connection."

"I'm an archaeologist; Matheson hunts for mineral resources and oil. There *is* no connection," said Rafi, shaking his head.

"Did you tell *anyone* about the tomb?"

"He didn't even tell me, his loving wife and help-mate," said Peggy.

"I didn't tell anyone; I swear it," said Rafi. "I wasn't expecting to find anything in Ethiopia except some anecdotal stuff about the Beta Jews or some old church records at best. This all came out of left field. When I found the tomb I was a little freaked-out actually. I didn't know *what* to do. I still don't."

"How did you figure out that the mural in the tomb was this Kotto River place?"

"I listed the salient features, the jungle, the three prominent hills and the three-forked waterfall, and we ran a regional African computer model based on Google Earth. I was skeptical, like you, Doc. We weren't really expecting a match."

"We?"

"A friend of mine in the geology department. A geomorphologist named Yadin Isaacs. He ran the computers."

"Did you tell him why you were running the model?"

"I made a joke about King Solomon's Mines and the queen of Sheba. He thought it was funny."

"Any connection between Matheson and this guy?"

"Not that I know of." Rafi shrugged.

Peggy tapped at the keyboard for a few moments, then sat back, shaking her head. "It's right there on his CV," she said. "'Winner of the Sir James Matheson Grant for Outstanding Achievement in the Field of Geology,' three years running."

"Bingo," said Holliday. "People like Matheson have tentacles into all sorts of places. Your pal doesn't want to bite the hand that feeds him, so he passes on some potentially interesting information and doesn't think about it again." Holliday paused. "How long ago was this?"

"Seven months."

"Plenty of time to put Ives into the field," said Holliday. "It was no coincidence at all." He shook his head.

"It looks like we've got some competition. Lethal competition."

Sir James Matheson, Ninth Earl of Emsworth, referred to as Lord Emsworth of Huntington in the annual reports of Matheson Resource Industries, stood in his private office and stared down at the large-scale topographical maps laid out on the granite conference table. Matheson, in his early sixties, had a broad forehead, thinning gray hair swept back, with the leathery face and broken capillaries of a longtime smoker and drinker. When Matheson spoke there was a faint trace of his West Country origins, but that was the only hint of his somewhat less than lordly beginnings. Major Allen Faulkener, Matheson's director of special projects, stood beside him.

"What are the transportation options?" Matheson said. "The material is worth nothing in the middle of a jungle."

"Only the river at this point," said Faulkener, tapping a spot on one of the maps. "The Kotto River could take barges of ore all the way down to the Ubangi and from there down to Mbandaka and the Congo River."

"Where they'd have to be guarded all the way to Brazzaville and the railway, which we'd probably have to refurbish for the buggers."

"Yes, sir."

"And if we had our own refinery and smelter?"

"We could easily build an airstrip and ship the finished goods from there."

"But not without this lunatic Kolingba knowing."

"No, sir, and not without his Two-IC knowing, either."

"I was never actually *in* the army, Faulkener, so terms like Two-IC don't impress me."

"Yes, sir."

"You mean his second in command, this Gash fellow. The American."

"Rwandan by birth, sir. He did spend time in the United States."

"Can we deal with him?"

"Perhaps at some later point," suggested Faulkener. "Right now his loyalties lie with Kolingba. His cash cow, so to speak."

"Has he been approached?"

"Only obliquely. He met with one of his bankers a few days ago in Banqui, the capital city of the Central African Republic. The banker sometimes works for us. He asked Gash's opinion about the possibility that a change of leadership might be more fruitful—that is, profitable."

"And?"

"Gash quoted the adage about birds in the hand being more valuable than those in the bush. Our man didn't pursue it."

"Can we deal with Kolingba at any level?"

"I doubt it, sir. He is a practitioner of Bwiti."

"Bwiti?"

"It's a religion, sir. He thinks he's the high priest. He takes huge doses of a plant-based drug called Tabernanthe iboga. It gives him visions, which he then acts on as domestic policy. He once had an iboga dream or a vision of boiling a traitorous man alive, his cousin, actually."

"And he acted on this?"

"The very next day, sir, along with the man's wife. In a fifty-gallon drum, as I understand it."

"He's mad, then," said Matheson.

"As a hatter, sir." Faulkener nodded.

"Oh, well," said Matheson. "I suppose he really will have to go; there's no other option." He stared down at the maps. "What about Harris, by the way?"

"He dealt with Ives, but as the Americans say, he's dropped the ball. Witnesses who have to be dealt with. The Israeli archaeologist who put us onto the whole thing in the first place, as a matter of fact."

"He's out of it, then?"

"I'm afraid so, Sir James, unless he suddenly gets very lucky."

"Then find me someone else to deal with Kolingba," said Matheson quietly. "And do it quickly. Too many people know about this already."

"Yes, sir."

8

Oliver Gash—the former Rwandan refugee turned Baltimore narcotics kingpin, turned secretary of state and foreign affairs for an insane African king—hadn't risen to his exalted position by being stupid. Even as a runner for the gangs in McElderry Park he knew the value of good intelligence. The cops used paid informers, so he did, too, except he paid his people better. By the time he was moving real weight through the I-95 corridor he was using encrypted satellite phones, GPS, social networking sites with peepers and listeners on his payroll from the state's attorney's office to the police garage. If something was going down he wanted to hear about it *before* it happened. As Solomon Kolingba's second in command, if somebody was even *thinking* about doing something he wanted to know about it first.

Right from the start he'd had trouble with the whole Limbani thing. In public Kolingba insisted that Limbani died in a cell in Ouanda Djallé prison three years ago.

Nobody was about to call Kolingba a liar but there had been persistent reports of the doctor's survival almost from the beginning. At first Gash had put it down to wishful thinking and mythmaking, but now he wasn't so sure. Only a few moments ago one of his "listening posts"—a man named Aristide Lundi who operated a banana beer and palm wine stand in Bangara village—reported that a half dozen men in camouflage fatigues had appeared out of the jungle. Two of them had gotten drunk and told Lundi that they were members of CALA, the Central African Liberation Army led by Amobe Limbani. Their hope, of course, was that Lundi would give them their beer out of fear but Lundi also reported that the six men were definitely members of the Yakima minority and spoke the Dendi dialect common to those people.

Bangara was almost a hundred miles away from Fourandao, but it was also on the Kotto River—too close for comfort as far as Gash was concerned. It was the fifth time in ten months that he'd heard about the phantom Central African Liberation Army, but it was the first time he'd heard Limbani's name attached to it.

He listened to the sound of snoring coming from Kolingba's office next door. He was having his "refresher," the long afternoon nap that allowed him to stay up until all hours of the night expounding on everything from Galileo's fundamental errors of mathematics to the proper way to cook hyena meat. An evening with King Kolingba was usually as exhausting as it was boring, but they had to be endured. Gash stood up, strapped on the holstered .45 automatic that went with his colonel's uniform and went across the plaza to the hotel. He needed a good stiff drink and a moment to think about Dr. Limbani and his liberation army.

Konrad Lanz got out of the cab in front of the address he'd been given, paid the driver and watched as the cab drove away. There were spotlights in the shrubbery, aimed upward at all five stories of the Cheyne Walk town house. His prospective client clearly had a great deal of money—always a good sign. Lanz pushed open the wrought-iron gate, went up three steps and rang the bell. He could faintly hear chamber music coming from inside. Brahms's Piano Trio in C minor, Op. 101. A good choice for entertaining a German mercenary. The door was opened by a butler in full livery and the music got louder. Lanz could tell that the music was live. Piano, violin and cello. As a child, he'd heard a recording of his grandfather performing the piece. The old man had unfortunately been first violin for the Berliner Philharmoniker under the Nazi Wilhelm Furtwängler. He'd been killed during a bombing raid in March 1944.

"Yes?" the butler asked.

"Major Faulkener asked me to come," said Lanz in unaccented English. "My name is Lanz."

"Of course, sir. The colonel is in the study. Please follow me."

Lanz stepped into a marble-floored foyer. Under the sound of the Brahms he could hear the chattering of conversations and clinking glasses that suggested a cocktail party down a hall and to his left. The butler went to the right around a flight of centrally positioned stairs and paused in front of a closed door. The butler knocked, opened the door and stood aside. Lanz stepped into the study.

The room was large and masculine. The ceiling was paneled in dark oak, and waist-high built-in bookcases ran around the room, interrupted by a pair of tall windows on one end and an ornate wood-burning fireplace at the other. There was a Georgian kneehole desk to the left of the fireplace with a matching secretary beside it serving as a wet bar. A gigantic Oriental carpet covered almost the entire floor. The rest of the furniture was dark green leather, and the gilt-framed paintings above the bookcases were all oils. Lanz recognized several military paintings, including a portrait of Lawrence of Arabia by Augustus John. Money and good taste—a rare combination in the twenty-first century. A man in a dark suit with a full head of silver hair and a well-trimmed mustache sat in one of the leather club chairs smoking what Lanz assumed to be an expensive cigar. There was a crystal glass of some sort of amber liquid sitting on a lacquered end table. Presumably this was the mysterious Major Faulkener, the man who'd sent him the ten thousand euros as an enticement to get him off his Tuscan farm.

"You'd be Lanz," said the man.

"That's right."

"Faulkener. Drink?"

"No, thank you."

"Have a seat."

Lanz sat down across from the silver-haired man.

Major Allen Faulkener did a quick assessment of the man who'd just sat down opposite him. Konrad Lanz was dressed like a Tuscan farmer, which he professed to be. He wore a slightly worn but quite expensive linen shirt, a narrow suede tie and a creased, chocolate-colored leather bomber jacket that looked as though he'd had it for years. The shoes were expensive but thick-soled and practical.

Lanz looked to be in his early fifties, with the rough, tanned look of a man who spent a great deal of time outdoors—once again, the image of a Tuscan farmer. Except the creases, lines and permanent tan didn't come from life under a benevolent Italian sun. The weathering on this man's face was equatorial and harsh, the parchment crinkling around the cold, ice blue eyes coming from squinting down the barrel of a gun. Even in his sixth decade the man's belly looked flat and hard and there were thick cords of muscle in his neck. The scarred, sinewy hands looked like they could crack walnuts or splinter teeth. According to the pedigree Faulkener had assembled, Konrad Lanz had fought as a mercenary in every African war since the Congolese Kisangani Mutinies in the late sixties, starting as a wet-behind-the-ears eighteen-year-old looking for adventure. He'd found it.

"How is Tuscany?" Faulkener asked pleasantly.

"Hot," answered Lanz.

"You've lived there a long time?"

"Yes."

The battered, energetic figure of Sir James Matheson stepped into the room. His face had the unhealthy flush of high blood pressure and there were dark bags under his eyes. Matheson closed the door behind him and turned the latch. Lanz stood up and so did Faulkener.

"Mr. Lanz, this is, uh, Mr. Smith."

Lanz turned to Faulkener, a look of weary irritation on his face. "Actually it's lieutenant colonel, Major Faulkener, and I haven't spent the last eight hours driving to Milan and flying here to be treated like an idiot." Lanz turned back to Matheson. "You're Sir James Matheson, Ninth Earl of Emsworth, majority shareholder in Matheson Resource Industries. Your address and a computer reverse directory told me that much. The ten thousand euros tells me you have a serious problem that you need solved militarily." Lanz paused. "How am I doing, Lord Emsworth?"

"Bravo, sir!" Matheson said. He went to the bar, poured himself a tumbler of neat Talisker single-malt and sat behind the desk. Lanz and Faulkener took their seats again. Lanz could still faintly hear the chamber music. The three-piece orchestra had switched to Beethoven's "Triple Concerto" in C major, Op. 56. Another German. Lanz wondered if Matheson had chosen the music on purpose. Looking at the man he rather doubted it; somehow the industrialist didn't look as though he had that sort of subtle nature.

"You know of Solomon Kolingba, I'm sure," Matheson said.

"The breakaway dictator in the Central African Republic." Lanz nodded.

"Indeed," said Matheson. "What is your opinion on the stability of his regime?"

"Politically or militarily?"

"Either."

"I have no idea." Lanz shrugged. "At a guess I'd say he'll be like most upstart dictators in Africa. He'll have his day in the sun but he doesn't even have the veneer of sanity, so eventually he'll be deposed himself. It's inevitable."

"Deposed from within?" Matheson asked, sipping his Talisker.

"As opposed to what?" Lanz asked, although he had a fairly good idea where this was heading.

"As opposed to a coup d'état from an outside source," said Faulkener bluntly.

"A mercenary force?" Lanz asked.

"That's why you're here, Colonel Lanz," said Faulkener crisply. Lanz could feel the silver-haired man itching to use the word *Oberstleutnant*, or better yet, *Obersturmbannführer*.

"I have no idea about Kolingba's military strength."

"We can give you all of that," said Faulkener. "But if Kolingba is killed and the garrison is taken the coup would be a fait accompli. The regular army is a farce, small-time warlords at the very best."

"You have someone to replace Kolingba with?"

"Several candidates. His second in command is the most likely," replied Faulkener.

"He has no loyalty to Kolingba?" Lanz asked.

"He's a very greedy man," said Matheson. "His only loyalty is to himself."

"In my opinion once Kolingba is removed everything else will fall into place," said Faulkener.

"But if I am to do this thing, it is not your opinion that is important, Major Faulkener; it is mine."

Faulkener's face reddened but he remained silent.

"What's the first step?" Matheson asked.

"A reconnaissance," said Lanz.

"To Fourandao, the capital?" Faulkener said.

"Certainly." Lanz nodded.

"We expected that," said Matheson.

"We have a cover prepared," said Faulkener. "There's not much in the way of tourism in Kukuanaland, so we've made you an official with an NGO specializing in foreign aid. We've got a passport, contact numbers, a complete legend that will play out if anyone investigates."

"I know nothing of foreign aid," said Lanz. "Nor do I have any interest in learning. I am a soldier. I'll provide my own cover."

"As what, may I ask?" Faulkener said, reddening again. Lanz was nothing but a hired gun, but he seemed to have taken over the meeting completely.

"As a dealer in small arms," said Lanz, smiling. "Something General Kolingba and I have in common."

"When?" Matheson asked.

"As soon as possible."

"Excellent!" Matheson said. He tossed off the last of the Talisker. "How much?"

"For the reconnaissance and my report?"

"Yes."

"One hundred thousand euros. Fifty thousand now, paid into my account in Liechtenstein, the balance when you get my report."

"A little steep, don't you think, Lanz?" Faulkener said.

"You're asking me to step into the lion's den, Major Faulkener. I think the price is fair. If you don't think so I can always go back to Tuscany."

"The price is fine," interrupted Matheson. "Go to Fourandao. Get me that report as soon as possible."

9

For all its storied, bloody history, Khartoum is a relatively young city. Established in 1821 by Ibrahim Pasha as an outpost of the Egyptian army, Khartoum grew into a major trading town for slave traders. Nestled on a peninsula where the Blue Nile and the White Nile converge, the city was strategically located, and in 1884 the self-styled Mahdi, or Messiah, of the Arab people laid siege to and eventually massacred the Anglo-Egyptian garrison under British General Charles George Gordon. The British got their revenge thirteen years later when General Herbert Kitchener routed the Mahdist forces in the town of Omdurman on the other side of the river. Patriotic to a fault, Lord Kitchener laid out the new city of Khartoum with a street plan designed like the Union Jack.

Like many African cities Khartoum has two faces: the oil-rich city of lavish resorts, exotic architecture and luxurious apartment buildings and, at the same time, a city of terrible poverty, with children selling stale food products in the souks, or markets, massive inflation and unemployment, lack of fresh water or sewage treatment, an active criminal trade in women and children and a massive black market trade in just about anything you could name.

"This can't be right," said Peggy, looking out the grimy window of the Land Cruiser. They were on an unpaved street in south Khartoum. Most of the buildings were low, cheap industrial structures made from concrete blocks with flat, rusty, corrugated iron roofs. The majority looked empty, what few windows they had filthy and broken. At some time in the past there had obviously been a flood, as the marks of the high-water line could be seen clearly on the buildings.

"It's what it said on that bit of hotel stationery in Ives's dispatch case," answered Rafi. "'Trans,' which we can assume means transportation; 'Mutwakil Osman, end of Al-Hamdab Street, over railway tracks. Look for old abandoned Petronas station on left.'" Rafi pointed. "There's the Petronas station, there's the end of the street, and we passed over the railway tracks a half dozen blocks ago."

"There's nothing here except the Nile River and some barges," said Holliday, pulling the Land Cruiser to a stop. Directly in front of the truck the road ended in a patch of weeds that turned into the rough, sloping bank of the Nile. A set of rickety wooden stairs led down to a narrow concrete walkway and several wooden docks that jutted out into the sluggish, wind-ruffled water. Several gigantic barges were moored to the docks, most of them clearly used for dredging Nile mud. Two others were fitted with large ribbed Quonset huts that appeared to be World War Two vintage. Holliday climbed out of the truck. Rafi and Peggy followed. It was hot but the light, faintly aromatic breeze coming off the river was refreshingly cool.

"Surely he didn't take a boat," said Rafi, frowning.

"Is the Kotto River a tributary of the Nile?" Peggy asked.

"No, but it's the same drainage basin. In the Sudan it's called the Bahr al-Arab," explained Rafi. "I suppose you could take a boat of some kind but it wouldn't be easy."

"Crocodiles?" Peggy asked.

"Hungry ones." Rafi grinned, throwing an affectionate arm across Peggy's shoulder.

"Let's check it out," suggested Holliday. He headed down the wobbly steps to the rough concrete pier. The breeze was stronger here and there was something else in the air: the familiar smell of gasoline.

Rafi and Peggy came down the steps after him. They walked along the pier until they reached the first one of the barges fitted with a Quonset hut. There was a door set into the side of the hut with a cardboard sign duct-taped to it that read, OSMAN AIR SERVICES.

"I don't see a runway anywhere," said Peggy.

They trooped down the single-width gangplank to the Quonset hut. Holliday rapped on the door. It rattled on its hinges. Overhead a bright, iridescent Nile Valley sunbird flitted toward the riverbank.

"Dakhaltum!" called out a muffled voice. Holliday could make out the sound of something like a lathe and the muffled clatter of a generator.

"It either means come in or go away," said Peggy.

"It means enter," said Rafi. "It's Sudanese. Open the door." Holliday lifted the latch and stepped inside.

The front half of the gloomy curved structure was fitted out as a combination living space and machine shop. There was an area for welding, a lathe, a drill press, racks of welding and a brazing rod and something up on trestles that looked suspiciously like an elongated sheet-metal banana covered in rust-colored primer paint. The other side of the space was given over to a narrow cot, a kitchen table, cupboards, a small stove and a large laundry sink. The back half of the Quonset hut was blocked off by an unpainted plywood bulkhead. In the center of the bulkhead was a rolling garage-door mechanism with an overhead set of rails.

A man in a white apron was standing at the stove stirring something steaming in a small aluminum pot.

"Aasalaamu Aleikum," said Rafi.

"Wa-Aleikum Aassalaam, effendi,*"* replied the man in the apron. He smiled pleasantly. "Chunky chicken," he said, gesturing toward the pot with a wooden spoon. "Care to join me? It's Campbell's." The man was short, slim, dark-skinned and wearing an ornately embroidered pillbox-shaped *kufi* on his head. He appeared to be in his middle forties. His accent was from somewhere in the American South.

"Mr. Mutwakil Osman?" Rafi asked.

"I went to the Riverside Military Academy in Gainesville, Georgia," said the man in the apron. "You have any idea what it was like being named Mutwakil in Gainesville, Georgia? My friends call me Donny."

"Donny Osman?" Peggy laughed.

"Hey, it's better than Mutwakil, believe me."

"You're American?" Rafi asked.

"Born and raised. My parents were both Sudanese. I've been living here since 2002." He shrugged. "Things weren't the same for Muslims after nine/eleven." He grimaced. "Especially if you fly airplanes for a living. I had a little puddle-jumper air transport company. It went bust in six months." He shrugged again. "Anyway, that's my story." He poured the soup into a bowl, carried the bowl over to the little kitchen table and began to eat. "What can I do for you folks?" He eyed them carefully, paying particular attention to Holliday. "Nobody comes here by accident."

"Archibald Ives," said Holliday flatly.

"Archie? Sure, what about him?"

"What's the connection?"

"What business is it of yours?"

"We found your name among his personal effects," said Holliday bluntly, looking for a reaction.

"Personal effects?"

"He's dead. Murdered."

The Sudanese man's face fell. "I knew it," he said softly.

"Knew what?" Holliday asked.

"Knew it was trouble right from the start."

"What was trouble?"

Osman put down his soup spoon and sighed. "I've been taking people into dangerous places for years," he said. "But this time it was *too* dangerous. The whole thing smelled, you know?"

"What whole thing?"

"Matheson for one, Kukuanaland for another."

"Because of Kolingba?"

"Limbani as well." Osman nodded.

"What about Limbani?" Rafi asked.

"Limbani's like Kolingba's white whale, or Marley's Ghost from *A Christmas Carol*."

"Explain," Holliday said.

"Limbani haunts Kolingba. He got away during the coup and ever since then Kolingba's been worrying about Limbani organizing some kind of rebel army in the jungle like Fidel and Che. He smokes that iboga stuff or snorts it or eats it or whatever you do and he has visions of Limbani and his hordes coming out of the woodwork like cockroaches."

"Limbani's a myth?" Peggy asked.

"Who knows?" Osman shrugged. "The point is, Kolingba's got patrols of his thugs roaming around in the bush shooting anything on two legs. There's a hundred-thousand-dollar reward for Limbani's head on a stick."

"And you took Ives there?" Rafi said.

"Archie seemed like a big boy—was a big boy. I thought he could take care of himself. He said it was his big chance. The strike that he could retire on."

"Well, he's retired now; that's for sure," said Peggy.

"Where exactly did you take him?" Holliday asked.

"Pretty much the end of the world," said Osman. "Seven hundred miles southwest of here. Just before the Bahr al-Arab River turns into the Kotto River there's a little place called Umm Rawq. That's where I took him. He didn't tell me where he was going other than down the Kotto for a few days."

"What's in this Umm Rawq place?" Holliday asked.

"A fish market, a dock, a store, a village, or what's left of it."

"Why Umm Rawq?"

"It's right on the border and he could rent a boat. That's the last time I saw him, heading upriver in the local steamer."

"Was there anybody with him?"

"A guide. A local. I think his name was Mahmoud."

There was a pause. Finally Peggy spoke. "How exactly did you get him to this Umm Rawq place?"

Osman smiled. He got up from the table, went to the big garage door and pushed it upward. The door rattled along the rails and they saw what was on the other side of the plywood bulkhead.

"I'll be damned," whispered Holliday. "She must be fifty years old."

"Sixty-six," said Osman proudly. Moored in a water-filled dock cut into the rear of the barge was a pure white Catalina PBY flying boat, its hull riding easily on the river, its single high wing making the aircraft look like a gigantic graceful bird about to take flight. The triple-bladed black-lacquered propellers on the twin engines gleamed. "I bought her from the South African Air Force nine years ago and flew her up here from Johannesburg." He stepped out onto the dock and looked up at the aircraft affectionately. The others followed him through the open doorway. "I spent a year refitting her, getting parts and restoring her. She and I have been partners ever since."

"She's beautiful," said Holliday, meaning it. The flying boat was a wonderful piece of history elegantly salvaged.

There was a long silence as the group stood there admiring the aircraft. Far out on the river a Nile sight-seeing boat went by, the booming electronic voice of a tour guide echoing over the water.

"This is what you call a Bono moment," said Peggy.

"A what?" Rafi asked.

Holliday sighed. "I think she means this is a moment of conscience."

"You'll have to explain that," said Rafi. "Pop stars aren't my forte."

"It means we're in a bit of a moral quandary," said Holliday. "Right now Kolingba and his little crime patch are a bit of a joke. Give him a trillion-dollar mineral find and he won't be a joke anymore."

"What are we supposed to do about it?" Rafi said. "I'm here for the archaeology, not a pitched battle."

"What *do* we do, Doc?" Peggy asked.

"We either do nothing, or we try to find Limbani and make it an equal playing field." He turned to Osman. "You'll take us to Umm Rawq?"

"Sure." Donny Osman nodded. "I'm in."

"Me, too," said Peggy.

Rafi sighed. "I just wanted to find King Solomon's Mines and now I'm going into a war zone."

10

Konrad Lanz ducked through the oval doorway of the ancient Air Mali Ilyushin Il-18 and stood on the stairs for a second, looking out over the Fourandao airport, officially known as Kolingba International, even though the single cracked concrete runway was less than twenty-five hundred feet long and the bedraggled-looking terminal wasn't even equipped with radar.

The terminal was a single, squat building made of concrete blocks, a rudimentary tower jutting up from the center of the structure. To the left was a fuel dump, and a small parking lot lay on the right. To the side of the doorway into the terminal Lanz could see something that looked very much like a Soviet BTR-40 armored personnel carrier, but he guessed it was more likely a Type 55 Chinese knockoff.

He went down the stairs, following the dozen or so other passengers on the flight from Bamako as they headed for the terminal. Lanz had been in dozens of airports like this and he knew their strengths and weak-nesses. As he passed the armored car he saw that it was, as suspected, the Chinese version of a BTR-40. Two men lounged in front of the machine, both in jungle fatigues, paratrooper boots and aviator-style mirrored sunglasses. Both carried Tokarev submachine guns that dated back to World War Two.

Like the weapons, the armored car was older than both the men leaning on it. Rust stained the front end, a headlight was missing and the windshield was so filthy it was opaque. The vehicle also had a decided list to the right, indicating to Lanz that either the tires were soft or the suspension was blown. The Chinese vehicle might as well have been on a stand with a brass plaque, because it obviously hadn't moved in a very long time. It stood to reason; the Chinese were free enough with their ordnance and their vehicles, but maintaining them was a different story. Running vehicles like the Type 55 required a parts depot, mechanics and a motor pool, the dull everyday workings of a real army, something that dictators like Kolingba had very little interest in. On the other hand a pair of Kamov Ka-52 "Alligator" attack helicopters on a hardstand next to the main terminal looked extremely well maintained.

Lanz stepped into the terminal. There was no doubt about immigration and customs protocol. An open area under two slowly spinning ceiling fans with two wooden desks and two wooden examination tables was obviously for locals returning home, while a closed door had a sign over it that said, FOREIGN VISITORS ONLY. Lanz opened the door and stepped inside.

There were three uniformed men in a small, window-less room with a gray tiled floor. The uniform was the same as those of the men lounging around in front of the armored car outside. One of the men sat behind a scarred wooden office desk, while a second man stood beside him and the third man stood in front of the exit door leading out of the room. There was a wooden examination table to the right of the desk. The two standing men wore mirrored aviator sunglasses, while the man behind the desk did not. The two guards carried what looked like Tokarev TT-30 automatic pistols in cheap belt holsters. A framed photograph of Solomon Kolingba hung on the wall behind the man at the desk. There was a wooden bench running along the wall opposite the desk.

Lanz stepped up to the desk and waited silently. The man behind the desk stared up at him. He was in his forties, the first gray showing at his temples. He wore round, stainless-steel-framed glasses. The name strip on his fatigues read, SAINT-SYLVESTRE; not surprising, since the Central African Republic had once been part of French Equatorial Africa.

"Passport."

Lanz reached into the inner pocket of his cream-colored linen jacket and took out a passport. It was dark blue with CANADA stamped in gold above the Canadian coat of arms. He handed it over.

Behind the desk Saint-Sylvestre leafed through the blank pages. "Canadian?"

"Yes."

"Your name is Konrad Lanz?"

"Yes."

"Not a Canadian name."

"My parents were Austrian. I immigrated as a child."

"You don't travel a great deal, I see."

"On the contrary," said Lanz. "I travel a great deal. You will notice the day of issue was only two months ago."

"A brand-new passport."

"The previous one was full." In fact, Lanz had a number of passports but Canadian ones were easiest to get and he preferred to use brand-new documents when traveling to a country he had never visited before. God only knew which countries a madman like Kolingba disliked or had been offended by in his addled psyche.

Lanz had spent a week researching Kukuanaland and its leader, and from what he had gathered there was no doubt that Freud would have had a field day deconstructing the self-made general's life and lunacies. According to various reports, his mother had been a prostitute who may or may not have been functionally retarded. His father had apparently been one of her clients. Kolingba had two sisters and three brothers, all

of whom died violently and under mysterious circumstances.

Kolingba's moods and behavior were notoriously un-
predictable and violent; the citizens of Kukuanaland lived
in perpetual fear. On the other hand, the general's second
in command, Oliver Gash, was an enigma, appearing on
the eve of the so-called "revolution" to offer his support.
Lanz's sources indicated that Gash had some sort of
vague criminal past in the United States; Lanz wasn't sure
which of the two men was the more dangerous.

"Why have you come here?" Saint-Sylvestre asked.

"Business."

"What kind of business?"

"None of yours," answered Lanz, wondering how far
the man behind the desk could be pushed.

"The Department of the Interior is concerned with
everyone's business, Mr. Lanz." Saint-Sylvestre smiled.

"I thought you were immigration, not the secret
police."

"In Kukuanaland they are one and the same," said
Saint-Sylvestre. "And there is nothing at all secret about
our police." The man's smile hardened into something
else. "We are a very open country, you see."

"Commendable," said Lanz.

"So, I ask again, what is your business here?"

"Guns," said Lanz.

Saint-Sylvestre blinked behind the steel-framed
glasses. "I beg your pardon?"

"I'm an arms dealer. . . . Mr. Saint-Sylvestre, I specialize in small arms of all types up to and including man-portable antitank systems like the American LAWs or the Russian RPG-7."

"Actually, it's Captain Saint-Sylvestre, Mr. Lanz." He paused. "What makes you think your services would be of interest to us?"

"Because the pistols your two guards are wearing were designed in the nineteen thirties. So were those submachine guns the guards outside were carrying."

Saint-Sylvestre glanced down at the passport in his hands and changed the subject. "You were in Mali."

"That's right."

"Did you do any business there?"

"None to speak of. I made a few contacts."

"And one of them suggested you visit us? Anyone in particular?"

"A man named Ives," said Lanz, throwing his line into the water. "Archibald Ives." There was no reaction from Saint-Sylvestre other than a brief note he jotted on a pad close to his right hand. The ballpoint he used was a Montblanc—his own, or booty from an unwary foreigner who'd passed through the bleak little room that was Saint-Sylvestre's fiefdom?

"And are you bringing any of these weapons into the country?" Saint-Sylvestre asked, nodding toward the single suitcase Lanz carried.

"Just the catalogs," Lanz answered.

"The suitcase," said Saint-Sylvestre, indicating the examination table. Lanz lifted the case and spun it around. The guard standing beside Saint-Sylvestre ran the zipper around the edges of the case and threw back the top. Saint-Sylvestre glanced inside. Toiletries, neatly packed summer-weight clothing and a half dozen thick catalogs: Armament Technology Incorporated of Canada, Browning, Bushmaster, the Czech Republic's eská Zbrojovka Uherský Brod, China's Norinco, Russia's Rosvoorouzhenie.

Captain Saint-Sylvestre picked up a catalog at random and leafed through it, then dropped it onto the table. Using the Montblanc, he turned over the clothes in the suitcase. He found only a library-edition copy of Carl Hiaasen's most recent novel. He picked it up. "What is this?"

"A very funny book about the cult of celebrity in the United States."

"You don't have this cult in Canada?"

"It's hard to tell." Lanz shrugged. "There are no celebrities in Canada. They all go to the U.S."

"The book is funny?"

"Very."

"The author is a celebrity?"

"I suppose," said Lanz.

"Then he ridicules himself?"

"I don't really care." Lanz sighed. He was getting bored with the man's convoluted interrogation. "I bought it to read on the plane."

Saint-Sylvestre dropped the book back into the suitcase and changed gears again. "Empty your pockets, please."

Lanz did so. Saint-Sylvestre picked up his wallet. He examined all the credit cards and counted the cash. There was four thousand dollars in U.S. hundred-dollar bills.

"A great deal of money."

"I'm a great believer in cash."

"So am I," said Saint-Sylvestre. He counted out ten hundred-dollar bills, folded them and slipped the money into the breast pocket of his uniform. He looked up at Lanz and smiled.

"Tax," he explained.

"That's what I thought." Lanz nodded.

"No cell phone?"

Lanz shrugged. "Would I get a signal?"

"No camera?"

"I didn't come here to take pictures."

"It is a very beautiful country," said Saint-Sylvestre. "There are many attractions for the visitor. Many colorful birds and exotic animals."

"I'm sure."

"Although the jungle can be very dangerous. Sometimes fatal," said Saint-Sylvestre. "I strongly advise you to stay in Fourandao. For your own safety."

"Of course," said Lanz. Now, what was *that* all about?

"You may go," said Saint-Sylvestre. Lanz nodded, repacked his suitcase and put everything back in his pockets, including his wallet.

"Perhaps you could recommend a hotel," said Lanz.

"There is only one. The Trianon."

Lanz nodded. The guard at the exit door stepped aside. Lanz picked up his suitcase and left. Saint-Sylvestre watched him go. Finally he spoke to the guard beside him in rapid-fire Sango.

"Tondo ni wande," he instructed. *Keep watch over the foreigner.*

"En, Kapita," said the guard. He followed Lanz out the door.

11

Michael Pierce Harris sat in his room at the Khartoum Hilton and listened to the distant satellite-echoing voice of his boss.

"What's the present situation?" Major Allen Faulkener asked from his London office.

"They're getting ready for some sort of expedition, that's for sure," answered Harris. "They've been picking up everything from bug spray and hammocks to machetes and malaria pills."

"The pilot, Osman?"

"Stripping down the engines on the Catalina."

"Do you have any idea about their ETD?"

"Tomorrow, maybe the day after. Osman's filed a flight plan for Umm Rawq."

There was a brief silence. Finally Faulkener spoke. "There's a Matheson twin Otter at the civilian airport in Khartoum. Take it down to Wau, on the border, in the morning. I'll have a half dozen men on standby. That should be enough."

"Enough for what?" Harris asked.

"They're following in Ives's footsteps," said Faulkener, his voice rising and falling spectrally on the carrier wave. "Make sure they stumble and fall. Fatally."

Returning from his regular afternoon stroll through town, Konrad Lanz stepped into the Bar Marie-Antoinette at the Trianon Palace Hotel and let his eyes adjust to the gloom. The long, narrow space off the lobby was empty except for Marcel Boganda, the bartender. Late sunlight leaked weakly through the partially opened louvers on the window that looked out onto the Trianon's colonial-style veranda.

The room was straight out of Rudyard Kipling, complete with a gently rotating wooden fan whickering overhead, a few old, cracked brown leather banquettes and club chairs scattered randomly. The centerpiece, the bar itself, was forty feet of art deco, deep red burled bubinga hardwood, the slab surface of the bar top as dense as marble. The bar was Marcel's pride and joy; every drink was served with a coaster and every condensation ring was wiped up almost before it had a chance to form.

Marcel was in his fifties, round faced and short haired. He wore tortoiseshell glasses and dressed in evening clothes from the time the bar opened at noon to closing time at midnight. He was a formal, distant man and rarely spoke unless he was spoken to. It was only by accident that Lanz had discovered from a waiter in the dining room on the far side of the lobby that Marcel actually owned the Trianon.

Crossing the room Lanz took a seat on one of the tall, high-backed leather-covered bar stools at the veranda end of the room. He put his Carl Hiaasen book down on the bar and waited. It took a moment or two but eventually Marcel wandered down and took Lanz's order: a chilled green-and-yellow bottle of Congolese Ngok beer with its lurid crocodile logo. Marcel poured the pale, corn-colored lager into a tall glass, letting the short head rise, just so. Lanz took a sip and sighed happily.

"Hot out there," said Lanz.

"Most usually is, sir," said Marcel. "It is a hot country."

"Lived here all your life?" Lanz asked.

"I went away to school, sir. To France. The Sorbonne."

"And you came back here?" Lanz asked, surprised.

"This is my home," said the bartender simply, shrugging his shoulders.

"Kukuanaland?"

"Fourandao, sir."

"What do you think about Kolingba?"

"I try not to," answered Marcel. Lanz wasn't entirely sure but he thought he caught a tinge of irony in the man's voice.

"Does he ever come here?"

"No, sir. Our president is not a drinker."

"How about his second in command, this Gash fellow?"

"Chocolate bourbon on the rocks from time to time," said Marcel. "Why do you ask me so many questions, sir?"

"I'll be honest with you, Marcel. I need an in to the president."

"In my experience, sir, people who preface a conversation with 'let me be honest' are anything but, and what precisely do you mean by an 'in'?"

"I'm an arms dealer, Marcel. I sell guns and ammunition, mostly to small African countries like this one, usually to their rebel factions, sometimes to warring religious and ethnic groups."

"We have no rebel factions, sir, nor do we have warring religious or ethic groups."

"What about this Limbani character?" Lanz said.

"Dr. Limbani has been dead for quite some time," said Marcel. But there was a faint flicker of apprehension and a little twitch of the eyes that went with the statement. Lanz decided to leave it for the moment.

"Where does Kolingba get his weapons?"

"I couldn't say," said Marcel.

120

The bartender was looking very uneasy now, and Lanz decided to back off completely. "Well, if you think of a way I could get in to see the man, let me know," he said.

"Of course, sir." There was a pause. "Will that be all?"

"Another beer, Marcel."

After Lanz finished the second beer, he picked up his book and left the bar. In the lobby he spotted a lone man sitting in one of the fan-backed wicker armchairs, smoking a cigarette and reading a copy of *Centrafrique-presse*. He was the same man who'd followed him on his afternoon walkabout. Lanz smiled. Saint-Sylvestre's surveillance was nothing if not obvious.

Lanz went up the broad, sweeping staircase to the mezzanine, then walked up three more flights to his small room under the eaves. It was simply furnished with an iron bedstead, a mattress that had seen better days and a simple spindle-legged desk with an old-fashioned brass swan-neck lamp. Lanz dropped the book onto the desk and stepped across to the window, which gave him a view over the square and into the compound directly opposite the hotel.

The compound ran a hundred and fifty feet on a side, the walls quarried cut stone, the large gate wood-strapped and hinged with iron. Guard towers, tin roofed and constructed from plywood, had been added at each corner. The so-called "presidential residence" was up against the east wall, and there was a rudimentary barracks building kitty-corner to it. A smaller brick building that sat directly across from the residence was almost certainly a guardhouse. The barracks looked as though it could hold between a hundred and a hundred and fifty men.

A tin-roofed shed had been built against the wall next to the guardhouse—obviously the motor pool. Lanz counted two bumblebee-striped Land Rovers with tinted windows, three armored personnel carriers and an even dozen "Mengshi" Chinese Humvee knock-offs painted in jungle camouflage, .50-caliber machine guns mounted just forward of the sunroof hatch. Considering all the other Chinese equipment he had seen, the machine guns were probably W-85s. Fourandao had a population of less than five thousand; the compound's ordnance was easily enough to protect the town from direct assault as long as there was no air element.

Lanz went back to the desk and sat down. Taking up the book, he carefully stripped off the celluloid library cover and the original jacket. He set the book aside and laid the dust jacket illustration-side down on the desk.

Lanz had been a soldier since his compulsory military service in the late seventies. He'd worked with every sort of intelligence tool, from satellite imagery and phone taps to photo intelligence and drugged "persuasion" of the enemy. Of all these techniques he'd never found anything more useful and more accurate than the evidence of his own eyes.

On the inside of the dust jacket was an accurate scale map of central Fourandao, the information gathered during his afternoon strolls during the past few days. The map was drawn lightly in pencil directly from memory after each of his daily constitutionals.

Fourandao was laid out in an elongated grid centered on Plaza de Revolution de Generale Kolingba, the old city square directly in front of Lanz's hotel. There was one main street running north and south, intersected by the road from Bangui that followed the west–east course of the Kotto River. On the outskirts of town the road from Bangui became Rue de Santo Antonio, and the north–south street was Rue de Liberdad. Two banks sat on the Rue de Liberdad—Banque Internationale pour le Centrafrique and Banque Populaire Maroco-Centrafricaine—and one on the square, the Bank of Central African States. Of the three, two were known to have been heavily involved in money laundering and financing for blood commodities. The Bank of Central African States occupied the only building of over four stories in Fourandao, the upper floors containing the People's Republic of China consular offices, the Kukua-naland Department of Customs and Excise and the Department of the Interior.

The two main streets were the only ones that were paved; the interconnecting grid of residential streets were dirt tracks. Lanz could detect no sewer system of any kind, which meant that the interconnecting streets flooded during the rainy season. Except for the buildings on the square Fourandao relied heavily on tin-roof and concrete-block construction. In most cases the quality of the concrete blocks had been poor, and without any foundations or drainage the majority of the buildings were crumbling at their bases. The only exception to this was a walled and guarded group of three modern blocks of flats that appeared to be built out of concrete. From what he could gather from eavesdropping in the bar of the hotel these flats were occupied by government bureaucrats in favor with Kolingba.

On his walks Lanz had noted evidence of malnutrition and rickets among the population, and on several occasions he'd seen huge rats nesting in the garbage-choked ditches. Dense foliage encroached on the edges of the town, and he'd seen several native women carrying bundles of firewood out of the jungle. Fourandao was as close to the edge of civilization as it was possible to get. There was no police force, since that function was operated out of Saint-Sylvestre's euphemistically named Department of the Interior, no fire department, no city hall or any other civil authority. Kukuanaland was a country in name only; in reality it was nothing more than a criminal fiefdom that probably didn't stretch much beyond the town limits.

Smiling to himself, Lanz began neatly filling in the

street names he'd gathered that day. Every battleground had its weaknesses and he was reasonably sure he'd discovered Fourandao's.

Oliver Gash sat in Captain Jean-Luc Saint-Sylvestre's office overlooking the Plaza de Revolution de Generale Kolingba and studied the huge aerial photograph of Fourandao that took up the entire wall behind the policeman's massive African mahogany desk, rumored to have once belonged to Mobutu Sese Seko, the long-dead dictator of Zaire, who had in turn purchased it from the estate of the late General Gnassingbé Eyadéma, the long-standing "president" of Togo. Both Gash and Captain Saint-Sylvestre were smoking Marlboros, the cigarette of choice among those in Kukuanaland who could afford them. Gash had once joked to General Kolingba that they should advertise in tourism magazines abroad, touting Kukuanaland as a vacation destination for smokers. Kolingba had taken him seriously and Gash had to spend weeks talking him out of it.

"So what exactly does he do on these little walks?" Gash asked.

"He walks." Saint-Sylvestre shrugged.

"No camera?"

"None that we can see."

"Anything in his room?" Gash asked.

"Nothing incriminating. He has a number of weapons catalogs."

"Did you run a background check?"

"Of course. He could be what he says he is—at first glance he appears to be an experienced mercenary who knows Africa well."

"But you have doubts," said Gash. It was a statement, not a question.

"I always have doubts, Dr. Gash. It is my business to have doubts. Our friend Lanz doesn't ring quite true. Why does a mercenary soldier suddenly switch to being an arms dealer? Why would a supposed arms dealer travel here knowing perfectly well that we are supplied by the Chinese and have been since the beginning? There are no fools in the arms business and if a man is an arms dealer he is a fool. Ergo, I don't believe it."

"All right," said Gash, stubbing out his cigarette in a huge ceramic ashtray on the desk in front of him. "What *is* he doing here?"

Saint-Sylvestre smiled. "At a guess I would say he's on a reconnaissance mission."

"To do what?"

"To facilitate a coup d'état," said the policeman mildly.

"Dangerous words, Captain," responded Gash. "Talk like that could get you into serious trouble."

"I'm not promoting the idea, Dr. Gash; I am merely giving my opinion." Saint-Sylvestre was well aware that he had to take a very circumspect path with Gash. The man was an uneducated savage, but he had what the Americans called "street sense" and a certain animal shrewdness that was sometimes mistaken for intelligence. Worst of all Gash had the killer instinct of a sociopath, which would have been Saint-Sylvestre's diagnosis had he been a doctor. In some ways Gash was even crazier than Kolingba.

Gash lit another cigarette, smirking as he did so. "All right, then, Captain, in your *opinion*, who is he working for?" In Baltimore it would have been easy to figure out which of your rivals was strong enough to make a play for your turf; here the same rules didn't apply.

"I'm not sure. Originally I thought it might be one of our neighbors—Chad, the Congo, Cameroon—but I don't think that's the case."

"Why not?"

"He's white, for one thing. I seriously doubt that the government of Chad would hire a white mercenary, not to mention the fact that they've got too much to lose internationally. The same is true of the Congo—to be seen as an aggressor now would be all the excuse the U.N. would need to send in troops. Cameroon doesn't have the money to launch a serious invasion and they'd have to go through the rest of the country to get to us. It doesn't make sense."

"What does?"

"He came here from Mali, but he wasn't hired there.

He also mentioned a man named Archibald Ives. I asked a few questions. Ives was a geologist."

"Was?"

"He's dead. Murdered in the Sudan."

"There's no oil in the CAR is there?" Gash asked.

Saint-Sylvestre shook his head. "Not a drop. They gave up looking for it years ago."

"What, then?"

"He was a primarily a mineral geologist, a prospector. If he was in Kukuanaland there's no record of it, so that means he came in illegally, probably through the Sudan."

"Looking for what?"

"I spent some time thinking about that," said Saint-Sylvestre, leaning back in his chair. "Any geologist in his right mind wouldn't come into Kukuanaland on a whim. He must have known what he was looking for. The only way he could have known that would be through remote sensing, probably from a satellite."

"The Americans? The CIA?"

"No, they wouldn't risk the political blowback if they were found out, and we don't have anything they want anyway. Kukuanaland is hardly strategic."

"They'd like to wipe us off the map; I know that much," said Gash. "That creepy secretary of state keeps on making all these war-criminal claims about the general."

"You don't need a geologist for that," said Saint-

Sylvestre. He shook his head. "No, somebody was looking for something and they found it. This Ives fellow was sent in to corroborate whatever their remote sensing told them. Lanz is here because the only way these people can get what they want is by getting rid of General Kolingba."

"A mining company?" Gash said.

"A big one." Saint-Sylvestre nodded. "Big enough to have access to a remote sensing satellite. Big enough to finance a small war."

"So we bring Lanz in and you interrogate him."

"To what end?" Saint-Sylvestre said. "We'd find out who the company was, but not what they're looking for, because I guarantee that Lanz doesn't know. If Lanz fails in his mission they'll just send in someone else."

"So what do you propose?"

"We continue surveillance; let him think he's getting away with it."

"And?"

"Eventually he'll pack his bag and go. And I'll be right behind him." Captain Jean-Luc Saint-Sylvestre sat back in his chair and smiled.

12

Peggy sat in the copilot's seat of the Catalina's skeletal cockpit and stared down at the mottled green landscape three hundred feet below. Doc and Rafi were asleep on the piles of equipment in the rear of the big amphibian. "You never think of the Sudan as being green," she said. "It's all about Darfur and droughts." She tripped the shutter release on the Nikon and took a half dozen more shots.

"Southern Sudan is a whole different thing," said Mutwakil Osman, the Catalina's pilot. "Twice the size of Texas and about a third of the population—less than seven million people."

"It looks beautiful," said Peggy.

"Not for long," said Osman. "When big corporations have their way it'll be clear-cut, strip-mined and turned into an oil field within ten years." He glanced over the side. "There's the river." Directly in front of them the sun was beginning to slide out of sight, turning the horizon into a flaring line of golds and reds that stretched into darkness on either side. "Just enough light to put her down."

Osman gently pushed the oversized wheel forward, then toed the left foot pedal. The plane went into a long sliding turn down the wide expanse of the silvery river snaking beneath their wings.

There was a faint vibration throughout the hull as the aircraft touched the surface of the river, slicing into the dark water and sending up a rooster-tail spray that rose up on both sides of the cockpit like a curtain that dropped away as Osman throttled back on the engines. Peggy noticed a half dozen dugouts on the water, the men slapping at the surface of the river with their paddles.

"A welcoming committee?" Peggy asked.

"Croc beaters." Osman grinned. "Hit one when you land and it could flip the old girl on her ass."

Osman guided the plane toward a narrow wooden pier. Docked there was an ancient river barge steamer that made the *African Queen* look like a speedboat. The steamer was about sixty feet long, twenty-five feet wide and had shrouded paddle wheels on either side of the deck. Rising above the tarred hull was a squat engine house and above that was a rickety-looking wheelhouse. At one time or another someone had attempted to paint the superstructure of the steamer white but the sun and the rain had steadily done their work and where any paint was left the color was a dejected gray. The entire vessel seemed to sag in the middle like a tired old horse.

"What on earth is that?" Rafi said, poking his head through the bulkhead door.

"That's the *Pevensey*," said Osman. "She delivers supplies up and down the river. You'll be taking her to the first cataract."

"I'm surprised she floats," said Rafi.

Osman killed the engines and they coasted the last hundred feet, sliding up on the shallow, sloping mud beach beside the pier. "Welcome to Umm Rawq," Osman said. He reached out and slipped a CQ radio frequency card out of a holder beneath the fuel gauge. He handed it to Peggy. "Hang on to that. If you ever need a lift sometime, just give me a call." He gave her a grin, then went off to speak to the captain of the *Pevensey* while Peggy, Rafi and Holliday began to explore the village.

Umm Rawq was a sordid little place with a single street of mud-brick hovels and a sheet-metal shanty selling banana beer and *Batman Forever* glasses from McDonald's. The whole village smelled of fish. An unseen radio boomed out tinny Afropop, and children played in the muddy, rubbish-littered road. None of the children were older than three or four, and the only male in the village was the gray-haired old bartender. The only other adult males they'd seen since landing were the crocodile beaters.

"Not the most hospitable place in the world," Doc said.

"It looks like the Lord's Resistance Army has been through here," said Peggy. "They take all the children over eight or nine and the able-bodied men. All in the name of God. Rape, murder, mutilation."

"I thought they were in Uganda?" Rafi said.

"They're spreading all over central Africa now. Here and the Congo as well."

"I've seen enough of Umm Rawq," said Holliday. They returned to the dock just in time to see Osman before he headed back toward Khartoum. The crocodile beaters had landed their long, narrow dugouts and were busy taking supplies from the Catalina on board *Pevensey*.

"I had a talk with Eddie," said Osman. "He was only going as far as Am Dafok this trip but he's willing to take you as far as the first cataract."

"Eddie's the captain?"

"Edimburgo Vladimir Cabrera Alfonso, to be precise," said Osman with a smile.

"Edimburgo Vladimir?" Peggy said.

"He's Cuban. His mother liked the name Edinburgh, as in Scotland, so she called him Edimburgo, but when she went down to the registry office the official said Edimburgo was an 'enemy' name, so she had to tack something revolutionary on to balance things out—hence the Vladimir. Cabrera is the father's name.

Alfonso is the mother's, which is how they do it in Cuba. His friends call him Eddie. He was over here as an 'adviser' during the Angola crisis in the nineteen seventies and he defected. He's been here ever since."

Eddie turned out to be six-foot-six, coal black, completely bald and as muscular as a stevedore. He flashed a million-dollar smile, and the twinkle in his eye made Holliday like him immediately. Eddie moved with the grace of a dancer, which as it turned out was how he'd been trained—ten years with the Cuban National Ballet, then off to Angola. He wore a black KA-BAR bowie knife the size of a short sword in a sheath on his hip.

The interior of the *Pevensey* was as ramshackle as the outside of the boat. Two passenger cabins were tucked behind the engine room, both the size of confessionals, and there was a "lounge" behind the wheelhouse with a grimy porthole on either side. A carpet the color of mold sat atop the worn decking, accented by a red velvet couch that had turned pale pink over time and that obviously doubled as the captain's bed.

While the croc beaters loaded all their supplies on deck, Captain Eddie ushered them into the lounge and offered them drinks, which turned out to be a choice of either Mamba malt liquor or 112-proof Red Star Chinese vodka. Holliday, Rafi and Peggy chose the malt liquor as the lesser of two evils. Eddie lit a long Cohiba cigar with a battered Zippo and poured himself a generous tumbler of vodka, then settled himself into an old wooden office chair. Along with a homemade chart table and the couch, the office chair was the only furniture in the little room. Behind the tall Cuban's head, resting on three pegs in the wall was an old, well-used-looking AK-47. The room was lit by a large window covered with a pair of grimy, tacked-on homemade cardboard shutters.

"Memories of better times?" Holliday asked.

"Old times, not necessarily better ones, señor." He turned away and addressed his other guests in the crowded little room. "So, *mis comandantes*, Donny tells me you wish to travel into Señor Conrad's Heart of Darkness."

"Something like that," said Rafi.

"That would make of me the Helmsman." Eddie smiled.

"A literate Cuban," said Peggy with a brittle tone in her voice. Holliday knew that Celia Cruz, one of Peggy's best friends in high school, had come over on the Mariel boatlift and had lost her mother and her father in the process.

Eddie slid the cigar from his mouth and gave Peggy a baleful look. "There are many things that Fidel did badly, señorita, but educating his people was not one of them. The country of my birth has a ninety-nine-point-eight percent literacy rate; your country cannot say the same, I'm afraid. There are also no student loans— university in Cuba is free."

Peggy frowned and took a pull at her bottle of Mamba.

"My cousin sometimes has strong opinions," said Holliday.

"Perhaps your cousin should judge the man in front of her and not the nation's politics. I am not Fidel." Captain Eddie stuck the cigar back into his mouth and once again Holliday saw the twinkle in his eye. "I have a much better tan, yes?"

Even Peggy couldn't help laughing.

"You must not take life so seriously, *amorcita*," said Eddie. "After half a century of Fidel, Cubans would have all slit their wrists by now if life was a serious thing. Havana is a city where the flushing of toilets is rationed and it is all the fault of 'embargo.' Everything is the fault of 'embargo.' Cockroaches are the fault of 'embargo.'" Eddie grinned broadly. "But our prostitutes on the beach at Veradero all have university educations." Holliday laughed along with the others, but he could see the evening disintegrating into tipsy stories about the ills of the Castro regime.

"How long will it take us to get to the first cataract?" Holliday asked, getting down to business.

"A night, a day and another night," said Captain Eddie, taking a big swallow of the Chinese vodka. "*Pevensey* is not as swift as she once was."

"And from there?" Rafi asked.

"From there I do not go," said Captain Eddie. "Beyond the first cataract is the province of the Lord's Re-sistance Army and Joseph Kony, their madman leader." He smiled and sucked on his cigar, then blew a huge cloud of smoke into the air. "It is also said the ghost of Dr. Amobe Barthélemy Limbani walks there as well."

"You don't seem to be the kind of man who'd be-lieve in ghosts," said Holliday.

"Travel up and down this river long enough, señor, and you find yourself able to believe anything."

"How soon can we get going?" Rafi asked.

Captain Eddie puffed his cigar thoughtfully and then emptied his glass of vodka. "Give me time to get steam up. An hour."

"You travel the river at night?" Holliday asked, surprised.

Eddie smiled. "It is the best time," he said. "Some-times the safest. What you can't see cannot see you in return. Mostly."

True to his word Eddie had the *Pevensey* fully loaded, boiler hissing, and pulling into the downstream current of the river almost exactly an hour later. Two crew members kept the boiler fueled, while the third member of the crew stood in the bow using a long pole to check for clearance. Peggy and Rafi had taken one of the two cabins, and Holliday stood beside Captain Eddie at the wheel. There was a simple marine telegraph to the right of the wheel with settings for "full ahead," "dead slow" and "stop," and a chain dangling down from the ceiling that was connected to the steam whistle on the roof of the wheelhouse. Night had fallen and the only light came from the red glow of Captain Eddie's ever-present cigar.

"You're like Churchill with that cigar," said Holliday, looking out onto the dark river ahead.

"He was a connoisseur, that man," said Eddie. "A man of *muy* good taste. He smoked La Aroma de Cuba and when they stopped making those he smoked Romeo y Julieta."

"You know a lot about Churchill?"

"I know a lot about cigars. My father ran one of the biggest Habanos factories until the day he died. He knew Churchill personally." Eddie reached into the breast pocket of his shirt and handed a cigar across to Holliday. "Please, señor, have one. It is a Montecristo No. 3."

"I'm afraid I quit smoking many years ago." Holliday sighed. "Although it's very tempting."

"If one does not give in to temptation occasionally, how can one appreciate the strength of will it takes to resist it?"

"You sound like a Jesuit professor I know at Georgetown University."

"There, it is God's will that you smoke this fine cigar," said Eddie. Holliday took the cigar and rolled it around in his mouth. The Zippo flared between Eddie's fingers. He let the kerosene smell fade, then applied the flame to the tip of the cigar. Holliday took a light pull. The taste was honey and rich earth. He could almost believe the stories of such cigars being rolled on the thighs of young virgins. "Not only virgins," said Eddie, reading his mind. "Pretty ones." Both men laughed and the engine chugged its regular coughing beat. The jungle on either side of them was dense and dark, wetland vines and roots spilling over into the water. Holliday could feel a steady tension rising out of nowhere, and then he realized he was thinking of being nineteen years old and crouching in the belly of a PBR going upriver on the Song Vam Co Dong in the Angel's Wing, listening to the jungle and knowing he'd never hear the one that killed him.

"Bad memory?" Eddie said.

"Old memory," Holliday replied.

"In the jungle?"

"Yes."

"The worst fighting is in the jungle, always. I have asked myself many times why that is and I cannot think of an answer."

"I think it's because the jungle has no history," said Holliday. "Things live and breed and die all in a day in the jungle and no one remembers. I was on patrol once and we found what was left of an old French fighter from the nineteen fifties, a Dewoitine, I think it was called. The jungle had almost swallowed it up completely; there were vines growing out of the pilot's eye sockets."

"What was your rank?" Eddie asked.

"Then? I was a PFC. I came out of it a lieutenant."

"And now?"

"Lieutenant colonel," said Holliday.

"Not very far up the ladder for a man of your years."

"I opened my mouth when I should have had it closed." Holliday laughed. "You don't get to be a general by having opinions; you get to be a general by following orders. In my army, at least."

"Mine, too, I am afraid. I never rose above *primer teniente*."

"More opinionated than me, then," said Holliday.

"There is a phrase in English, I think: 'to suffer fools badly'? I was very bad at this and there were a great many fools among the Cubanos in Angola and Guinea-Bissau, I can assure you."

One of the boiler crew, a gray-haired man named Samir, knocked on the wheelhouse door. He rattled off something in Arabic, got the nod from Eddie, then vanished into the darkness.

"What was that all about?" Holliday asked.

"Samir is our cook. He was inquiring about breakfast and asking for permission to take a piece of chicken as bait."

"Bait for what?"

"Moonfish, perhaps a turtle if we are very lucky." Eddie dragged on his cigar, lighting up his dark, laughing eyes. "They only bite on white meat, of course."

"Of course," said Holliday, and they continued down the dark jungle river.

13

". . . This was certainly true in my case, and I can still remember very little of the intervening years until I came to myself once again as Reinhart Stengl Hartmann in this home for the aged overlooking the mountains of the Oberammergau. May I never leave it or see Africa again except in my dreams."

Sir James Matheson, Ninth Earl of Emsworth, sat in his London office and closed the old copybook, pushing it to one side of his desk. He reclined in his chair, listening to the distant traffic noise from the Strand. It was this book, with its spidery, old-man's handwriting, that had introduced the enormous strike—confirmed by the late Archibald Ives—in the first place. The copybook had been lost among the archival files of a minor takeover that had occurred almost thirty years ago, when his father, the eighth earl, was still running the company. Had Matheson Resource Industries not decided to digitize their files, and had a bright junior director not noticed a minor concession within what was once the Ubangi-Shari precinct of French Equatorial Africa, Sir James might have let the opportunity of a lifetime pass him by.

Reinhart Stengl Hartmann, dead for decades and forgotten long before that, had begun his career as a young man in the goldfields of South Africa's Witwatersrand. With only minor success, Hartmann decided to try his luck elsewhere, finally settling on the operation of a rubber plantation in what was then the Congo Free State. With the annexation of the Congo by King Leopold of Belgium in 1908, Hartmann was forced to move once again, this time to Ubangi-Shari on the other side of the Congo River. He operated as an ivory trader there until the 1920s and then, acting on a tip from a native guide, he traveled into the jungle interior, once again prospecting for gold. According to official reports made by the French governor of the province at the time, Hartmann did in fact find gold, but not in spectacular amounts. With the man branded a failure, the governor and just about everyone else forgot about Reinhart Stengl Hartmann.

Matheson, on the other hand, had years of experience reading ledgers, spreadsheets and every other sort of business document, and to him Hartmann's tactics were as transparent as glass. Hartmann's African concern operated under the name of Kotto Fluss Bergau—Kotto River Mining. On paper it appeared that all the shares of the company had been owned by Hartmann, but a closer look revealed that a majority of stock was held as collateral for large personal loans to Hartmann by a second company, this one operating out of Switzerland under the name Edelstein Malder Genf SA—Gemstone Brokers of Geneva.

Edelstein Malder Genf did business with only one other company: Makelaar Steen Amsterdam—Gem Brokers of Amsterdam, and they were doing a great deal of business. Matheson had laughed out loud when he made the final connection. Hartmann hadn't struck gold on the Kotto River; he'd found diamonds, and lots of them, although not quite enough to wake the sleeping bloodhounds of De Beers.

Over a period of fifteen years Hartmann managed to accumulate a huge fortune, but his only obvious use of the money was the building of a bizarre estate in the middle of the jungle that looked remarkably like the home of a wealthy Bavarian farmer. Called Lowenshalle—the Lion's Lair—it overlooked the Kotto River and the mist-clouded, three-forked waterfall a mile or so upstream.

Hartmann's covert diamond trading practice was interrupted only by World War Two, but by 1950 a series of severe heart attacks made his life in Lowenshalle impossible. Within a few months he had abandoned everything, smuggling his last consignment of diamonds in the false base of an oxygen bottle as he returned to Europe. In Lowenshalle his few native servants drifted away, returning to their villages. The estate was stripped of any obvious valuables and the jungle quickly began to inexorably swallow up everything that Hartmann had built.

Back in Europe, Hartmann consolidated his holdings into a single limited trust, then settled into a retirement home in the Bavarian village of Garmisch-Partenkirchen, where he spent his last few years writing out the story and the secrets of his life in what would become almost a hundred copybooks like the one on Matheson's desk. Upon his death, with no heirs, the notebooks became the property of Hartmann's trust, and the trust in turn became the property of Matheson Resource Industries when, decades later, it purchased Kotto Fluss Bergau from the Swiss bank that managed Hartmann's interests. At no time, since the initial incorporation of Kotto River Mining and its attendant distribution companies, was there anything mentioned in writing or in rumor of any mining operations on the Lowenshalle estate or anywhere nearby. Like so many other stories hidden in the vaults and safety-deposit boxes of so many banks around the world, it would have probably stayed that way until the end of time if it hadn't been for a few simple twists of fate.

"Almost enough to make you believe in God." Matheson grunted softly to himself. There was a gentle double tap on his door. "Enter," he said. The door opened and Major Allen Faulkener stepped into the room.

· "Yes?" Matheson said briskly.

"I thought you'd like to know," said the security officer, "Harris is in play."

"Let's hope he doesn't bugger it up this time," said Matheson. "If he'd done it right on the Khartoum highway we wouldn't be in this position now."

"He's got six of the Sinclair woman's 'specials' with him, and they've got their orders. If he does bugger it up he knows what'll happen to him," said Faulkener.

"Excellent." Matheson nodded. "Once we've dealt with Holliday and his interfering friends perhaps we could give some thought to President Kolingba's successor."

The smell of cooking fish was mouthwatering. Samir, in his role as chef, had rolled the thick deboned catfish steaks in cornmeal and dropped them into a quarter inch of dark palm oil. The oil seethed in the bottom of a big cast-iron frying pan on one of the two burners on the wood-burning cookstove that stood on a firebrick base on the forward deck of the *Pevensey*. The other burner was being used to brown thick circles of sweet potato. The elderly Sudanese man deftly flipped the slabs of fish and potatoes with a homemade sheet-metal spatula. A pile of kindling in a sagging wire basket was stacked beside him along with a hatchet in case he needed to feed the stove.

While Samir cooked, his boiler room partner, Bakri, took over in the wheelhouse and Jean-Paul, the third member of the crew, poled the river, calling out the depth of water under the steam barge's flat-bottomed keel. It was early and mist still twisted in ghostly trails over the river, the sun a bright hammered bronze disk rising over the ragged fog hanging above the lush jungle trees to the east.

"We'll find some shade in a few hours and wait out the worst of the sun," suggested Eddie. Samir flipped a golden brown catfish fillet and a scoop of sweet potatoes onto a tin plate and gave it to his boss, but Eddie gallantly handed it over to Peggy instead. She ate a tentative morsel of the fish and her eyes widened.

"It's delicious," she said. She speared a fried piece of sweet potato onto her fork and popped it into her mouth. "Wonderful!" Samir smiled happily and began filling the rest of the plates.

"The giraffe catfish isn't like the mud-fish bottom-feeders in America," said Eddie. "It prefers to eat plant material, so the taste is usually fresher." He laughed. "In Cuba now they think the catfish is an agent of the devil god, Babalu Aye, because he can walk overland on his fins, but they eat him anyway."

Holliday sensed it before he heard it, and heard it before he saw it. As he took his plate from Samir some instinct and perhaps a fleeting glint seen out of the corner of his eye made him suddenly tense and twist around on the plastic milk crate he was using as a seat. He squinted, looking for something he wasn't quite sure was there, and then he saw it: a phantom in the mist above the trees, the first flash of sunlight reflecting off the windscreen of a low-flying aircraft. A small plane, maybe a Cessna Caravan, tricked out with floats and painted dark green to blend in with the jungle treetops.

A split second later he spotted a bright double flash from under the wings followed by a strangely clipped, hollow *whoosh*, like the abruptly terminated sound of a bullet striking water at high speed. The sound was horribly familiar: a pair of underwing Hellfire air-to-ground missiles being fired—forty pounds of fire-and-forget high explosive coming at them at roughly a thousand miles an hour.

"Incoming!" Holliday bellowed. And almost before the warning was out of his mouth the Hellfires struck. Used by a skilled operator, the AGM-114 Hellfire could be aimed through the open window of a moving vehicle. In the case of the two missiles aimed at the *Pevensey*, one struck the rear wall of the lounge behind the wheelhouse and the second exploded in the boiler room simultaneously, putting a ragged hole the size of a car door through the bottom of the old barge.

Bakri, standing in the wheelhouse, was vaporized on the spot. As the *Pevensey* suddenly lurched with the impact of the two missiles, Jean-Paul, standing in the bow with his pole, was thrown into the river, and Samir, crouched in front of his frying pans, had his ribs crushed as the stove tipped over on him, then was turned into a human torch as the furiously boiling cooking oil spilled onto his head, neck and chest. Samir's thin cotton clothing and his hair burst into flame as the blackened, crackling firewood spilled out of the overturned stove and he died, his bubbling scream choked off as his mouth and throat filled with the burning oil.

Sitting on the starboard side of the barge Holliday instinctively threw himself toward Peggy and Rafi, his outstretched arms bowling them over as a hail of cast iron, glass and wood debris flew over them. *Pevensey*, helm gone, swung hard into the current, then almost tipped over as the surging water poured into the gaping hole in her bottom.

Holliday had a brief glimpse of the aircraft as it roared overhead. He hit the river, automatically assessing: a Cessna Caravan 208. Nine passengers, but six or seven was more likely with the Hellfire payload. The water closed over his head as he was pushed down toward the stony bottom, his vision cut in half by the silt-heavy current. Then he remembered.

Crocodiles.

The Nile version, up to twenty feet long and sometimes weighing as much as a ton—bronze, the green-yellow-and-dirty-purple prehistoric horrors—could travel up to forty miles an hour if they were hungry enough. They had sixty-eight cone-shaped teeth and a bite force of five thousand pounds per square inch. They sometimes hunted in packs of five or more and had been known to take down a four-thousand-pound black rhinoceros. An average-sized human being would be little more than a hors d'oeuvre.

Holliday flailed his way frantically back to the surface. He was being swept along with the current along with the remains of the *Pevensey*. He shook the water out of his eyes and spotted Rafi struggling to drag an unconscious Peggy toward the shore. Captain Eddie was already there, hauling himself up the muddy bank. The half-submerged wire kindling basket whirled by and Holliday reached out and levered the hatchet out of the top piece of firewood. On the shore Captain Eddie yelled out a warning.

"*¡Detrás de usted!* Behind you!"

A huge, surging creature was powering its way toward him, massive armored tail swirling, its dead dinosaur eyes barely breaking the surface of the swiftly flowing river. Almost immediately Holliday realized that the grotesque creature had its attention elsewhere—it was racing toward Peggy as Rafi and Captain Eddie tried to haul her out of the water.

Holliday twisted away to one side like a matador playing a bull and backhanded the blade of the hatchet into the creature's eye. The crocodile reared up, making a terrible, deep-throated bellowing sound. Holliday managed to jerk the hatchet out of the animal's eye and struck out for the shore as the wounded creature rolled away from him. He reached the shallows and staggered to his feet as Captain Eddie came back down the bank and held out one hand.

"I would advise you to be a little quicker, señor," said the Cuban. He jerked Holliday up onto the muddy shore, sweeping the big bowie knife out of its sheath. As Holliday stumbled up the bank he turned and saw Eddie lunging forward and driving the heavy blade up to the hilt high between the eyes of the already half-blinded giant that had been seeking its revenge.

The crocodile squirmed and shivered as the knife went into its brain and then suddenly went rigid. Eddie pulled out the blade, reached into the water, grabbed one of the creature's stubby legs, then half flipped the body, exposing the pale, eggplant-shaded belly. He pushed the bowie knife into the crocodile's throat and sawed downward, esophagus, heart, lungs, liver and intestine spilling out into the shallows like a hideously foul-smelling stew. He used his boot to push the disemboweled creature's corpse into the current.

"That should keep his friends busy for a while," said Eddie, grabbing Holliday's elbow and helping him up the riverbank. At the edge of the dense jungle Rafi was bending over Peggy, who was sitting up and coughing, her back against the thick trunk of a tree that overhung the river.

"She's okay," said Rafi. "Half-drowned but okay."

Eddie watched the remains of *Pevensey* washing up onshore like flotsam. He turned back to Holliday. "You have some serious enemies, señor. Perhaps you should have warned me."

"Sorry about that," answered Holliday, hands on knees as he tried to catch his breath. "I didn't think they wanted me that badly."

"I think you were wrong, *Comandante*," said Captain Eddie. "I think they want you very badly indeed."

Holliday climbed to his feet, his clothes smeared with mud, stinking but alive. "Where's the widest part of the river closest to here? I need about fifteen hundred feet, say half a kilometer."

"We've just been attacked with rockets and nearly eaten by crocodiles," said Peggy, her voice weary. "Why would you want to know something like that?"

"Because that's how much water a good floatplane pilot in a Caravan needs to land," said Holliday.

"Twenty kilometers behind us or thirty ahead," said Captain Eddie, wiping the blade of his knife across his jeans. He slid it back into its sheath.

"How long to get to us here?"

"By boat, four hours, more likely five at this time of day. Twice that by land. There are very few trails, so they would have to stay close to the river, follow its turns."

"Are they likely to find boats?" Holliday asked.

"Perhaps a dugout or two, small ones, not what they

need. There are no villages along that part of the river," answered Eddie.

"So we've got eight hours, maybe, until nightfall."

"For what?" Rafi asked, crouched beside Peggy.

"To get ready," said Holliday.

14

"Point me toward a good hardwood," said Holliday, standing in the narrow clearing between the riverbank and the jungle.

"A tree, señor?" Eddie asked a little skeptically. There were thousands of trees all around them.

"A tree." Holliday nodded. "A hardwood in particular."

"Miss Blackstock is leaning against one," said Eddie, pointing. The tree in question was sixty or seventy feet tall, its summit lost in the jungle canopy overhead. Its roots were splayed and thick, raising the trunk like the legs of a massive spider. The leaves were broad, round and a deep, rich green. The branches hung down like a heavy curtain. "It is an iroko tree. There has been much poetry written about it. It is also in danger of extinction."

"Looks like it's flourishing to me." Holliday shrugged.

"It is pollinated only by the strawberry fox-eared fruit bat. The bat is being killed off by farmers velar-cutting for their crops."

Holliday approached the tree and looked up through the tangle of limbs. Rafi and Peggy followed his gaze.

"What are you looking for?" Rafi asked.

"A dead branch."

"I thought we were trying to get away from the guys on the floatplane," said Peggy.

"They've got weapons and we don't," said Holliday coldly. "One way or the other they'll catch up to us and kill us, so we have to kill them first."

"With a dead branch?" Rafi said.

"With *that* dead branch," said Holliday. He reached up with the hatchet and hacked off a leafless branch about three fingers thick. He pulled it down, trimmed one end and held it up against himself to measure. The branch was a little shorter than he was, making it about six feet long.

"We're going to beat them to death with clubs when they go to sleep?" said Peggy.

"Why don't you and Rafi help Captain Eddie see what he can salvage from *Pevensey* and I'll show you," suggested Holliday, pointing to the Cuban, who was pulling wreckage out of the river.

Half an hour later, after borrowing Eddie's knife, Holliday's six-foot stave was further sculpted. Both ends slightly notched, the ends a little more than half an inch thick now, the center a little more than half an inch in diameter. The "front" of the stave was sapwood, with the heavier heartwood on the "inside," creating a natural laminate. With that much done Holliday went down to the riverbank to see how his companions were doing.

Eddie and the others had retrieved most of the material that had washed up onshore or was easily accessible without arousing the interests of the half-submerged fleet of crocodiles cruising on the edge of the main current. While Eddie and Rafi carried the heavier things higher on the bank Peggy sorted out what they had already gathered. It was an eclectic collection.

Letting his eyes run over the exhibition of junk spread out in the little clearing, Holliday took a quick inventory. There was a pair of two-by-fours with pieces of wallboard and nails still clinging to them—Holliday guessed they were uprights for the boiler room enclosures. The window frame and cardboard shutters; two unopened gift boxes of Ginsu steak knives, twenty-four knives in all; a full-sized ax embedded in a log; a soggy-looking roll of duct tape and an old bamboo fishing rod with a reel of black nylon line still attached.

"Just about everything I need," said Holliday. "Maybe we really can even the odds a little." He turned and found Captain Eddie beside him.

"Anything I can do, *compadre*?"

"A fire," said Holliday after thinking for a moment. "A small one, but nice and hot."

*   *   *

"Going through the files, I can come up with only four really viable candidates to replace Kolingba," said Allen Faulkener, dropping a stack of blue-and-red-striped top secret folders on Sir James Matheson's desk. "The obvious choice is Dr. Oliver Gash, late of Baltimore, Maryland, also known as Olivier Gashabi, a refugee from Rwanda in the early days of the genocide. He has the brains, the connections and the innate greed to run Kukuanaland as we see fit, given the right incentives. Number two is Dr. Amobe Barthélemy Limbani, the governor of the Vakaga prefecture before its abrupt name change to Kukuanaland. He presents several serious drawbacks in that he may well be dead; if he's not we haven't been able to find him; and last but not least, if he is alive and if we could find him he might well not be bribable."

"Everybody has a price," said Matheson. "And if he's not bribable he's got something in his past that makes blackmail possible."

"Not in Limbani's case. He appears to be clean as a whistle, and besides, there are other problems that may be insurmountable."

"The third possibility?" Matheson said.

"Ah, the dark horse." Faulkener nodded. "Francois Nagoupandé. He was vice governor of Vakaga and the man who betrayed Limbani. He lives in a compound in Bamako, Mali, on his ill-gotten gains. He's terrified that

Kolingba will try to assassinate him, so he's surrounded by bodyguards. Best of all he is a Banda, not a Yakima like Limbani—in fact, his ethnicity was the reason he was appointed vice governor."

"Is he approachable?" Matheson asked.

"Yes," said Faulkener. "We have done so already."

"And his response?"

"Anything that can remove the Kolingba threat and promises a uniform with lots of medals, and he's your man. Rather like an Idi Amin in the rough."

"He wants money, too, I presume."

"By his standards a great deal, but to MRI it would be pocket change. We also have to promise him an escape route and a bank account in Switzerland when the inevitable revolution arrives. He's an idiot, but he's no fool, if you know what I mean."

"We'll have to strike a special company. Something with a very large initial offering that has long since fallen into decline. One of the early copper mines in the Philippines. Preferably something suitably colonial. Dutch or Belgian. I want us to have absolute control and no transparency."

"I'll see what I can find," said Faulkener. "What about Nagoupandé?"

"I'd like to meet with him as soon as possible," Matheson said.

"Easy enough to arrange, I should think," said Faulkener.

"Send him the private jet," said Matheson. "That

should impress him." His smile broadened. "Perhaps we should get him fitted up at Gieves and Hawkes, then bring him to the meeting when Lanz is ready."

"Medals?"

"As many as you can find. Make him look like a bloody king."

There was a good reason for the logo of Blackhawk Security being the proud carved bow figurehead of a Viking longboat: Lars Thorvaldsson, the founder of Blackhawk, had considered himself a modern-day Viking. Lars had made billions over the years, and had always said he'd found inspiration from his Viking ancestors. According to him, he was directly related to Leif Erikson, through his father, Erik Thorvaldsson, otherwise known as Erik the Red.

It was Lars who came up with the motto, "We founded America; now we keep her safe," and as the company grew so did the Viking tradition. Blackhawk's first television advertisement aired during the halftime break for the Super Bowl VI in 1972, showing a wooden ship with a Blackhawk figurehead landing on the Duluth waterfront, along with a Viking in a horned helmet blowing the traditional Gjallarhorn, the calling horn of the traditional Norse sagas.

With the death of Lars Thorvaldsson in 1989 and the subsequent purchase of the company by the multinational corporation owned by Kate Sinclair combined with the beginning of the elder Bush's Iraq war, Blackhawk Security grew even larger, and so did the Viking tradition. There were seminars on Viking core values of strength, honor and pride for senior executives, Viking workshops of various kinds for midlevel employees, Viking reenactments for the whole family and Viking summer camp for the kids. Kate Sinclair even built the World of the Vikings theme park near the Mall of America, not far from Lars Thorvaldsson's original office in Bloomington, Minnesota.

In light of their heavy Viking indoctrination, it was hardly surprising that the seven-man Blackhawk intrusion team, led by Michael Pierce Harris, had decided that they would approach their objective in the "old Viking way." Perhaps they even saw themselves as the mythical "gray ghosts," the dusk trolls who came out of the fading light wearing their Galdrastafir, the runish emblems that made them invisible. Whatever it was they were thinking, it didn't work.

They came in two dugouts, three in one, four in the other, with Harris the last man out of the second canoe. The light was failing, just as Holliday had hoped. At a glance the clearing looked empty, although it was obvious from the tracks up the muddy bank and the salvaged wreckage that this was where the survivors of the Hellfire attack had climbed out of the water.

All seven men, Harris included, were wearing full jungle camouflage BDUs, paratrooper boots and jungle camo slouch hats. They were armed with Heckler & Koch MP5s, Browning Hi-Power semiautomatic pistols and eight-inch KA-BAR knives. Several also carried M67 hand grenades on Sam Brownes looped over their shoulders. Harris carried a Glock 9 instead of a Browning.

The seven men came up the muddy riverbank yelling loudly. The quickest one up the slope died first. A two–foot-long arrow shot from Holliday's rudimentary English longbow caught him just left of the heart and penetrated to his spine. The arrow had been fletched with duct-tape feathers and the point was just fire-hardened wood. Nevertheless at one hundred and eight foot-pounds per square inch of force it was just as lethal as the MP5 he never got to fire.

Numbers two and three stepped on muddy cardboard packing laid out on the riverbank, dropping down into a shallow pit onto twenty-four Ginsu steak knives.

The fourth man made it to the top of the bank, where Holliday's second homemade arrow pierced his groin, slicing into his bladder and intestine. Lying flat in the jungle foliage a few yards to the right, just out of the clearing, Captain Eddie saw that the man was still alive and dangerous. He hurled himself forward out of the bushes in a diving tackle, hitting the wounded man waist high. He drove the bowie knife underhanded into the man's belly, then sawed upward under the ribs, slicing into the right lung and finally piercing the heart.

Seeing the odds so drastically reduced within less than a minute, Harris veered into the jungle, trying to put as much distance between the clearing and himself as quickly as possible. The remaining members of Harris's team were right behind him, the Viking code forgotten. With an arrow already notched and drawn Holliday let fly. The hardened point of the arrow struck Harris between the first and second cervical vertebra and without the cutting point of a steel head the arrow slipped sideways and punctured the internal carotid artery before jerking upward and piercing the tongue. Harris was paralyzed instantly, fell to his knees and watched mutely as his lifeblood poured from his mouth onto the dark rich earth of the jungle floor.

In the clearing Holliday tossed the longbow aside and pulled the MP5 out of one dead man's loosened grip. He fired a burst in the direction of the fleeing men, but managed only to clip the foliage above their heads.

There was a sudden, stunned silence. Rafi and Peggy stared at the bodies, paying particular attention to their own grisly handiwork. Captain Eddie went from dead man to dead man, stripping their weapons, their floppy slouch hats and finally their paratrooper boots.

"Their shoes?" Rafi queried, stunned at the Cuban's methodical concentration.

"The floor of the jungle can be very dangerous for your feet," said Eddie.

"He's right," said Holliday, who was pulling the

bodies from the hidden knife pit. Each knife came out of the dead flesh with soft, almost obscene sucking noises. Holliday began stripping both men. "Give us a hand," he instructed. "The quicker we get this done the sooner we can get out of here."

They gathered up anything useful, left the bodies and headed down the riverbank to the two dugouts. As they climbed into the crudely built canoes it began to rain.

"Wonderful." Holliday grunted, pushing his dugout away from the shore. "Just what we needed."

15

Captain Jean-Luc Saint-Sylvestre sat in his bedroom and stared through the viewfinder of the Canon EOS 5D at the hotel across from him. The Ali Pasha Hotel was on Clapham Street, just off the Brixton Road in south London.

The policeman could imagine the interior: six floors of tiny rooms and toilets the size of cupboards. Narrow stairways, peeling wallpaper and groaning pipes. Bedbugs, roaches and mice. Ten thousand places in London just like it. Anonymity defined.

The whole area was unofficially known as the capital of Afro-Caribbean England and it was easy enough for Saint-Sylvestre to fit in as long as he kept a check on his university-educated accent.

As well as being the densest part of black London, Brixton was also the crime capital of the city. Behind the colorful facade of the fresh fruit and vegetable stands and the street-long markets for African and Caribbean clothes, you could trade in just about any vice the human mind could think of, from heroin to hookers, smuggled cigarettes to smuggled women, blood diamonds to body parts, machine guns, stolen goods, counterfeit handbags, wristwatches and haute couture.

From your heart's desire and passions to your soul's blackest cravings—all were the stock-in-trade of Brixton. All of which made Brixton a logical end for Saint-Sylvestre's pursuit of the still enigmatic Konrad Lanz.

During Lanz's six-day stay in Kukuanaland he had made four official attempts to see Kolingba and gone for five afternoon walks. He had remained in the Trianon hotel during the evenings, sometimes eating in his room and sometimes in the Marie Antoinette Bar.

During these evenings he spoke only to Marcel Boganda, the bartender, a longtime paid informant of Saint-Sylvestre's. According to Boganda their conversation had never gotten onto subjects of any more interest than the weather. Although Saint-Sylvestre had heard or seen nothing to dispute Oliver Gash's presumption that Lanz was in Fourandao to reconnoiter a coup d'état, neither had he heard or seen anything to support it.

Saint-Sylvestre had been a policeman in the Central African Republic a great deal longer than Gash had been a resident there, and something about the Rwandan/American refugee triggered the policeman's distrust.

If there had ever been a man more of an opportunist than President Kolingba, it was his newly minted second in command Oliver Gash, and if Gash wanted to know about an upcoming coup it was only to decide which side he should take or whether he should flee to his secret accounts in a number of Switzerland-, Panama- and Liechtenstein-based banks, all of which Saint-Sylvestre knew about.

Saint-Sylvestre also knew about Kolingba's secret accounts, and was well aware that one of his own people at the Department of Internal Affairs had similar documentation regarding the African leader. On more than one occasion during Saint-Sylvestre's long career it had occurred to the policeman that the government of the Central African Republic in general, and Kukuanaland in particular, was no more nor less corrupt and corruptible than any other nation; it was simply smaller and more overt. Like an expectation of personal privacy, in Kukuanaland there wasn't the slightest expectation of a government that was incorruptible.

Corruption had been expected on the African continent with the first delivery of foreign-aid powdered milk and penicillin. There were three thousand tribes and two thousand languages all fighting for their existence and no moral code whether Catholic, Lutheran, Baptist or otherwise had ever made more than the most superficial inroads into that wretched, poor and terrible place. Joseph Conrad knew what he was talking about when he reached the end of that river in the Congo and found nothing but "The horror! The horror!"

And now it seemed there was more to come. In the four days since Konrad Lanz's arrival at Heathrow he had met five people at his somewhat sordid headquarters at the Ali Pasha. Of the five, four had been cast from the same mold: hard, tough-looking men with an animal sense about them, even in the bowels of a megacity like London.

One of them had even been recognizable from the photo files Saint-Sylvestre kept at the airport. His name was Stefan Whartski, a Pole who'd started his mercenary career as a transport pilot during the Eritrean civil wars of 1980 and 1981. With men like Whartski talking to Lanz, it looked more and more as though his intuitions had been correct—he was watching a coup d'état in the making.

The fifth Saint-Sylvestre called Mr. X. It was this man who was now meeting with Lanz for the second time, and he was something else altogether. Tall, distinguished, wearing his Bond Street suit like a uniform and with a military bearing that would have looked better on the parade ground than crawling through the jungle swamps outside Fourandao. This was the money man at ground level, not the principal perhaps but a conduit leading to him.

Lanz and the mystery man suddenly came out of the hotel and stood talking for a moment, bathed in the security light over the main door of the grimy six-story building. Saint-Sylvestre twisted the big telephoto lens.

After a thousand surveillances like this one, reading lips was second nature to him.

Mr. X: "You've checked the money, then?"

Lanz: "Yes. Quite correct."

Mr. X: "You'll be there tomorrow?"

Lanz: "You said seven thirty."

Mr. X: "Yes. Wear a tie, please."

Lanz: "Anything you like."

Mr. X: "All right, then."

Lanz: "Sure you won't come for a bite? They do a very nice butter chicken."

Mr. X: "That sort of thing never agrees with me. Indian food, I mean." He paused. "Must get home to the wife and kiddies."

Lanz: "Of course."

The two men parted without shaking hands. Mr. X climbed into a black Jaguar XJ sedan while Lanz headed for the High Street. Saint-Sylvestre took out his cell phone and hit the speed dial. A tentative voice answered on the second ring. "*Selam*, 'alo?" Tahib Akurgal said.

"It's me," the policeman said without identifying himself. God only knew what sort of lists the night clerk at the Ali Pasha Hotel was on.

"Yes?"

"What did you hear?" Saint-Sylvestre said. The first question he'd posed to Tahib, the hardworking medical student who worked nights at his uncle's hotel, was, "How much did the gray-haired man with the German accent pay you to report anyone asking questions about him?" Tahib had balked. Saint-Sylvestre said he'd double the amount and if he found out that Tahib was playing both ends against the middle he'd slit the throats of every single member of Tahib's family, young or old, saving Tahib for last. Tahib was now on Saint-Sylvestre's payroll at a hundred pounds a day.

"They are going to meet his lordship at seven thirty tomorrow evening."

"His lordship?" Was Mr. X spoofing his boss or was something else going on?

"That is what the other man said, effendi."

"Did the other one say where this meeting was to take place?"

"Yes, he even made sure that Lanz-*bey* wrote the address down."

"What is it?"

"Number nine Grantham Place, flat six, London W-one."

Westminster. Mr. Lanz and Mr. X were playing for high stakes. Grantham Place was to the Ali Pasha like heaven was to hell.

"I'm coming across the street, Tahib. I'll need the key."

"No, sir, please, Lanz-*bey* will kill me if he finds out!"

"Lanz-*bey* is eating butter chicken at a curry house up the road, probably the same Curry Capital he's had dinner at for the past three nights."

"Please, sir," Tahib groveled. "I cannot."

Saint-Sylvestre smiled. "Yes, sir," he said. "You can, and you will. Another hundred pounds."

"This would be in addition to the regular hundred pounds?" The groveling was gone. The policeman had done a little scratching into the night clerk's background and discovered that Tahib's father was a major dealer on the Istanbul gold market in the Kapali carsi, the Grand Bazaar, which by definition meant he was a criminal. Like father, like son. A doctor perhaps, but a doctor with a criminal mind.

"Yes, in addition to the regular hundred pounds."

"Perhaps you would like a key to the adjoining room in case of an emergency, effendi."

"You're wasting my time, Tahib. Don't do that."

"No, sir, of course not. I shall await your arrival, effendi."

Saint-Sylvestre took the tiny Chobi miniature camera out of his backpack and slipped the half-inch square device into his shirt pocket. Three minutes later he was letting himself into Konrad Lanz's hotel room with the key provided by Tahib Akurgal.

The room was on the top floor of the hotel, facing an alley lined with industrial-sized rubbish bins and the back sides of buildings facing the next street. There was a zigzagging, rusting and ancient fire escape with a landing outside of Lanz's window that appeared to be painted shut.

The room contained a narrow bed, a writing desk that had been moved from against the wall to stand alone under the only overhead light, and two chairs—a Victorian-style captain's chair with scrolled arms and legs and a plump upholstered club chair with a chenille throw covering the worn, pale burgundy velvet upholstery.

The only other furniture was an IKEA-style side table for the swaybacked bed and a pressboard chest of drawers. Lanz's suitcase was sitting open on the chest, an expensive-looking Mulholland Brothers shaving kit in plain view.

Saint-Sylvestre crossed to the desk. There was a yellow lined pad of neatly made notes, a fine-tip felt pen and the cover of the Carl Hiaasen book Lanz had brought to Fourandao.

Saint-Sylvestre was impressed by Lanz's ingenuity; working from memory every day, Lanz had put together an exceptionally detailed map of the center of the town, including the location of electrical transformers and telephone lines along with their switching stations. Particular attention had been paid to the presidential compound, noting the number of guard towers and the number of shifts at each tower. The offices of the Department of the Interior were correctly located on the plaza, as were the three blocks of flats directly behind the plaza, most of which were occupied by favored friends of Kolingba who occupied most of the government bureaucratic offices for Kukuanaland. The map also noted army patrol routes and times and noted manpower for each.

The notes on the yellow pad reflected the maps, and Lanz's simple shorthand for various terms was easy enough to decipher. The mercenary had correctly judged that the compound held around two hundred men, with a hundred on duty at any one time.

The rare comings and goings of the president and Gash were also noted. There was a page of notes devoted to nothing but ordnance, armor and airpower, all of it accurate. Lanz hadn't missed a trick.

On another page there was a list of names and ranks as well as figures that were most likely pay scales. And lists of equipment. Each of the separate pages had an estimated figure totaled in euros at the bottom. The last page had a simple formula that Saint-Sylvestre recognized without any trouble:

2 comp X 200 (2 Maj.) PSF

8 plat X20 (8 Lieut)

40 sq. X 10 (20 sgt.)

Two majors for two companies of two hundred troops provided by an unnamed private security force, divided into eight platoons of twenty headed by eight lieutenants, further divided into forty separate squads of ten, each with its own sergeant: Lanz's prescription for taking over Fourandao with four hundred highly trained and well-armed soldiers. The final grand total for men, equipment and transportation was slightly in excess of one million euros. A country taken for one million, three hundred thousand American dollars.

Saint-Sylvestre began to photograph the documents with the tiny Chobi camera.

Who would pay that much money for a backward, corrupt and hostile piece of jungle territory surrounded by plague, genocide, mass rape and murder in the middle of Africa? And even more important, why?

16

He smelled the rich scents of bouillabaisse wafting up from the restaurant below and heard the soft patter of a summer shower on the roof of the little hotel on Chartres Street in the French Quarter of New Orleans. He kept his eyes closed, knowing it would all slip away if he opened them, and let the warm breeze coming through the jalousie windows dry the sweat on his bare skin. He listened to his heartbeat slow, and faintly heard a trumpet far away playing "Tiger Rag." He knew where he was and knew who was on the bed beside him even though it couldn't be. He was posted to Fort Polk and she taught school in the city but that was years ago.

"Stay," he whispered, reaching out a hand and feeling nothing. "Stay for just a little while," he pleaded. "Please, Amy."

But Amy was gone, dust and memory for many years. Alive only in dreams, but in those dreams so achingly alive. He woke in the little tent and wiped the tears from his eyes, glad the Cuban he was sharing space with hadn't seen.

The tent was a jungle camo Marmot Limelight, courtesy of the murder squad that had been sent to kill them. Holliday stared up at the curved roof. The sound of the rain was real enough. Strangely, so was the smell of cooking food. He roused himself, sitting up and scrubbing the troubled sleep from his face. Sometimes he hated the memories of his wife for their persistence and the deep, aching pain they caused, and sometimes he wondered how he would live without them, worried that if they faded he would fade along with them, just like the old song MacArthur quoted from in his famous speech. Maybe that was what he was *supposed* to do.

He crawled out of the tent and stood up. There was mist on the river and in the trees. The rain whispered, hissing as it fell through the canopy of leaves. Birds called to one another noisily. Eddie was squatting over a fire he'd built in the sheltering boughs of a tree close to the riverbank. A large green-and-white-mottled fish with enormous eyes had been slit and cleaned, then spitted through the gills on a green sapling hung above the coals. The Cuban looked up as Holliday ducked under the overhanging branches of the tree and joined him. They were screened from the river itself by a heavy stand of high reeds, making them virtually invisible to anyone going past.

"More memories, *mi coronel?*" Eddie asked.

"You see too much, my friend," said Holliday. "The fish smells good."

"Puffer," said Eddie. "*Es muy sabroso*, good eating."

"I'm starved," said Holliday, and realized it was true. Eddie picked up a length of twig and gently pulled it along the scorched scales of the big fish. The skin peeled back easily, showing the thick white flesh below.

"Almost ready," said Eddie.

On cue Peggy, rumpled and still half-asleep, poked her head out of the tent opening and looked around blearily. She shivered in the damp air even though it was already getting hot. She dragged herself across the tiny little patch of open ground behind the reeds and slumped down beside Holliday. A moment later Rafi appeared and joined her. Eddie took the fish down from its skewer and sliced it into large pieces, putting each one into a large flat leaf. He handed them around. "Eat with your fingers. My restaurant is like Havana where they chain down the spoons."

Peggy scooped up a handful of the white, flaky flesh and popped it into her mouth. She chewed and swallowed. "Not bad for the middle of the African jungle." She nodded. "Too bad there're no condiments."

"Aha!" Eddie said. "I found this just for you!" He leaned over and handed Peggy one of the big leaves folded into a packet. She opened it and found a pile of little woody flecks.

"What is it?"

"Try a little. A very little," said Eddie. Peggy picked up a few flecks on the tip of her finger and tasted them. She winced, coughed, squeezed her eyes shut and moaned. "Hot-hot-hot-hot!" She waved her hands. "Water!"

Eddie tossed her one of the bottles of water they'd found in the Blackhawk team's supplies. She twisted off the cap and drained the bottle, then sat back gasping, tears running down her face.

"What the hell was that?" She gasped.

"*Capsicum annuum*, African piquin pepper." Eddie grinned. He pointed with his knife at a densely branched plant with big purple flowers that was growing in a patch of foliage on the other side of the fire. "It grows all over here."

"She's used to the stuff that comes in little bottles on the restaurant tables." Holliday laughed.

"Phooey," said Peggy. She tore off another chunk of fish from the piece on her broadleaf plate and ate it. They sat in silence, eating the fish and looking out toward the river half-hidden in the mist.

"We have to make a decision," said Holliday, finishing the meal and licking his fingers one by one.

"About what?" Peggy asked.

"About going on," he answered.

"I don't understand," Rafi said.

"This is no wild-goose chase anymore," said Holliday. "It's serious."

178

"I always thought it was serious," retorted Rafi.

"We were looking for King Solomon's Mines, Rafi. That's like looking for Noah's Ark on Mount Ararat or the Holy Grail behind the rose-red walls of Petra. All archaeological expeditions are wild-goose chases when you get right down to it, but this goose has become too dangerous to track down anymore. People are trying to kill us."

"Not for King Solomon's Mines," said Rafi.

"No, they're after something else and we're getting in the way. And they're serious. Ask the late Mr. Archibald Ives about that."

"So we just give up?" Rafi said.

"It's not a matter of giving up, Rafi; it's about getting out of the line of fire," answered Holliday. "These people are firing air-to-ground missiles at us. We're being given a warning. I think it's one we should heed."

"*¡Silencio!*" Eddie barked, suddenly alert, his head tilted toward the river, his eyes closed.

"What is it?" Peggy said.

"Listen!" Eddie hissed. "And keep your heads down." He scooped a double handful of earth up and dropped it on the fire, covering it. He dumped another load down and tamped it with his hands.

"There," whispered Holliday. "I hear it now. Upriver from us."

Eddie scuttled across the little clearing and down to the reeds. Holliday followed him.

"Stay here; stay out of sight," he cautioned. Rafi nodded.

"It's getting closer," said Eddie, peering through the reeds as Holliday joined him.

Voices in the mist, strange, high-pitched like a children's choir. And then a heavy echoing sound like the muffled beating of a giant wooden drum.

"It is the *Guenmilere*, I think," said Eddie, listening.

"The what?"

"The *Guenmilere*, it is a thing from Santeria, a *canto*."

"A chant?"

"Yes, a chant."

There was a few seconds of silence.

"¡Coño!" Eddie whispered.

The source of the strange voices came into view, two massive pirogues, or river dugouts, each made from the straight, heavy trunk of a single ash tree, each sixty or seventy feet in length and fitted with a large banana-shaped outrigger. In each of the long, narrow boats forty paddlers worked, all boys between the ages of eight and twelve, each with a very adult Kalashnikov AK-47 assault rifle strapped across his back. In the center of each boat was a pile of supplies tied down under tarpaulins.

And they were singing, the familiar song turned into sinister cadence, each brief line punctuated by a grown man in the bow of the boats beating on the hull with a

long, heavy club. As the adult beat the side of the boat
he let out a heavy, drawn-out grunt:

> Onward Christian Soldiers
> HUH!
> Marching as to war,
> HUH!
> With the cross of Jesus
> HUH!
> Going on before.
> HUH!
> Christ the royal Master
> HUH!
> Leads against the foe;
> HUH!
> Forward into battle
> HUH!
> See his banners go.

The two boats slipped through the current, surging
with each stroke of the paddles, the children bowed
over as though weighed down by the AK-47s on their
backs and chained like slaves by the hammering beat of
the clubs.

"Child soldiers," said Holliday. Children torn from
their families and forced to watch and perform atroci-
ties, and then enlisted in an unholy army and turned
from children into savage, monstrous killers. He'd seen

them in Somalia and in ones and twos in Afghanistan, where they were usually more orphan than soldier, but never in numbers like this, uniformed and well armed. "Who are they?"

"Lord's Resistance Army," answered Eddie. "Out of Uganda originally, led by a *demente* named Joseph Kony." They watched as the huge dugouts moved downstream, vanishing into the mist again.

"What are they doing here?" Holliday asked.

"Who knows," replied Eddie. "They fight for anyone now if the price is right. I do know one thing, though, *mi coronel.* Those two pirogues are just the vanguard. There will be more behind them. On the river and through the jungle. You have no choice anymore."

"Choice?"

"There is no turning back now, Señor Holliday. If we are to live we must go on."

17

The living room of the flat was white and very modern. A white leather couch, several matching club chairs and a glass-and-steel coffee table sat in front of the white brick hearth of the fireplace. Above the fireplace was a large triptych of Francis Bacon paintings commemorating the death of Bacon's lover, George Dyer. Bacon's stark representation of a man writhing and twisting on a beach had been purchased at Sotheby's for sixty-seven million dollars.

Although he'd owned the painting through the Bambridge Trust for the past three years, Sir James Matheson had never seen it before. He decided that he rather liked it, probably because it so blatantly illustrated violent, passionate emotions that the billionaire industrialist was reasonably sure he didn't have. Being his father's son and spending thirteen years in the English public school system had taken care of that.

With Matheson were Konrad Lanz, Major Allen

Faulkener and the guest of honor, Francois Nagoupandé, fully outfitted in the uniform of a general in the Royal Army. The left side of his chest was weighed down with as many service ribbons and medals as Faulkener could find, including the French Croix de Guerre, the India General Service Medal, the Naval Fleet Reserve Medal, the Victoria Cross, the George Cross, the Order of St. Michael and St. George, the Distinguished Service Medal, the South African Pro Patria Medal, and a very handsome Knight Grand Cross of the Order of the Roman Eagle of which Benito Mussolini had been a proud member until his death in 1945. Nagoupandé, who now insisted on being introduced as Brigadier General Francois Nagoupandé, didn't have the slightest idea what any of the decorations meant and he didn't care. As long as he had more medals than Kolingba he was happy.

During his time in London, Faulkener had seen to it that a numbered account was established for him at the Gesner Kantonalbank in Aarau, Switzerland, with a million-dollar deposit as a retainer for Nagoupandé's services as a consultant. Nagoupandé was provided with several bodyguards and a satellite television to keep him occupied during the day, as well as several attentive young women to keep the despot-to-be happy during the evening hours. Except for his fitting at Gieves & Hawkes, he had not left the confines of the safe house rented in Belgravia. Food was brought in by the bodyguards from various pubs and restaurants in the area.

Faulkener carefully went through the basic plan of action outlined by Lanz in a typed forty-four-page report.

"At twenty-four hundred hours on the day of the incursion," Faulkener began, "half the four-hundred-man force will land at the Fourandao airport using a Vickers Vanguard aircraft leased from Lebanese Air Transport out of Mopti Airport in northern Mali, which is the assembly point for the entire force. Two of the companies at the airport will be referred to as Vanguard One and Vanguard Two, one hundred men to each company.

"Vanguard One will be responsible for seizing the Fourandao airport and any operational equipment they find on-site, including two Kamov Ka-50 Werewolf attack helicopters known to be based there. Vanguard Two will be responsible for destroying the microwave repeaters at the airport as well as the satellite uplink. Except for the low-signal shortwave signal from the presidential compound in the city, this will effectively cut off Kukuanaland from the rest of the world, including Bangui, the capital of the Central African Republic.

"With this accomplished, two twenty-man platoons, one from Vanguard One and the other from Vanguard Two, will remain behind to secure the airport and a possible line of retreat, although it is unlikely that this will be necessary. These two platoons will be code-named Van A and Van B. Following this, the remaining men of Vanguard One and Vanguard Two will enter Fourandao from the north following Avenue Forno da Cal, as shown on the map, a copy of which will be provided to each man.

"The objectives of Vanguard One and Vanguard Two are the Plaza de Revolution de Generale Kolingba, the offices of the Kukuanaland Ministry of the Interior (located above the Bank of Central African States on the north side of the square) and the walled blocks of flats directly behind the Trianon Palace Hotel. These flats likely house the bureaucratic cream of the Kukuanaland crop and are well guarded. The guards are to be killed on sight, but the occupants of the buildings are to be kept in their flats. Any attempt by any one of the occupants to escape should be stopped with all necessary force.

"One hour before the arrival of Vanguard One and Vanguard Two at the Fourandao airport, the rest of the force will arrive on the Kotto River seven miles downstream from the Fourandao pier at the southern end of the town. They will arrive on the Kotto River in two refitted Short Shetland WWII transport amphibians carrying one hundred men each. They will have the code names River One and River Two and will also assemble in Mopti, three miles north of the town on the Niger River.

"From their landing sites, marked with GPS coordinates on their orders, River One and River Two will travel upstream to the city in ten-man Zodiac Minuteman inflatables, which will be referred to as Zodiac A through V for the purposes of radio transmission. Zodiac A and Zodiac B to remain with the two aircraft on the river. Zodiac A and Zodiac B will contain the pilots, copilots and flight engineers for both planes.

"On arriving at the Fourandao pier, squads Zodiac C through Zodiac V will reassemble into their requisite companies, radio confirmation of their arrival to Vanguard One and Vanguard Two, and having done so will travel north on Rue de Liberdad to the Plaza de Revolution de Generale Kolingba and seize and hold the southern side of the plaza and the surrounding streets.

"Since the beginning of the incursion takes place well beyond the eighteen-hundred-hour curfew in Fourandao it can be assumed that anyone you meet will be part of the enemy forces and the incursion force will act in accordance with this fact. Anyone assumed to be a civilian during the period of the incursion is to be treated in the same manner.

"On consolidating the incursion force and with the synchronizing of the four company commanders' watches the main attack on the presidential compound will begin, commencing with a mortar attack from zero minutes to zero fifteen minutes. At the same time LAWs rockets will be fired at the corner guard towers of the presidential compound walls and there will be a concerted attempt to use LAWs rockets to destroy the shortwave antenna tower on top of the compound's main building.

"Concurrently sharpshooter teams from all four companies will fire on any members of General Kolingba's compound forces trying to escape from the compound. It is known that there are a number of armored personnel carriers within the compound. Any of these not destroyed in the initial mortar attack must not be allowed to leave the compound and any attempt at this is to be stopped with as much force as necessary, including the use of RPGs, LAWs rockets and the distribution of M-21 antitank mines at the intersection of all streets leading away from the compound.

"There have been a number of rumors that there is an escape tunnel leading from the presidential residence to a building outside the compound. While doing his initial surveillance, Colonel Lanz saw three buildings that seemed in extremely good repair when compared to their neighbors, and one of which, a pharmacy, appeared to be either under surveillance or being guarded by two men in a vehicle wearing plain clothes.

"A study of the methods employed by General Kolingba's second in command, Olivier Gashabi, a.k.a. Oliver Gash, point to an escape tunnel as a very real possibility. Immediately at the beginning of the mortar attack on the compound it is suggested that the pharmacy building be destroyed with the use of incendiaries and RPG fire. Even then a watch should be kept on the ruins.

"It is estimated that half to two-thirds of the forces within the compound will have been killed or wounded within the first hour after the commencement of the attack. Any attempt to surrender is to be forcibly refused, even if the surrender is offered by Kolingba himself.

"It is estimated that there are three thousand members of the Kukuanaland armed forces scattered in small garrisons around the territory, while all command and control functions, including resupply of these garrison troops, is done from Fourandao.

"The four-hundred-man incursion force is neither strong enough, large enough nor well enough supplied to hold off a consolidation of these garrison forces for very long, so it is imperative that the head of the snake, so to speak, be killed immediately and completely. The incursion force has no ability to take prisoners or guard them. The destruction of the compound forces must be one hundred percent."

"What about the civilian population?" Matheson asked.

"The civilian population is entirely cowed by Kolingba. The man is a despot. If he is killed the initial response of the local population will be one of relief."

"The bureaucrats in the flats?"

"They are to be kept under house arrest," replied Faulkener. "Brigadier General Nagoupandé assures me that there are enough members of his loyal government in exile to fulfill any functions presently being handled by the occupants of the three buildings."

"And after the brigadier general has formally taken the reins of power?" Matheson asked.

"That will be entirely up to Brigadier General Nagoupandé," answered Faulkener, his voice bland and without emotion. He knew precisely what would happen to them, because Nagoupandé had described in vivid detail what he would do to each and every one of them, man, woman and child. There was no need to burden Matheson with the same lurid and obscene information.

"Quite so." Matheson nodded. "How long is our force supposed to last before they are relieved?"

"Six days," replied Faulkener, his tone brisk. "This is the amount of time we project it will take for news of the brigadier general's return to travel by word of mouth throughout Kukuanaland."

"Jungle drums?" Matheson smiled, lighting a cigar.

"A company called InterMedia did a study several years ago that showed in countries with difficult-to-reach populations, such as those in Africa, Kukuanaland in particular, word of mouth is still the optimum method of communication. According to the study we can expect seventy-five percent penetration within four days and eighty percent within six."

"And the result of this happy news?" Matheson asked.

Nagoupandé spoke for the first time that evening. "I am Banda; you knew this?"

"Certainly." Matheson nodded.

"That is a ratio of exactly five to one," said Nagoupandé. "With those odds and the knowledge that Kolingba is dead and I am in power there will be *un révolution de machetes*, as our French colonial masters called it, a revolution of machetes. A great deal of Baya and Yakima blood will be spilled and the small garrisons will be overrun. In a few weeks there will be a People's Banda Army and I shall be at its head. Any Yakima still alive will almost certainly flee."

"Limbani among them?" Matheson asked.

"Limbani is dead," said Nagoupandé flatly, his black eyes going cold. Matheson drew in a sharp breath and concentrated on the tip of his cigar to hide the sudden apprehension he felt. Faulkener had convinced him that Nagoupandé was just another greedy dictator-in-waiting, ready for his fifteen minutes of fame before he sank back into obscurity, but just now in the certainty of the man's voice he wasn't quite so sure.

"You're positive?" Lanz said. "I don't like the idea of having to deal with someone else's army coming out of the jungle at the last minute."

"When you were on your spying mission in my country, did you see any sign of his presence?"

"No. Not a thing. Just a look on a bartender's face when I mentioned his name."

Nagoupandé laughed. "Marcel Boganda." He nodded. "He is an informer for Jean-Luc Saint-Sylvestre, the head of the Department of the Interior. He was head of the secret police back in the days that I was Limbani's assistant. Boganda was one of the *araignées* in Saint-Sylvestre's web."

"Saint-Sylvestre." Lanz nodded, smiling wanly. "The name of the customs official at the airport when I arrived."

"He is shown the passenger lists long before the flight arrives. When he sees a name on the manifest he does not recognize he sometimes investigates," said Nagoupandé. "A careful man, our Jean-Luc."

"All of this is fluff and flummery," said Matheson. "The only real threat is from Limbani. He is the only one who has the resources and the education to effect a real revolution in Kukuanaland."

Nagoupandé looked at Matheson indifferently. "Your prejudices are showing, sir. You have me in your mind as another savage from the Dark Continent wishing to rape his country and then retire in luxury and obscurity in some safe haven like Dubai or Switzerland. I am not your average African despot, however. I have an undergraduate degree in anthropology from the Université de Paris and a master's degree in political science and economics from the Ruprecht-Karls University of Heidelberg. I returned to my country because I thought I could do something to change it, to make it a better place for my people. I thought that the French had corrupted paradise and that with some time and patience and effort it could be paradise once more. I was wrong. Corruption is a disease that once contracted cannot be cured. Kolingba is only a symptom.

"So take what you want, but pay me well, Sir James, and I will be your puppet for as long as you require. Cheat me or betray me and you will live to regret it. The only codicil is that you bring me Solomon Bokassa Sesesse Kolingba's head on the end of a spear." Nagoupandé smiled pleasantly. "Savage enough for you, Sir James?"

Matheson was quiet for a long moment, smoking his cigar and staring at the painting on the wall that had cost him twice what the "destabilization" of Kukuanaland would amount to by the time all was said and done. There was perhaps ten billion pounds of profit to be made from this worm-in-the-apple of a country and with the shell company Faulkener was negotiating for through the bank in Aarau. Return enough for the risk and all the blood to be shed.

He turned his glance away from the painting and looked at Nagoupandé. The man looked ridiculous in his brigadier general's uniform, but Matheson knew that the uniform was not for the man's vanity but worn as a symbol of his power to his people, not far removed from the tribal scars some African chiefs still scored across their faces. The more scars, the greater the power.

Matheson knew exactly what Nagoupandé's background was, and in the end his fine speech didn't matter. Nagoupandé was smart enough to do as he was told, because he was easily replaced—one puppet dancing on its strings was much like any other.

"Yes, Brigadier General Nagoupandé, savage enough." Matheson paused. "Quite savage enough."

Grantham Place was a pricey cul-de-sac off Old Park Lane, and number nine was a large block of Victorian brick flats pierced on three sides by porte cocheres that led into an inner courtyard. It looked very much like a brick version of the Dakota in New York City, a building Captain Jean-Luc Saint-Sylvestre of the Kukuanaland secret police was quite familiar with, being a fan of both Roman Polanski and John Lennon. Of course, in Kukuanaland, the assassin Mark David Chapman would have been summarily executed on the spot and then torn limb from limb.

Flat six was on the second floor; that was easy enough to discover by visiting the English Heritage head office in Holborn, as was the original floor plan for the flat, a six-bedroom monster with two maid's rooms and four bathrooms.

The long-term lease was held by something called

the Bambridge Trust and was represented by a law firm in Edinburgh, Scotland, which paid the rent in full on January 1 of each year. They also paid for regular cleaning and maintenance, and contributed ten thousand pounds a year to English Heritage—beyond which the English Heritage partners knew nothing about the Bambridge Trust, nor did they wish to know anything.

At six thirty p.m., dressed in a well-cut Savile Row suit, Saint-Sylvestre rode the tube to the Hyde Park Corner station, then walked down Piccadilly to Old Park Lane and returned to the main entrance to the Grantham Place building. Nothing had changed since his first visit. He bent down, pretending to lace up his shoe, then turned back down Old Park Lane and stepped into a pub unimaginatively called the Rose and Crown. He took a table with a view through the big bow window to the street. He ordered a Heineken and a steak-and-kidney pie with chips, then settled down to wait.

At six forty-five the parade began with his Mr. X and none other than Francois Nagoupandé in tow dressed in a brigadier general's uniform. Two bodyguards rode along with Mr. X and the ex–lieutenant governor under Amobe Limbani. Twenty minutes later a black Rolls-Royce Phantom whispered down the narrow street, and, craning his neck, Saint-Sylvestre watched as a figure recognizable from the London *Times* as well as *Country Life* and the *Wall Street Journal* appeared. Sir

James Matheson, CEO of Matheson Resource Industries and one of the richest men in the world.

Twenty minutes later a cab dropped off Konrad Lanz at the Grantham address. An interesting assortment of witches around the Kukuanaland cauldron, thought Saint-Sylvestre. Of them Nagoupandé was the most interesting. Kolingba inevitably underrated him, but ever since Kolingba had seized power Saint-Sylvestre had spent a great deal of effort trying to track him down, to no avail. For the man Kolingba called a blundering bureaucrat and a buffoon, Nagoupandé was surprisingly clever at keeping himself hidden.

Nagoupandé's attendance at this evening's meeting confirmed everything that Saint-Sylvestre had been thinking. Matheson had found something in the hinterland and he was willing to pay whatever it cost to overthrow Kolingba and install Nagoupandé to get it. For a moment the secret policeman wondered, not for the first time, whether carrying too many secrets around in your head like he did was inevitably self-destructive.

If Nagoupandé were allowed to take power, Saint-Sylvestre knew that the dictator's new broom would sweep the country clean, searching every nook and cranny. Perhaps it was better to go with the devil you knew than the devil you thought you *might* know. For now, at least, Saint-Sylvestre was still Solomon Kolingba's man.

Saint-Sylvestre nursed several pints, then left the

noisy pub and took up a station in the outdoor café of the Rendezvous Mayfair casino a little farther up the road. Grantham Place itself was blocked by the rear wall of an apartment block on Brick Lane, so if they exited the building he was sure to see them.

At eleven thirty Nagoupandé and his bodyguards left Grantham Place, minus Mr. X. Lanz was next to leave half an hour later, and fifteen minutes after that the Rolls-Royce appeared and Mr. X and Sir James Matheson departed. By rights the flat should have been empty, but Saint-Sylvestre waited another half hour to be absolutely sure. At a quarter to one he finally left the café, walked half a block and turned down Grantham Place.

He knew there was a porter's lodge halfway through the porte cochere on the Old Park Lane side, but at the Grantham Place entrance there was a ten-foot-tall scrolled and spiked wrought-iron gate instead, the original iron locks replaced by modern Yales. Saint-Sylvestre took his tubular electric pick and a torsion bar out of his pocket, looked around and then fitted the torsion bar into the lock, pressing down the tumblers.

He then inserted the pick on the end of the electric unit, hit the button three or four times to get the pins lined up, then twisted the torsion bar to the left. The gate swung open. Saint-Sylvestre put the electric pick and the torsion bar back in his pocket, pulled the gate open fully and stepped through into the empty interior courtyard. He walked across to the interior door and repeated the process with the pick gun when he was sure the way was clear.

Pocketing the little device, he climbed three steps and turned down a short hall that led to the elevator lobby. There was a sleepy-looking security guard behind an elegant reproduction Louis Quinze desk reading the *Daily Mirror*. As Saint-Sylvestre appeared the man's head came up out of the paper and stared.

"His lordship forgot his reading glasses," explained Saint-Sylvestre with a smile. The security guard nodded and went back to his paper. Saint-Sylvestre climbed into the empty elevator and rode up to the second floor. A few moments later he had successfully bypassed the lock on flat six and let himself inside.

The flat was expansive, just the way the floor plan had indicated, furnished in an anonymous ultramodern style that reflected nothing about the people who occupied it. All there was to show that it had recently been occupied was a fresh cigar butt in a huge cut-glass ashtray in the living room and a collection of used drink glasses piled into the dishwasher in the kitchen.

Presumably the cleaners would be in to give the place the once-over before it was used again. It looked as though his efforts had been wasted. He checked every room and came up empty-handed. Then he pulled open the louvered doors on the coat cupboard in the entrance hall and found a single object out of place, along with the scent of an expensive aftershave.

If memory served, the aftershave was a scent developed by the Sultan of Oman back in the 1960s—Amouage Die Pour Homme, probably purchased in an effort to impress Nagoupandé, since it cost something like two or three hundred dollars an ounce. But the object that had caught his interest was a business card: Leonhard Euhler, Gesler Bank, 11 Rathausgasse, Aarau, Switzerland.

18

They paddled west, letting the current do most of the work. The dugouts were tethered bow to stern using the horizontal slots normally used for making portages overland down steep grades. As the current increased in speed it seemed to Holliday that the river narrowed, the banks stony rather than the low muddy beaches that had been the norm up until now. There were fewer eddies and backwaters and no crocodiles at all; the water was too swift and there was little for them to eat.

Even the sound of the river was different, deeper and louder, the roar echoing off the hills that were beginning to rise from the jungle. As the sun rose behind them on the morning after seeing the child warriors, Holliday saw the shimmering magic light of a rainbow in the distance.

"Waterfall ahead," he called, turning back to warn Rafi and Peggy in the trailing dugout. "Next time I spot

a likely place we'll get off the river and take a look."
There was no way of telling on which side they'd make
landfall, so Holliday and Captain Eddie kept them centered in midriver, feeling the strengthening of the current with each stroke of the paddle.

Fifteen minutes later Eddie called out and pointed to
the starboard shore with his dripping paddle. *"¡Ahí!"*
There.

Two hundred yards ahead on their right-hand side
Holliday saw the spot Eddie had pointed out, a tiny
patch of light green, a little paler than the surrounding
foliage. Holliday jammed his paddle on the left and the
bow of the lead dugout swung around, taking them out
of the current at a shallow angle. He and Eddie paddled
hard, Rafi and Peggy following suit. Just as they approached the little beach Holliday reached back and
pulled the quick release on the tether that bound the
two crude boats together. Both dugouts made it to a
barely visible swirl of calmer water and they drove the
boats up onto the rough sand.

Holliday and Eddie stepped out of the lead dugout
and pulled it even higher out of the water. Then the two
men dropped down onto the sand for a much-needed
break. From where they sat they could hear the steady
distant thunder of the waterfall.

"We are not the first to stop here," said Eddie, reaching into the long grass at the edge of the tiny strip of
sand as Rafi and Peggy pulled their dugout completely

out of the water. The Cuban held up a crushed green tin of Sparletta cream soda.

"The kiddie soldiers?" Peggy said.

"*¿Los niños? Sí.*" Eddie nodded.

"Who are they going to fight for, I wonder," said Holliday.

"Presumably Kolingba, or someone against him." Rafi shrugged.

"It could be that they are only on a raid," said Eddie. "Borders mean nothing to them. They could be, how do you say, *reclutamiento*, recruiting. They go to the villages, take the children. If the parents object they kill them. Sometimes they kill them anyway."

"I don't care what they're doing," said Holliday. "The question is, How do we get ourselves out of their way? Right now we're trapped. They're ahead of us and behind us."

"We could hide the boats and wait for the ones behind us to go past, then go back upriver," suggested Rafi.

"They'll have scouts on land as well as in boats. The jungle is their home. They would almost certainly find us," said Eddie.

"There's no way of telling how far ahead they are," said Holliday. "Or if they've already arrived at their destination."

"How would we know?" Peggy asked.

"First we must portage the boats below the falls.

203

Maybe they will have left some sign?" The Cuban held up the can. "A trail of Sparletta, like the two children of *la bruja* and her *casa de pan de jengibre*."

"'Hansel and Gretel.'" Peggy laughed.

"Sí." Eddie nodded. "They cook her in the oven, yes?"

"Yes," said Holliday grimly. "And that's what those kids with the AK-47s will do if they catch us. Rafi and I will see how far it is to the fire. Peggy, you stay here with Eddie and watch our backs. Maybe unload some of the gear from the boats to make them lighter."

"Will do," said Peggy.

Holliday and Rafi followed the narrow trail into the jungle. It had clearly been used as a portage for a very long time: logs, some old and rotten, lay half buried in the dark, rich soil at six- or seven-foot intervals to make it easier to slide the dugouts overland. As they made their way down the pathway the trees around them broke into chatters and screams of animals warning one another of the approach of possible predators. Beyond those warning calls there was the normal chaotic sound track of the jungle: the shivering whisper of breezes through the high canopy, the eerie singing of insects calling to prospective mates and the barely audible slip and slide of other creatures, climbing, twisting and digging their way through ground and trees.

"It's never quiet, is it?" Holliday said.

"Spooky," answered Rafi, his voice edgy. "Especially

when you stop and imagine what kind of things are alive all around you and how easy it would be for them to make a meal out of you if they were given half a chance. This morning I woke up and saw a centipede on the ridgepole of the tent that had to be six or seven inches long. Nasty bastards, and they bite, too." He shook his head. "I'm just a desert kind of guy, I guess."

"Right." Holliday laughed. "A desert kind of guy who likes his on-campus Aroma Espresso Bar venti caramel macchiatos, stirred, with extra caramel sauce and toffee nut instead of vanilla."

"How did you know that?" Rafi asked, looking a little affronted.

"Peg does about a five-minute skit of you ordering. It's like something off an old episode of *Frasier* except in Hebrew."

"Well, at least I don't whine because they closed all the Starbucks outlets in Israel."

"I could never figure that out," said Holliday. "Starbucks is like the plague—it's everywhere except Israel."

"The secret power of the Viennese coffee cartel," said Rafi.

The trail came to an end and they stepped out onto a slab of stone half the size of a city block. Directly in front of them they could see a steep, treacherous set of rapids that no one in their right mind would attempt to run.

"Not your Lost Templar's vision of Eden," said Holliday.

"It's too soon to be the Kazaba Falls," said Rafi. "We've got a long way to go yet."

The frothing pool beneath the rapids turned into a misty reed-edged lake a thousand feet in diameter feeding into the low-banked river again, far below. The jungle was like an unbroken, undulating carpet of yellow and green that stretched to the horizon. Holliday took the military binoculars he'd liberated from the assault team and looked downriver. In the middle distance and close to the winding river he could just make out several thin curls of white-gray smoke rising above the jungle. It was either a riverside village or the camp of the child soldiers. The river at that point appeared to be less than two hundred feet wide. There wasn't the slightest chance of slipping by keeping under cover of the opposite bank. He handed the glasses to Rafi.

"Maybe it's just a downstream village," suggested the archaeologist.

"I doubt it. That smoke is about five miles off. The kiddie soldiers are a day and a half ahead of us. They would have raided the village by now if they were still on the water and you'd be seeing a lot more smoke. If they haven't raided the village that means they're in the jungle somewhere between here and there."

"So what do we do?" Peggy asked.

"Get rid of the dugouts and anything else we can't

carry," said Holliday. "Take the tents, the dry food and the weapons. That's about it."

Peggy and Rafi started going through the packs while Eddie took Holliday aside.

"Those men who attacked us by the river. They had *granadas*, yes?"

"That's right," said Holliday. "Two of the men had a half dozen each."

"I need four," said Eddie. "And some of those plastic drinking glasses."

"What for?"

"A welcome present for whoever our friends are back there," he said, cocking a thumb upriver the way they'd come.

"A welcome present?"

"A farewell present, too." Eddie grinned. "*Hola* and *adios*." The Cuban laughed. "The hello will be *explosivo*; the good-bye will be *los ángeles cantando. ¿Lo captaste, mi amigo?*"

"*Lo entiendo, amigo,*" said Holliday, smiling. "I understand."

Jean-Luc Saint-Sylvestre had no affection for mountains. If he couldn't see the sun rise over some kind of horizon it made him nervous. He didn't like Switzerland at all, where sunrises were in very short supply and there were mountains everywhere.

He flew out of Heathrow in the early morning, caught the eleven-thirty train from Geneva to Zurich and arrived at exactly two thirty in the afternoon. He rented a Europcar VW Passat and drove the twenty-five miles to Aarau, a town of seventeen thousand clustered around the banks of the Aar River at the foot of the Jura Mountains. It was exactly what you'd expect of a classic Swiss town.

Saint-Sylvestre had a lunch of lamb and egg noodles in the Restaurant Laterne on the Rathausgasse, then walked two blocks to number eleven, the address on the business card.

The Gesler Bank was a small, discreet gray building with small shuttered windows and an arched doorway with a brass door. There wasn't even a plaque announcing the building's purpose, only a carved number 11 above the door. There was, however, a state-of-the-art CCTV camera on a bracket in the doorway arch angled to cover anyone pressing the white porcelain button on one side of the doorframe. Saint-Sylvestre pushed the button, ignoring the cameras. There was a brief pause and then the brass door clicked and came slightly ajar. Saint-Sylvestre stepped inside and the door closed behind him. He found himself in a glassed-in security portal, the brass door at his back and floor-to-ceiling glass panels all around him. Through the glass he could see into a small wood-paneled lobby, the walls hung with oil paintings, all portraits. A guard in a pin-striped suit sat behind a small desk. The guard leaned forward and spoke into a microphone.

"Ihr Unternehmen wenden, Sie sich bitte," said the voice, coming from a speaker above Saint-Sylvestre's head.

"I'm here to see Herr Leonhard Euhler," answered Saint-Sylvestre, speaking in French.

The man behind the table didn't hesitate for a moment and replied in clear French with a Paris accent. "What business do you have with Herr Euhler?"

"Private business. I am here under the authority of the Moroccan government."

"One moment," said the guard, still speaking French. Keeping his eyes on Saint-Sylvestre in the security portal he reached down to his belt and lifted up a little speak-to-talk unit, then clicked for an answer, which Saint-Sylvestre couldn't make out. "He'll be right down," said the guard.

There was a buzzing sound from within the glass booth that Saint-Sylvestre assumed came from some sort of built-in metal detector. A few moments later a narrow elevator door on the wall behind the guard opened and a slight man in his late forties or early fifties appeared.

He was medium height, and wore a dark suit, a pale blue shirt and a bright red tie. His shoes looked expensive. As he crossed the lobby Saint-Sylvester saw that he was round faced, with a high forehead, thinning hair and a thick toothbrush mustache that covered his upper lip above a wide smile. He wore stylish black plastic circular eyeglasses. He looked more like an aging, homosexual British bureaucrat than a banker. The diamond stud cuff links, the silk tie and the manicured and clear-polished nails were just a little too fey.

The security portal slipped open noiselessly and Saint-Sylvestre stepped out. "I am Dr. Euhler," said the smiling man, extending a hand. "How may I be of service?"

Why were all German-Swiss doctors? Saint-Sylvestre wondered. He shook the extended hand. "My name is Tarik Ben Barka," he said, speaking English and using the name that appeared on the passport a recent visitor to Kukuanaland had "lost," and which now carried Saint-Sylvestre's photograph. He took the sand-colored passport out of the inside pocket of his suit and extended it to Euhler, who waved it off.

"You are here on behalf of the government of Morocco?"

He could feel the man's pale blue eyes looking him over.

"Not exactly. I am here on behalf of several clients of the Banque Populaire du Maroc."

"They are Moroccan, these clients?" Euhler said.

"No," said Saint-Sylvestre. "They are not."

"Ah." Euhler nodded. "Perhaps we should continue our conversation in my office."

Euhler led Saint-Sylvestre to the narrow elevator, passing the guard at the table. Despite the tailoring of the guard's suit Saint-Sylvestre could detect the slight pull at the shoulders that marked a weapon sling; probably a German MP9 machine pistol or some other room sweeper like it.

The elevator was wood paneled and marble floored. It whined upward for a few seconds and then opened into a narrow hallway manned by another guard. Saint-Sylvestre followed Euhler to the end of the hall. The banker put his palm onto a biometric pad by the door, standing aside politely to let Saint-Sylvestre enter.

The office looked more like a Victorian living room than a banker's office. The chairs were ornate and velvet covered, the desk was a giant, deeply sculpted thing, and the display case behind the desk was filled with what appeared to be ancient pottery. The paintings on the walls were all baroque Swiss landscapes of the sort that Sherlock Holmes would have liked—all lonely meadows and craggy peaks in serried rows.

At first glance you could easily make the mistake that the man behind the desk was some airheaded romantic, someone who'd likely inherited his position from a relative who was one of the bank's directors and, considering that there was no ring on the third finger of his left hand, either a confirmed bachelor or more likely gay, as he'd thought before.

Saint-Sylvestre wasn't quite so sure. Gay or not, Euhler gave off the impression of someone acting out a role but whose mind was carefully ticking somewhere behind the jolly, smiling mask, assessing and calculating, thinking about each move like a master chess player.

"You are a Muslim, Mr. Ben Barka?" Euhler asked.

"Why do you ask?" Saint-Sylvestre said, taken a little off guard.

"I usually have coffee around this time along with an aperitif. I would not like to offend you by offering you liquor."

"Very thoughtful." Saint-Sylvestre nodded. "But I am of the Lemba religion. Coffee and an aperitif would be very pleasant, thank you."

Euhler beamed and called for coffee on his intercom, then stood and went to an armoire on the other side of the room. For the first time Saint-Sylvester noticed the lack of street sounds outside Euhler's office window and it occurred to him that the window was bulletproof.

"Kümmel?" Euhler offered, holding up a bottle of the caraway-and-cumin-flavored liqueur.

"Certainly." Saint-Sylvestre nodded. The coffee arrived, brought on a silver tray with a silver service and small porcelain cups by a male secretary. The secretary left the office and Euhler returned to his desk with the drinks in their tiny crystal glasses. He then went through the coffee-pouring ritual, offering Saint-Sylvestre sugar, which he accepted, and cream, which he did not.

Saint-Sylvestre sipped the kümmel while Euhler sat back in his ridiculous velvet-covered office chair.

"So tell me about these clients of yours," he said, smiling pleasantly from beneath his mustache.

"They would like to open accounts at your bank. Private accounts."

"All our accounts are quite private."

"There have been rumors of Swiss bank transparency, the so-called G-twenty blacklists," said Saint-Sylvestre mildly. He watched as Euhler's complexion reddened slightly.

"And after all the loud talking is over and the dust settles you will see that we are in fact on no one's blacklists, let alone the G-twenty, who I must say have enough to answer for on their own." Euhler shook his head. "The world is in a terrible economic slump and they look to place the blame on whomever they can. Switzerland is convenient. It is hardly our fault that our ability to manage financial affairs is better than theirs. It is nothing but jealousy, Mr. Ben Barka."

"My clients can be guaranteed complete discretion?"

"Certainly," said Euhler a little ponderously.

Saint-Silvestre allowed himself a long pause, then spoke. "You are aware of the situation in Cuba?"

"Fragile." Euhler nodded.

"'Explosive,' I think would be a better word," said Saint-Sylvestre. "The Western press applauds Raul Castro's opening of free markets in that country as a turn toward democracy, but it is not. It is an act of desperation. The country is bankrupt and the revolution is dead. The younger generation watches Miami TV on wall-sized televisions and lives almost completely within the black market. Corruption is rife."

Saint-Sylvestre smiled at Euhler and went fishing for a moment, an idea forming in the back of his mind. Then, clearing his throat, he spoke aloud several lines from William Butler Yeats's poem "The Second Coming."

Euhler's face lit up. "Ah, Yeats, one of my favorites," he said, cooing like a dove. He recited the next verse, then said dramatically, "I'm afraid those times have come 'round again."

Saint-Sylvestre nodded. "Which is why I am here, of course."

"I take it your clients are Cuban, then?" Euhler said.

"And have been since Angola," said Saint-Sylvestre. "They are farseeing men and women, most of whom have chosen Spain as their country of choice when the situation becomes too tenuous at home."

"Yes." Euhler nodded.

"The Spanish banking regulations are compliant with all forty of the G-twenty regulations regarding money laundering. The Moroccan banking system is not. They are referred to as 'serious shortcomings' by the G-twenty financial task force."

"Loopholes," said Euhler.

"Yes," answered Saint-Sylvestre.

"And Morocco and Spain are separated by a mere seven nautical miles." Euhler smiled.

"Quite so," said Saint Sylvestre. "Getting the funds to Morocco is easy enough, but once there my clients would like to see their funds invested in a broader number of opportunities than we can offer."

"Could you give me some idea of the amounts we are talking about?" Euhler said. The German had sniffed around enough and liked what he smelled.

"Approximately half a billion dollars, perhaps more." The object was to put him on an equal playing field with Matheson and MRI.

Euhler didn't even blink.

"Are these individual clients or are they willing to invest as a cartel?"

"Whichever is most beneficial," said Saint-Sylvestre. He was making it as easy as possible for the round-faced Euhler to take the bait. It was time to add the icing to the cake.

"If your bank works out for these clients, then perhaps we could discuss further business. We have a number of clients in similar situations who could benefit from a broader investment profile."

"This sounds extremely interesting, Mr. Ben Barka." Euhler nodded. "Perhaps we could discuss it further over dinner tonight."

"That would be most pleasant," said Saint-Sylvestre. "And please, call me Tarik."

"And I am Leonhard." The banker smiled. "But my friends call me Lenny." He opened a drawer in the desk, took out a card and used an expensive-looking fountain pen to scribble on it.

"I meet few men of culture in my work," said Saint-Sylvestre, sighing as he dangled the carrot. "Certainly not ones who can recite Yeats from memory."

"As I mentioned, he is a favorite of mine. I wrote several essays about him over the years at school."

"A prescient man," said Saint-Sylvestre. "In parts of Africa he would be thought of as a griot, a shaman, a foreteller of the future."

"A role which seems to fall to bankers now." Euhler laughed with a strange, strangled sound that was almost a giggle. He smiled again. "Perhaps you would like dinner tonight and we can discuss it?"

Saint-Sylvestre smiled. The banker was definitely wooing him. "That sounds very pleasant."

"There is a place nearby. Very modern. The Krone. The Crown. They do a very nice steak tartare, if you like that sort of thing."

"Very much," said Saint-Sylvestre, who loathed raw meat.

"I live in Zurich, but I have a pied-à-terre in Aarau on the Delfterstrasse."

"Like the porcelain," said Saint-Sylvestre, nodding toward the ornate display cabinet.

"Ah, yes," said Euhler, flushing a little. "A small hobby of mine." He handed over the card: *42 Delfterstrasse, Apartment 709.* "We can meet at the restaurant at seven, shall we say? Then perhaps go back to my place for a nightcap."

"Wonderful," said Saint-Sylvestre. "I'll see you at seven. We can continue our discussion."

"At the very least," said Euhler, his round, grinning face eager.

Carrot, hook, line and sinker; the only thing left was the stick.

19

After hiding the dugouts deep in the brush they went down the pathway to the big stone platform, then turned down a narrow path leading downward toward the distant bowl of the jungle floor. After fifty yards they reached the old portage point—a spindly tooth of rock, a knob worn by a thousand ropes used to lower dugouts to the course of the foaming river far below.

A few feet away a huge iron ring had been spiked into the rock wall of the cliff, a testament to later travelers portaging downriver. They found several more pop cans here and a discarded running shoe, the canvas rotted away and the rubber sole smooth and full of ragged holes. Peggy paused to take a photo of the empty shoe and Holliday could see that the image was souring in his young cousin's soul.

"It never ends," she said softly, looking out over the enormous expanse of the valley cut through by the dark artery of the river. "The whole continent is going to tear itself apart with genocide, corruption and greed. It really is the Dark Continent, not because the people are black but because no one from anywhere else can penetrate its heart."

"It's like Afghanistan," said Holliday, standing beside her. "I've often thought the best thing is just to leave places like that alone. They have their own laws, their own culture and their own way of life and we stole it all away and gave them Chicago Bulls T-shirts in return. They watch our television and see our lives and they can't have them and it festers in them like a wound. That's really why we have wars and revolutions—plain old envy."

"Pretty philosophical for an old soldier," said Peggy.

Holliday, his smile slight, answered her. "The first philosophical thought that comes into a warrior's head might as well be his death warrant. Think about war and you can't fight them anymore, because when you really think about war there's no good reason to fight one."

"That's a bit simplistic, isn't it?" Peggy asked.

"Wars are simple things, despite what politicians tell you. You want what the other guy wants . . . Louis Vuitton jeans, Gucci handbags, gasoline, you name it and you're willing to kill him to get it. Stealth fighters and nuclear submarines are hardly the tools of diplomacy; they're the modern version of the Neanderthal club. The club makers want you to go to war so they can sell a lot of clubs, so they're always whispering in your ear that their club's better than the other guys' and so on."

"But children?" Peggy said. "It's obscene."

"Now who's being simplistic?" said Holliday. "In the tenth century, twelve was considered the optimum age for marriage. In the Viking era if you were old enough to hold a sword and war shield you were a man. I bet this Waldo the Brain Smasher we're following was no more than twenty. The average age of a kid fighting in Vietnam was nineteen or twenty, the average age for the guys fighting in Iraq or Afghanistan even younger."

"He speaks like this all the time?" Eddie asked Rafi as they came down the path.

"What's that supposed to mean?" Holliday said.

"You sound like *el Comandante* giving one of his *oraciónes* in the Plaza de la Revolución in Havana." The Cuban laughed. "People are given lunches and beer to listen to him for five, six hours sometimes. You could make, how you say, a *comida*, a picnic. He could talk forever, that man—embargo this, embargo that—embargo was *el diablo* himself. It was very funny, really."

"He means you're doing it again, Doc," said Rafi.

"Doing what?"

"Giving a lecture." Peggy laughed. "You're back at West Point in a class full of fourth-year 'firsties' laying down the law according to Lieutenant Colonel John 'Doc' Holliday, U.S. Army Ranger."

Doc laughed at himself. "I guess I was at that," he said. It was true. He missed teaching, watching his kids get their chops together so maybe they could go out and fight the good fight and come out the other end intact, maybe thanks to him, even if it was only for a little bit of learning.

They headed down the long, steep, winding path that led down the escarpment, the thunder of the falls booming on their left and the looming jungle wall on their right. Holliday could see the mural in the Templar tomb in his mind's eye and wondered at the ethereal, slightly otherworldly aura that the artist had seen a thousand years ago and that was just as visible now.

When he was a kid he'd read Conan Doyle's *The Lost World* and a strange, never very popular comic book called *Turok, Son of Stone* about two young Indians trapped in a valley of dinosaurs, and he had that strange feeling of the past and future somehow touching each other across the chasm of years, and not for the first time since beginning their expedition.

As they all walked down the lowering path to the bottom of the valley he wondered for a moment if being left in that past might just be the best thing for him. Once upon a time it seemed that duty and honor had been part of life, as well as real pride in the things that he did well, but all that had gone, it seemed, and it didn't look likely to reappear anytime soon.

So what of Lucius Gellius Publicola, the disgraced

general sent on a suicide mission to replenish Anthony's war chest? Had he thought that great riches from this hidden jungle valley would buy his honor back? Or of Ragnar Skull Splitter and his men, making that same voyage nine hundred years later, looking for the treasure of the vanished Eighteenth Legion and its desperate, failed leader?

And what of Roche-Guillaume, the Lost Templar, three hundred years after Ragnar, more a historian than a soldier-knight, a man in many ways very much like him, given to philosophy and curiosity in equal parts? What had it been like to see and feel all these things, to climb out on that rocky slab above them now and see that timeless rainbow and wonder if it was leading him to the treasures of Solomon?

And what if it was all no more than someone's flight of fancy, Roche-Guillaume dreaming of the place he knew existed, but a place of failure he could not admit? What if they had all put themselves in potentially fatal harm's way for no more than a fantasy from seven hundred years before?

Eddie reached the bottom first with Holliday right behind him. There was a definite path where the child soldiers had pushed the dugouts through the tall grasses looking for a safer spot than directly beside the falls, and a second track, narrow and rough, probably used by animals.

Leaves and branches were broken off knee-high and

there were mounds of boar scat here and there. The child soldiers' launch point was of no use to them, so Holliday took a few steps down the boar trail. He'd never actually run into one of the creatures before but he was damned glad they'd brought along a couple of the sharpened spears they'd made, not to mention Eddie's gigantic knife.

"You'd better come and see this, *amigo*," said Eddie, stepping back from the base of the falls. He took Holliday's elbow and pointed.

"My God," he whispered, feeling a rush of adrenaline slam into his heart and tears gather in the corners of his eyes. The past *was* coming up to welcome him.

"What is it?" Rafi said as he and Peggy joined them.

The symbols were carved almost an inch deep into a massive boulder thrown up by the falls aeons ago. Whoever had etched the symbols wanted them there forever.

ᚠᚢᚱᚷᚲᛚ ᛟᚦ

"They're runes, an early form of Norse writing. It's a 'Kilroy was here' from a thousand years ago. Our friend Ragnar Skull Splitter doing a little graffiti."

"Can you read them?" Eddie asked Holliday.

"Only a couple. The one at the end is Thor, the Viking's chief god; the one that looks like an R means journey. I think it's some kind of prayer of thanksgiving for having made it this far."

"Amen to that," said Eddie.

"Arne Saknussemm," whispered Holliday.

"*¡Sí!*" Eddie grinned. "When I was a boy my father read this to me: *Viaje al Centro de la Tierra!* This Saknussemm, he was an *alquimista?*"

"Alchemist." Holliday nodded.

Eddie pointed at the carvings on the black, wet rock. "Like those, I think—his carvings led the others to the center of the earth."

"Nice dad," said Holliday. He couldn't remember his own drunken father ever having read a book to him.

"A nice man, yes," said Eddie, wistfully.

Rafi was beaming like a little kid. "It's wonderful! The runes are absolute proof of my theory!" He ran his fingers into the deep indentations that had been carved into the dark stone. He turned to Peggy. "Take a picture," he said eagerly. "This will put a few people's noses out of joint back at the university."

Peggy dug her Nikon out of her pack and Rafi arranged himself proudly beside the deeply etched lettering, like an old photo of a man on a safari, his foot planted on the head of a dead animal.

"For posterity." Rafi grinned. "And for the pages of the *Qedem* article I'm going to publish."

"Maybe you should get Eddie into the picture, since he was the one who found it," Holliday said. "Maybe give him some credit in the article as well."

"Uh, sure, that sounds good," said Rafi, his face falling just a little bit. "Come on, Eddie; get in here."

"No, thank you, *mi amigo*, this is your thing. I do not want to interfere. It was only luck that I saw it."

"Are you sure?" Rafi said without much eagerness in his voice.

"*Absolutamente*, I am sure." The Cuban smiled.

Peggy took several shots with Rafi in the frame and then a half dozen close shots, getting the sun shadows as deeply into the engraving on the stone as possible. When she was finished they turned back down the narrow old boar path heading deeper into the jungle, Rafi and Peggy in the lead.

"You should have had your picture taken," said Holliday. "You *did* find it first."

"Only an accident, *Doctoro*. It is for him, the adventure, the science of all this; let him have it. We are the lucky ones, after all."

"What do you mean?"

"For Rafi it is dates and kings and radiocarbon dating; for us it is the story, the *narración*. Rafi writes it in his notebooks; we feel it in our hearts. It is both our joy and our tragedy, yes, this imagination, this romance?"

"You should have been a poet, Eddie, not a soldier."

"All Cubans are poets, *amigo*." The big man laughed sourly. "You have to be when they only pay you five pesos a week."

They walked on ahead until they saw Rafi and Peggy stopped in front of an area of scuffed and deeply scratched earth. There were a few cloven hoofprints and the tracks of small, bare human feet, as well. The cracked surface of the disturbed, dry ground indicated that it had recently been used as a mud wallow by the wild pigs that employed the path as a highway through the jungle. The children's footprints were also indicative; they weren't far behind the child soldiers.

"Maybe we should turn off," suggested Rafi.

"The jungle's too thick. This is no canopy rain forest. This is the only way for now."

They kept on moving through the morning hours, the trail leading blindly down to the river once or twice, probably to water the animals who used it, then veered away, heading back into the deeper jungle but always moving west. By noon it became too hot to walk and when the trail led down toward the river again they paused to rest for a few minutes.

So far they hadn't seen any sign of the child soldiers. They had dried food from the attacking team's stores, but no one felt much like dehydrated beef Stroganoff or dried mac and cheese with "real" ground beef. Holliday let them light a small fire as long as the wood was tinder-dry and smokeless, and Eddie went down to the river with his spear to try his luck again. Rafi slept, Holliday tended the fire and Peggy went looking for subjects to photograph.

"Not too far," warned Holliday, "we may have to bail in a rush."

"Yes, sir, boss." Peggy grinned, with a mock salute.

A few minutes later Holliday heard his cousin's familiar laugh and a little while after that she reappeared, the Nikon over her shoulder and something cupped in her hands. Holliday poked at the fire with a twig to keep it burning and stood up.

"What've you got there, kiddo?"

"It's a baby!" Peggy chortled. As Holliday approached her she opened her cupped hands and showed him what she'd found.

"Oh, shit!" Holliday whispered.

"What is it?" Peggy said, startled by his reaction.

"Put it down!" The little creatures in her hand looked like a furry cross between guinea pigs and chipmunks.

"What do you mean?"

"They're boar piglets and that means the mother's around somewhere."

"But—"

"Put them down! Now!" Peggy froze, Rafi woke up with a jerk and somewhere down the trail they heard a sound like a giant steam locomotive. An angry steam locomotive.

Rafi stood up, blinking away sleep. "What the hell?"

Suddenly the locomotive was making sounds like a hundred hammers striking stone and the sounds were getting closer. Eddie appeared, grinning proudly, a two-foot-long fish with a nose like an elephant held with three fingers of his left hand crammed into its gills, the spear that had impaled the scaleless creature in his right hand.

The sow came down the trail from behind them, screeching her steam-engine cry at the top of her lungs, her sharp hooves pounding the dirt, her head high. The beast was black with traces of bristled rust at the shoulders and from where Holliday was standing he could swear the small angry eyes were as red as a demon's. Peggy stood frozen, eyes wide, staring at the furious mother of the infant piglets she held in her hands. It seemed incredible that the piglets and the massive mother were even of the same species.

The mother rushed headlong at Peggy, at least two hundred and fifty pounds of toothy, infuriated horror, the muscles in her back bunched and ready to head off any move her quarry could make.

Unlike the male of the species, the small horned female preferred to attack with her teeth and usually charged with her head high, looking for tender targets in the midsection, preferably stomach and groin.

Holliday had about a three-quarter view. He hauled the handgun he'd taken from one of their dead attackers and fired, striking the creature somewhere in the belly. The enormous pig never even slowed. She was halfway across the clearing now and there was no time for a second shot. Peggy was still frozen on the spot, the piglets squealing in her hand, smelling the approaching sow.

"Peggy!" Rafi bellowed, running toward her. Holliday made a running tackle, bowling Rafi out of harm's way just as the elephant-nosed fish Eddie had been carrying flew through the air and struck the creature heavily on the side of the head. Stunned for a second she came to a lurching halt, looking around, roaring insanely.

"¡Hola! ¡El cerdo grande, cago en tu leche el gordota! ¡Por aquí!"

The huge creature spotted Eddie, turned to him on her spindly legs and pawed the ground with her razor hooves. Eddie pointed the heavy spear toward the sow and made a lunging motion. The sow attacked, head high. Eddie waited until the last second, dropped to one knee, then pounded the blunt end of the spear into the ground at no more than a twenty-degree angle. He gripped the spear with both arms and tensed as the sow sprang forward, the end of the spear going under her raised snout and into the soft tissue of her chest. Eddie was bowled over onto his back but he managed to hang on to the spear. Squealing, the huge beast thrust herself toward Eddie, forcing her body down the pole, impaling herself even more horribly as she tried to bring her gnashing teeth to bear. She died, snorting and groaning weakly a few moments later, the beast's hot blood pooling on the front of Eddie's shirt, soaking it. The stink of the beast's death odor was pungent.

"How did you know where to stab it?" Holliday asked. "My shot didn't even slow it down."

Eddie staggered to his knees and pushed the sow aside.

"My older brother Domingo and I used to hunt them at our uncle's farm in Holguín Province," Eddie answered.

"I guess we lucked out," said Rafi.

"Don't be quite so sure," answered Holliday, hearing a series of familiar clicking sounds. Everyone looked in his direction as four young boys between nine and twelve stepped out of the jungle, their expressions flat and emotionless, the AK-47s in their arms rock steady. Holliday stared. They'd gone from Verne's *Journey to the Center of the Earth* to *Lord of the Flies* in the blink of an eye.

20

The Krone restaurant and bar was exactly as Euhler had described it, lots of glass and gleaming marble behind a classic facade of white half-timbered buildings on a white half-timbered street where even the cobblestone appeared to have been polished recently.

Lenny Euhler had changed out of his suit and was now wearing a pair of tight blue jeans, penny loafers and a pale blue roll-neck sweater. The eyeglasses had gone from black to bright red. He was sitting at the bar drinking a mojito and trying to look bored. There was already an empty glass beside him and a chewed lime wedge.

Saint-Sylvestre sat down beside the banker and gave the man his best smile. Euhler seemed relieved, as though he'd been thinking that he'd allowed his supposedly secret sexuality to interfere with business and consequently had lost a half-billion-dollar deal for having offended Saint-Sylvestre by showing his true colors.

Saint-Sylvestre added to poor Euhler's relief by putting a hand on his shoulder and squeezing lightly. Fat and bone. No muscle. The banker's eyes filled with tears of reassurance.

"Lenny! Been waiting long?"

"Just a few minutes, my dear Tarik," he said, gesturing toward the empty glass. "I've gotten a little ahead of you, I'm afraid, but good tables are frightfully hard to get here at this hour, so I thought I'd get here early and cross the maître d's palm."

"Don't worry, Lenny; I can assure you that I'll catch up."

A bartender stopped and asked him what he wanted and Saint-Sylvestre ordered a margarita. "To keep in the festive mood." He smiled.

"Excellent." Lenny beamed.

After ten minutes of banker's talk of interest rates and the global performance of one stock or another, their table was announced and they went into the restaurant, all crisp white linen and gleaming silver. Euhler had sautéed scallops on a mesclun salad to start and Saint-Sylvestre had the requisite steak tartare with a bright yellow egg yolk perched on the top. This was followed by tandoori chicken breast with wasabi for Euhler and a simple whitefish with almond butter for Saint-Sylvestre, trying to recover from the scoop of bloody ground sirloin with its single yellow egg-yolk eye. All of this was washed down with several bottles of

Castanar Riserva Barrique 2005, a Swiss red that was surprisingly drinkable.

As the meal progressed, Saint-Sylvestre sipping his wine while Euhler gulped his, the conversation went from the general to the specific, slowly but surely honing in on the potential for mineral investment in Africa, led in that direction by Saint-Sylvestre's gentle prodding. Given that he'd found Euhler's business card in the same anonymously owned flat as Sir James Matheson and Francois Nagoupandé, it seemed likely that Matheson was arranging some mineral licensing agreement with Nagoupandé in return for giving the newly created brigadier general Kukuanaland's and Kolingba's heads on the same platter.

The coincidence of Kukuanaland's coup and a sudden mineral find by Matheson would be a little hard for the world press to swallow, not to mention a crown investigating committee into Matheson's business practices being established just down the street at Westminster, so the mining magnate had to be using Euhler's services to distance himself from both the coup and the mineral find. The question was, How?

After a third bottle of wine and a two-octave rise in Euhler's voice, Saint-Sylvestre suggested that they return to the banker's apartment for the promised nightcap. Euhler was pleased as punch and insisted on walking through the cobblestone streets down toward the Aar River, for which the town was named.

According to Lenny, Aarau was located in something called the "golden triangle" of Zurich, Bern and Basel, making it one of the fastest-growing municipalities in the country. It also offered great prospects for people wishing to invest their money. Saint-Sylvestre made it quite clear that the investors he represented were interested in natural resources generally and gold, silver and platinum specifically. They were, according to Saint-Sylvestre, extremely practical people. Lenny gave him a melodramatic wink and squeezed his arm tighter. "I may have just the thing for you, Tarik, my dear."

Euhler's apartment turned out to be an ultramodern white concrete ziggurat overlooking the river and the foothills of the Jura Mountains. It was quite lavish for a pied-à-terre, with two bedrooms, two full bathrooms, one en suite, a living room, a dining room and a home office. Saint-Sylvestre was pleased to notice that there were no obvious security cameras, which was a bonus; he'd definitely been recorded at the bank, but only as one of a number of calls.

"Do much work at home?" Saint-Sylvestre asked mildly, peeking into the room. The computer was a top-end Acer Veriton with a landing pad for a number of specialty bank peripherals, including a real-time stock exchange ticker. The furniture was all steel and black and leather and the only decoration on the wall was a seventy-inch TV tuned to some digitized program that showed a waterfall in a forest somewhere.

The same thing appeared as a screen shot on the computer. Saint-Sylvestre noted that one drawer of the desk was actually a small safe, complete with a digital combination lock.

"Sometimes." Lenny nodded, leaning into the room behind Saint-Sylvestre, making sure their hips touched agreeably. "I have a direct link with the computer at the bank, so I can sometimes get a jump on my colleagues, especially as far as currency trading and precious metals are concerned." It was interesting that the alcoholic slur seemed to leave the man's voice when he talked about money.

"Presumably your password isn't something as easy as your date of birth." Saint-Sylvestre smiled. "I'd hate to think my clients' funds were so insecure."

"No cause to worry." Lenny smiled, leading him away from the home office to the living room. "As big as the Jura Mountains," he said, waving dramatically toward the view out his living room window.

Saint-Sylvestre let the obscure comment pass and followed Lenny into the living room. Lenny was clearly not a complex man when it came to decor. The living room was as white and leather and steel as the home office was black. On the wall above the gas fireplace was a large framed panoramic photograph of a series of mountain peaks.

"You are a climber?" Saint-Sylvestre asked.

"I was as a boy. I was president of the climbers' club

and the photographers' club at my boarding school for three years running." He pointed to the panoramic photograph. "That is called the Jura Ridgeway; you hike all the mountains of the Jura. It takes about two and a half weeks. I have some very fond memories of that time." Saint-Sylvestre could see tears well up in the drunken man's eyes and wondered if the banker hadn't lost his virginity to some strapping schoolmate in hiking boots and leather shorts. He stood up and went to examine the panorama. All the heights and longitudes and latitudes of each mountain were neatly inked in. Mont Tendre appeared to be the tallest. He went back to his seat on the couch.

"Which school was that?" Saint-Sylvestre asked.

"St. Georges in Montreux," said the banker. "I was sent there by my father for the English. A great number of the bank's clients are from England."

"That must explain it, then." Saint-Sylvestre nodded. "It was an English friend of mine who suggested Gesler Bank."

"Might I ask who?"

"I'd rather not betray any confidences." Saint-Sylvestre shrugged, sitting on the big white couch, playing coy. "Let me just say that he is presently in negotiation with another African client of mine."

"Isn't that interesting," said Euhler, getting up and going to a wet bar to the left of the gas fireplace. "I've just opened an account for such a man." Euhler brought

Saint-Sylvestre back a mojito. Saint-Sylvestre took a sip. Very heavy on the rum.

"Perhaps he knows more than you think," said Saint-Sylvestre, slurring his speech a little.

"Oh, and just what do you mean by that, my dear Tarik?" Euhler's eyes had darkened and he was definitely on alert, which was exactly what Saint-Sylvestre wanted. He learned many years ago that the art of interrogation relied on two things: not letting the subject know he or she was being interrogated and letting the subject ask the right questions, not the interrogator. A subject thinking he was in a position of power was a subject who would often pour his heart out to you without knowing he was doing so.

"Nothing, nothing," mumbled Saint-Sylvestre, trying to act embarrassed and sleepy. He slid across the couch until their thighs touched. Euhler ran a knuckle down Saint-Sylvestre's clean-shaven cheek. Saint-Silvestre resisted a shudder and closed his eyes.

"Oh, come now, we're friends," cooed Euhler. "If I am correct we may even have the same client's interests in mind."

"Francois Nagoupandé," said Saint-Sylvestre, jigging the bait on the end of the line. "His name is Francois Nagoupandé."

"And what does he think he knows?"

"He thinks he knows that Matheson Resource Industries is trying to cheat him out of his fair share of . . ."

"Of what, Tarik?" Euhler said, his voice urgent. And it wasn't the urgency that came from hoping that a secret hadn't been spilled. It was the urgency of greed. Euhler smelled something going on and he wanted a nibble at the cheese. The first thing that came to Saint-Sylvestre's mind was gold or silver, or perhaps even platinum or even diamonds—all four had been found in the Central African Republic over the years but never in any real quantity or quality.

The diamonds had been small and alluvial, washed down from the great basins of the Nile sources, and none of the precious metals had ever been found in amounts large enough to justify the cost of development or extraction. Certainly not enough to justify a military coup and putting a buffoon and puppet like Nagoupandé on Kolingba's throne. So what was going on?

"Of what?" Euhler repeated, a harsh edge in his voice now.

"Je ne sais pas," mumbled Saint-Sylvestre sleepily, reverting to sloppy French. "Too tired to think. Maybe *un petit somme*, a little nap; then I'll tell you what Nagoupandé said. Just a little nap first, Lenny, please."

Euhler was looking frantic. "This is important, Tarik, my dear friend. There are millions to be made here. For us over and above what we make for our clients. You must wake up."

"Give me a reason, my little Swiss friend."

"I'll show you," said Euhler. He left the room and came back a few moments later carrying something that looked like a stock certificate. He put it down on the glass-and-steel surface of the coffee table in front of the big white couch.

It was a stock certificate, bright orange and ornately engraved with an angelic figure with sweeping drapery seated on a rough slab of granite, looking back over her shoulder at a raised escutcheon that said, "Silver Brand Mining Company Limited." According to the information under the escutcheon there was ten million dollars' capitalization from ten million shares at a dollar each. The certificate had been sold to its owner on December 6, 1919. The registry was from British Columbia, Canada, and the place of registration had been Vancouver, British Columbia.

"Je ne comprends . . ." said Saint-Sylvestre, keeping up the sleepy mumbling ruse. "I don't understand."

"This company exists," said Euhler. "My client wishes me to see its majority owners and purchase their extant shares. They own seven of the ten million shares, while my client now owns virtually all of the rest. The company shares are worth nothing now. Only ten to twelve cents per share on the Vancouver Stock Exchange. My client will pay the owners fifty cents per share, half of the face value. He's not doing it himself, of course; he's using a proxy—me. The owners are two elderly sisters. They will receive two-point-five million dollars each for their shares. They think they have won the lottery, yes? Betty and Margaret Brocklebank. They already have the check; it only needs my signature and endorsement. They are twins, retired and living alone in Vancouver. I have only to have them sign the proxies over to me. They have already agreed."

"I still don't understand," said Saint-Sylvestre. "What does this have to do with Nagoupandé?"

"The shares must go onto the open market all over the world. We will announce a gold strike somewhere in British Columbia. The shares will rise and they will be purchased quickly as the price goes up. The gold find will turn out to be false and the stocks will fall, at which point my client will buy them for lower than the price they were when they went on the market. Nagoupandé will by then have been installed as head of state of Kukuanaland and whatever mineral is located there will be announced as being owned by Silver Brand Mining, a Canadian corporation. Any questions will take them to the directors of Silver Brand, who are all employees of Gesler Bank, but not actual shareholders in Silver Brand Mining. My client is safely hidden, yes? All we have to do is purchase enough shares at the fifty-cent margin to go along for the ride, as the Americans say."

"I would need some time to consult with my Cuban friends," said Saint-Sylvestre. "When do you sign over the proxy?"

"Nagoupandé is to be installed as head of state on

the thirty-first of this month. My client wishes to have the proxy in hand a week before that. I leave the day after tomorrow."

Saint-Sylvestre checked his watch. "A week from tomorrow, then."

"I suppose." Euhler reached out and stroked Saint-Sylvestre's cheek again. "Like another drink, Tarik? To celebrate our auspicious meeting?"

"The bathroom first, I'm afraid." Saint-Sylvestre smiled.

"There are two; you're welcome to use the en suite in my bedroom if you like."

"That might be fun," said Saint-Sylvestre. "Perhaps we could have our drinks in there."

"Wonderful." Euhler beamed. "It's just to the left. I'll mix."

"And I'll pee," said Saint-Sylvestre.

Euhler giggled brightly and headed for the bar. Saint-Sylvestre went through Euhler's bedroom—black satin sheets, a pedestal BeoSound 9000 audio center and a long, low chest of drawers. There was a modern headboard that also served as a bookcase. Saint-Sylvestre looked—mostly poetry and literary criticism. A lot of García Lorca, which stood to reason. He went into the adjoining bathroom.

The bathroom had a tub, a walk-in shower enclosure and a single, hand-painted porcelain sink. A flat-screen TV was mounted above the sink so you could watch the morning news or the stock ticker while you brushed your teeth. In the medicine cabinet he found hair darkener, an electric razor—Braun, of course—and a selection of pills, mostly for pain, allergies and sleep. There was also a box of a dozen Viagra. Saint-Sylvestre quickly checked through the painkillers and the sleeping pills: ten-milligram Percocet, Opana, the trade name for oxymorphone, which was even stronger than the Percocet; Seconal and phenobarbital for sleep; and even a selection of anxiety depressants, like Ativan, diazepam and even Zanaflex.

Euhler seemed to use the Ativan most of all and the prescription was almost out, so Saint-Sylvestre used the three-quarters-empty plastic bottle to load up with a random selection of all the other drugs, making sure he had big doses of the Opana and the phenobarbital. He snapped the lid on and then flushed the toilet.

Closing his eyes for a moment, he thought things through, then undid the top three buttons of his shirt and stepped back into the bedroom. Euhler was seated on the bed in light blue boxer shorts and knee-length black socks. He had a drink in each hand and also an erection. There was some bland music like Vangelis filling the room through the multiple B&O speakers.

"There you are," tootled the banker.

"Here I am," replied Saint-Sylvestre. He sat down beside the banker on the bed and Euhler handed him a drink. Saint-Sylvestre put his own drink on the bedside table. "Put your drink down and I'll give you one of my patented shoulder rubs," said Saint-Sylvestre. "You look just a little tense. Nervous."

Euhler laughed weakly. "I usually am in these sorts of . . . situations. A massage right now would be lovely." He handed his drink to Saint-Sylvestre, who put it down beside his own.

Saint-Sylvestre shuffled around on the bed so he was directly behind the banker, his strong black legs hanging over the bed, bracketing Euhler's. "No need to be nervous, Lenny."

The man still smelled of too much aftershave. Saint-Sylvestre leaned forward, pressing his back against Euhler's, gripping the shoulders skillfully and kneading them as Euhler groaned out his pleasure. Saint-Sylvestre tightened his thighs, pushing forward a little more, and the banker moaned. Finally the secret policeman wrapped one arm around the banker's neck, gripping his wrist with his free hand, and as he squeezed his own thighs between Euhler's he pushed forward even more.

"This feels like something an osteopath or a chiropractor might do." Euhler grunted. He didn't sound terribly pleased.

"Something like," agreed Saint-Sylvestre, expanding his lungs and chest.

"Not very romantic, really," said Euhler, a small note of complaint in his voice.

"No, I suppose not," said Saint-Sylvestre. He was

glad Euhler had the drugs. He could have done it with his bare hands but this was so much cleaner, and if any suspicions were eventually raised they would all lead to dead ends. The policeman steadily increased the pressure of his biceps below Euhler's left ear and the pressure of his forearm under the right ear. He then pushed his forehead into the back of Euhler's skull, the conflicting and tightening pressures cutting off all blood to the brain through the carotid arteries and the jugular veins. It took about three seconds in the full sleeper hold to put Euhler into unconsciousness and another twenty-second count to make sure he'd stay out for a minute or two. Five minutes in the hold could turn him into a vegetable, or worse, kill him.

Saint-Sylvestre leaned back then, bringing Euhler's body upright. With his right hand still wrapped around the man's neck he reached into the back pocket of his trousers and took out a pair of latex surgical gloves. It took a few seconds to get the gloves on and then he got down to work. He reached into the front pocket of his trousers and took out the pill bottle, snapping off the lid and letting it fall onto the floor.

With Euhler still held upright Saint-Sylvestre began feeding the pills from the bottle into his mouth and washing them down with the fresh mojito on the bedside table, lightly stroking the banker's neck to make sure the pills and the liquor stayed down. When he'd emptied the bottle of pills he wiped the bottle on his shirt, then let it drop to the floor beside the bed. He shifted out from behind the banker's half-dressed body and stood up, stretching. Euhler was snoring heavily. Saint-Sylvestre surveyed the room, then went through the routine he'd previously assembled in his mind.

First he did up his own shirt, then stripped off the rest of Euhler's clothes, leaving him naked, sprawled across the black satin bedspread. Saint-Sylvestre then pulled the coverlet down, tugging it under Euhler's body and leaving it in a black puddle on the floor at the end of the bed. The policeman then arranged a pile of satin-covered pillows against the headboard and dragged Euhler's flaccid body up the bed until it lay propped half-upright against the pile. Euhler's snoring now had a choking, dangerous edge and there were pauses in his breathing followed by deep gasping sounds. The drugs were taking him further into unconsciousness. Saint-Sylvestre glanced at the books on the shelf above Euhler's head and opened one at random. It was called *Spokesmen* by somebody named Thomas Whipple. He saw what he needed, smiled and tore out the last stanza at the bottom of the page. It was a poem by the American Carl Sandburg—"Death Snips Proud Men"—and seemed fitting enough.

The policeman stuffed the ragged bit of paper into Euhler's palm and closed his fist over it. He left the book on the bed, then left Euhler and the bedroom, returning to the living room and then the home office.

He sat down at the computer keyboard and pressed a random key. The waterfall animation disappeared and there was a dark blue screen and a line of text that said, *Password, please*, with a flashing cursor below it.

He found a pencil and a little pad of paper in the desk drawer and went into the living room. He stood in front of Euhler's prize photograph and jotted down both Mont Tendre's height—1,679 meters—and the coordinates below it—46°35'41"N 6°18'36"E.

He removed the extraneous material and came up with a string of numbers—167946354161836—which he then entered on the keyboard. The screen cleared again and took him to a directory, which he proceeded to copy onto a dozen CD-ROMs he found in a box in the desk.

He switched off the computer, then stared down at the digital combination lock on the desk safe. On the off chance it would work he entered 1679—the height of Mont Tendre. Nothing happened. He tried the reverse, 9761, and the door clicked open. There was a passport, several dozen Krugerrands, and a respectable stack of high-denomination euros.

The only other thing in the safe was a bundle of letters and photographs, tied up in a predictable red ribbon. The pictures were pornographic and the letters were as well; even though Saint-Sylvestre's German was mediocre he could figure out what *Ich möchte Sie saugen* and *lassen Sie uns wie Tiere bumsen* meant.

In the pictures Lenny appeared to be the submissive while his young, blond and very muscular friend was the dominant. The letters were all headed, *mein süßer liebster Liebling Lenny*, and signed, *Ihr liebevolles* baby, *Lutzie*. Love letters from one man to another. He went back into the living room and did some housekeeping, emptying glasses and putting them in the dishwasher as well as removing any other signs that Euhler had entertained a guest that night.

He returned to the bedroom and saw that Euhler had both vomited and lost control of his bowels. Either his heart had slowed to a stop under the effects of the multiple drugs or he had suffocated on his own vomit. One way or another, the banker was dead. Saint-Sylvestre dropped the letters and the ribbon on the floor beside the bed, leaving the impression that reading them had been Euhler's last act before ripping his maudlin little epigraph from the book collection, then downing the pills with his mojito—party boy to the end.

It all looked authentic enough and there was no reason to suspect foul play. An aging homosexual took his own life knowing that things were never going to get any better than they'd been with *Ihr liebevolles* baby, *Lutzie*. If Lutzie was very unlucky the police would track him down and ask a few questions, but that would almost certainly be the end of it.

Satisfied, Saint-Sylvestre used his cell phone to look

up flights from Zurich to Vancouver. He found a Swiss-air flight out of Zurich to Paris in an hour and a half, and a red-eye Air Canada flight that would get him to Vancouver at seven in the morning, Pacific time.

He picked up the old stock certificate off the coffee table, folded it and put it into the inside pocket of his jacket. He took one last look around, Euhler out of his thoughts, his mind now thinking about twin sisters in an old folks' home halfway around the world. He left the apartment, closing the door softly behind him.

21

The children marched them through the jungle in perfect military order, the smallest taking point thirty or forty feet ahead, one on their left, one on their right and the fourth coming up behind, the too-large weapon held firmly at port arms, ready to cut them down at the slightest indication of resistance.

It was he who had relieved Peggy of her camera and now wore it across his chest, looking like a sort of fearsome tourist child waiting for Mowgli or Baloo to appear on the trail before him.

They walked without speaking and when they communicated it was through hand motions and whistles. Their attention was on their environment and their prisoners, their faces devoid of emotion, or perhaps, thought Holliday, they had no emotion left.

When he was ten his uncle had bought him a perfect replica of a Buntline Special, the Colt Peacemaker with the twelve-inch barrel that legend had it Wyatt Earp used. The enormous handgun must have looked ridiculous to any adult, but there was no sense of that with their four young jailers. The AK-47s seemed horribly normal being carried by these kids. The four children guarding them would commit cold-blooded murder without hesitation. The oldest couldn't have been more than twelve.

They walked through the forest for an hour, and then two. At first Holliday thought they were heading for the distant trio of hills that seemed to struggle up out of the jungle but then they turned away. Coming over a small ridge he saw the river and between them and the water the smoking ruins of a village.

A few minutes later they reached the bottom of the rise and Holliday saw the first human remains, a human arm, male, sliced off close to the shoulder, marrow yellow where the bone had been crushed, blood in the dirt and sand congealing on the stump, the hand flexed as though clutching for a beggar's offering that would never come. A few yards down the path was a head, split almost in two with the sweeping cut of a blade, taking off the head at the eyebrows and opening it like a soft-boiled egg.

Rafi threw up and Peggy began to cry silently. Strangely Eddie began to sing; the tune was familiar— "Auld Lang Syne"—but the words were different. Spanish, crooned like a lullaby, whispered so softly Holliday doubted that anyone else had heard.

Por qué perder las esperanzas
de volverse a ver,
por qué perder las esperanzas
si hay tanto querer.

The words must have had some fierce meaning for the Cuban, because his jaw was hard and Holliday could see the big sinus vein bulging across his forehead: as they continued along the path and into the smoking remains of the village there was more and more carnage—an infant that had been covered in gasoline and then thrown into a campfire, several male bodies staked out on the ground covered with hacking bloody cuts, several men, women and girls strung up from tree branches with piano wire that had almost decapitated them, the smell of blood and feces everywhere and above it all the sound of wailing children. Holliday could see them down at the riverbank. They were tied together in a row, about fifteen of them, the rope then attached to the stern of one of their big dugouts. A dozen older children, fourteen or fifteen years old, were waiting at their paddles, apparently for some signal.

Their four guards led the prisoners around the smoldering wreckage of a large hut, probably the common "longhouse" or dormitory for single men. Beyond it was a Russian UAZ Jeep knockoff in old-style jungle camo. Sitting on the hood of the vehicle was a dragon-headed man wearing a blue-and-orange New York Knicks jersey and old-fashioned black-and-white high-tops with a pair of worn green-on-green fatigues pushed into them. Holliday could see a very expensive-looking cobra tattoo in three colors on his right shoulder.

Beside him on the hood of the vehicle was a bloody machete. He had a holster around his waist and Holliday could see the handle of a .45 automatic peeking out. The dragon head looked as though it had been carved out of soft, light wood, the scales on the head alternately painted green and gold, the face red and the eyes yellow. The long curling tongue that stretched out over the bright ivory animal teeth was black. Holliday had never seen anything like it.

"My God!" Rafi whispered.

"What?" Holliday asked.

"It's a figurehead; I swear it, a Norse figurehead."

"What's that supposed to mean, this guy is a descendant of our Viking pals back there?"

"It means it's part of a cargo cult tradition," said Rafi.

"You done your gabbin' now?" said a voice from within the mask. The man sitting on the hood of the Russian Jeep took off the mask and set it down opposite the machete. The blood was beginning to dry a rusty brown. The buzzing of flies was everywhere.

"Where did you get the mask?" Rafi asked.

"Not that it be any your business little mama's *mang sal* but I got it off the head of their witchie man. Right off his head!" The man in the Knicks jersey laughed. All his front teeth, top and bottom, were gold.

"Who are you?" Holliday asked.

"I am the man who holds your life in his hands, *Nduku*. The name my mother gave me was Jerimiah Salamango but I am now called Jerimiah Salamango of Christ, destroyer in His holy name. Rapist of temptress women in His holy name, deliverer of souls in His holy name, praise God! You understand this? I kill for my God as well as pray to Him on my knees five times each day. And this is the day that God hath made and we should rejoice in the shedding of blood for Him, praise God and hallelujah!"

"Why have you brought us here?" Holliday asked. The reek of the village was overpowering and the flies landing on him left sticky tracks on his skin.

"At first we saw your trail and then we saw the bodies of the men you killed and Jerimiah Salamango had curiosity about men who would take on a machine gun with spears and arrows. Then when my scouts reported back to me I thought I would make you my envoys, tells of Jerimiah's story across the land to put fear in everyone and say that he was coming. In the end that is what Jerimiah Salamango has decided to do. When it was told to me that your woman had a picture camera it was even better, because you can get Jerimiah Salamango's face on the *CBS Evening News with Katie Couric*. This camera makes video?"

"Yes," said Peggy.

"Jerimiah thinks you are very lucky that you are the operator of the camera or you would have been fed to my lions, my very young lions." He spread his hands, indicating the children around them. "My hungry lions."

"You're insane," said Rafi.

"You could be dead in a very few moments if Jerimiah loses his temper."

"Shut up, Rafi," Peggy said.

Salamango slid off the hood of the car and walked down a narrow pathway to the river that had obviously once been the main street of the village. The boy carrying Peggy's camera prodded them forward and they walked beside the man in the Knicks T-shirt through the smoldering lines of straw and mud huts and through the littered, shattered bodies and pieces of bodies.

"The trick is to make them kill their parents first. Beat their mothers' brains in, slit their fathers' throats, rape and then disembowel their sisters. Once they have done this for you to save their own lives they are yours, like property, like dogs. They will do anything for you and no order must need to make sense; it must only come from you like a man whistling for a dog that is his."

Holliday began looking around for some kind of weapon, even a rock would do, estimating his odds of poking the man's eyes out of his head or tearing out his tongue before he was swarmed and torn apart by his childish minions.

Only once or twice in his career—or in his life at all, for that matter—had he ever felt that sacrificing his life was a worthwhile and reasonable option; this was one of those times. To kill this man would be what Rafi called a mitzvah, an altogether good thing for the human race.

They reached the river. There were several fishing boats tied together, led by one of the outboard-powered dugouts the child soldiers had used to reach the river. In the fishing boats, crowded to the gunwales, were the rest of the people of the village, mostly old men, old women and very young children of both sexes. Everyone in the boats was wailing, screaming and crying. The smell of kerosene drifted over the river and Holliday knew what was going to happen. All around the boats Holliday could also see the cruising, scaly backs of swarms of crocodiles, waiting for the delivery of their prey. Waiting on the bank of the river were the rest of the jeering swarm of boy soldiers, gathered to watch the show.

"¡El bastardo sádica! ¡Se va a quemar a continuación, darles de comer a los cocodrilos! ¡Malos matar al puta madre!" Eddie muttered, furious, his dark eyes flashing with anger. His big fists clenched and the vein in his forehead was beating like a drum.

"Not if I kill him first," said Holliday.

"With what?" Salamango laughed, overhearing

them. "Do you know what those people out there in those boats said when we came into their village and began burning their houses and raping their daughters? They said that they were protected by the gods. They were protected by the *umufo omhloshana*; you know what that means?"

"The pale strangers," said Eddie.

"That's right, black man, Pale Strangers." Salamango let out a huge rumble of laughter. "Well, my friends, you are the only pale strangers I see around here and I don't see much protection going on." He barked an order and the boy with Peggy's camera came forward. Salamango gave another order and the boy reluctantly handed the camera over to Peggy and stepped back.

"You take the pictures when I tell you and you don't stop until I tell you; understand, little white woman? Don't start or stop before I tell you or I'll rip you in half where you stand." He grinned. "I want to make post-cards to send to the United Nations."

Rafi took a single lurching step forward but Holliday jammed his foot down painfully on the archaeologist's instep. Peggy was crying now, tears streaming down her cheeks.

"Why do you want to do this?" she asked. "Why?"

The man in the Knicks shirt stared down at her, lip curled. "I had a brother and his name was Felicianos and he was eight years old. They came into our village one night and killed almost everybody. They left Felicianos till the end and then they chopped off his *orgao* and threw it into the fire and then threw him in after it. They were FNLA, these people, Frente Nacional para a Libertação de Angola, Portuguese with American arms, because America was afraid that Angola would become Marxist."

"That was terrible, but no reason to do this," pleaded Peggy.

"I do terrible things to show how terrible I am," Salamango explained. "More terrible than the pigs who killed my brother by a thousand times. I do it for a million Felicianos."

Eddie spit on the bloody ground. "You do it because you like it, *cabrón*," he said. "I know your type; I've smelled them before. They stink of their own anger and take it out on the world."

"I'll second that," said Holliday.

Salamango sneered. "You people with your democracies and your communism, you don't understand how the game is played here. Here, in my Africa, the leader is the man who is feared among his tribe and any other tribe; the man who is feared is the man who kills; and the man who is feared most and has the most power is the man who kills most. It has been that way for ten thousand years and it will be that way for another ten thousand or until we are all dead. That is Africa, little girl, and anyone who tells you other than that is white or a liar, and probably both."

He turned and raised his fist. He called out a single word: *"Kuf-wa!"*

On the dugout the boy at the outboard tossed something into the nearest of the fishing boats. There was no immediate flame, just a heat ripple in the air that distorted the screaming figures on the first boat. The dugout set the fishing boats adrift and the first people, their clothes and flesh on fire, leaped over the side to be devoured by the waiting crocodiles. Within less than a minute the water around the flaming boats was a frothing red horror of blood and snapping bones.

And then it began.

The first dart, whether by accident or design, struck Salamango in the right eye, burying itself in the orb, leaving nothing outside the body except a narrow white cone of what appeared to be ordinary paper. The second dart struck him in the cheek, the long metal tip piercing from side to side with the cone on the left and the flattened diamond-shaped point coming out the other side. The points appeared to be coated with some sort of black, tarry substance.

Holliday turned on his heel and watched as all four of the armed children guarding them were also struck, each one more than once, the bright white cones appearing in faces, backs, chests and bellies.

The effects of the darts were instantaneous: paralysis, choking, convulsions, a strychnine-like arching of the back, foaming at the mouth and then complete loss of sphincter control followed almost immediately by death.

Holliday, Peggy, Rafi and Eddie were the only people left untouched. Out on the river, the dugout drifted. The boy who had torched the sailboats was draped over the gunwale as two crocodiles fought to pull his corpse into the water.

The sailboats themselves were smoldering hulks, their occupants either burned to death or dragged down to the muddy bottom by the giant reptiles. The whole thing had been silent and from the first dart in Salamango's eye to the last child's death had taken only seconds. Not a word had been said; not a shot had been fired.

With her camera Peggy began taking photos of the bizarre killing ground all around them. Suddenly she stopped; her hands were shaking too hard. Holliday followed her stunned gaze. Men began to appear from the jungle, scores of them, all dressed in ornately folded linen loincloths that looked like pleated kilts and sandals, their thongs crisscrossed up to the knee in a familiar design. They carried five- or six-foot-long bamboo tubes in their hands and short quivers on their belts for the long, cone-ended darts.

Some of the men wore crested wooden helmets with leather cheek flaps, the crests made from some kind of stiffened animal-hair bristle, while others wore simple linen coifs to match the kiltlike loincloths. The strangest thing about them was their color—a tanned light brown like heavily creamed coffee. Their hair was dark and straight, their features definitely Caucasian rather than negroid. Most startling of all, Holliday could see that some of the oddly dressed men had blue eyes.

"Umufo omhloshana," Eddie said quietly.

Holliday nodded. "The Pale Strangers."

22

There was a knock on Sir James Matheson's office door.

"Enter!"

Allen Faulkener stepped into the lavish office and stood in front of Matheson's desk. "Leonhard Euhler is dead," he said stiffly.

"Christ!" Matheson said. "How?"

"Some sort of homosexual tryst, as far as the Swiss police are concerned. Love letters, suicide note."

Matheson sat rigidly behind his desk, palms spread on its smooth empty surface. He thought for a moment, then leaned down, pulled open the humidor drawer of the desk and took out a Romeo y Julieta Short Churchill Robusto.

He closed the drawer carefully, then took a gold Dunhill cutter-punch combination out of his waistcoat pocket and prepared the cigar for smoking. He sat back in his chair and lit the cigar with a matching Dunhill lighter, all the while trying to maintain his composure in front of Faulkener. It didn't do to let the hired help see the master afraid, and for the first time in a long time that was exactly what Sir James Matheson was—afraid.

Matheson wasn't much of a believer in luck or happenstance. Whatever evidence the Swiss police had in hand he couldn't quite bring himself to believe that Euhler would pick this particular moment to snuff out his lights for some idiotic love affair. He could sense the first small cracks in his plan, but if his intuition was right, who was responsible, and how did he stop the cracks from getting worse?

"No signs of foul play?"

"Apparently not. Pills, the love letters, as I mentioned. The man who wrote the letters died in a car accident."

"Recently?"

"Six years ago."

Why would a man, poof or not, kill himself over the death of a lover six years ago? It was making less and less sense. Everything was pointing to the Kolingba operation.

"I'll want to see the autopsy report, the police file and any surveillance tapes that were made."

"I've already checked, Sir James. There were no cameras at his residence but there are interior and exterior cameras at the bank."

"Speak to Herr Gesler personally; tell him that since

Euhler was handling some delicate business for us I would very much appreciate receiving copies of the tapes as soon as possible. If he balks, lean on him a little; remind him of the dossier on his personal affairs that is in our possession. Get the tapes for the day before the man's death and for the day after." Matheson paused. "He was supposed to get the proxies on the mining company you found; did he do so?"

"Not that I am aware of, Sir James."

No, of course not; there'd be no point in killing him if the proxies had been exchanged. Someone else was trying to get them. But who? Nagoupandé? He didn't have the brains of a gnat, and Matheson seriously doubted that the man would be able to imagine such a conspiracy, let alone orchestrate it.

Kolingba was probably incapable as well, but his personal Rasputin, this Oliver Gash, might, although he doubted it somehow; Gash's dossier portrayed him as a criminal with a criminal's shrewdness and without the real sophistication to manage a massive short-selling stock fraud. It simply wasn't his thing. He took another puff on the cigar, enjoying its rich, sweet flavor for a few brief seconds. Time to get down to brass tacks. The proxies.

"Find out the position of the proxies. If Euhler did not have them signed you will go to British Columbia yourself and obtain them. I have copies here."

"Yes, sir."

"Have we heard from Harris and Mrs. Sinclair's hooligans in Africa?"

"No, sir. Not a word."

"Then presume that he's been wiped off the slate and that Holliday and his archaeologist friend are still at large. We're looking at far too much media exposure if they're allowed to survive. Find someone better than Harris to stop them."

"Yes, sir."

"How much longer for our Austrian friend Lanz?"

"The new moon is next week."

"His minders are keeping an eye on him?"

"Yes, sir."

"All right, get me those tapes and find out about the proxies. Without them I might as well be investing in a dustbin full of ashes."

"Yes, sir." Faulkener left the room.

Matheson sat back in his chair. He was breaking half the securities and exchange laws in this country and any others where he expected to trade Silver Brand Mining, and if he was caught at it they'd put him behind bars for the rest of his life. His financial crimes made Bernie Madoff look like an amateur. On top of that he could be charged with conspiring to commit murder both before and after the fact, not to mention toppling a foreign head of state and bribing his replacement. To make things worse it now looked like there was some mysterious competitor for Kukuanaland's spoils.

His smile widened and he pulled heartily on the stubby little Churchill Robusto. He hadn't been this sick with fear and this excited since he'd lost his virginity to his father's mistress at the age of fourteen. He took the sweet-tasting cigar out of his mouth and blew a plume of aromatic smoke toward the ornate plaster ceiling of his office. These were the moments a man lived for!

A single figure stepped out of the jungle, his face covered by an ornate wooden mask, its edges trimmed with stiffened gold rattan like a lion's mane, a round cockerel crest topped with rigid bristle, bloodred like that of a helmet worn by a Roman centurion.

The red wooden eyes of the face bulged and the mouth was a boxy square, wooden bars where the teeth should be, much like a gladiator's protective head covering. He wore the same white cloth kilt as the others, complete with a short quiver full of darts, but this man's skin was coal black. His feet were covered in heavy sandals, leather strips crisscrossed almost to his knees.

In one hand he carried one of the long blowgun tubes and in his right hand he carried something very much like the crook and flail of an Egyptian pharaoh: sacred signs of power, divinity and kingship. Like the scepters found in King Tutankhamen's arms, these were also solid gold. A heavy gold arm ring was set with enormous uncut diamonds and emeralds.

As he approached Holliday and the others the man in the ornate mask slipped the gold flail and crook into the waistband of his kilt and raised his hand to remove the mask. As he did so one of the lighter-skinned men stepped forward, head bowed, and took the mask from him almost reverentially. Like the flail and crook, the mask, too, was clearly some sign of high office.

The face of the man, now unmasked, was dark eyed and intelligent. He smiled, and as he did so Holliday could see an old-fashioned silver amalgam filling in his left bicuspid. Whoever he was, this man was no jungle savage.

He stopped in front of Holliday and extended his hand. "Good afternoon, Colonel Holliday, my name is Dr. Amobe Barthélemy Limbani. Perhaps you could introduce me to your friends."

23

Captain Jean-Luc Saint-Sylvestre's experience of the United States was limited to a fourteen-day package holiday to Miami he took out of simple curiosity one August. His experience of Canada and Vancouver amounted to even less: a few satellite TV interviews he'd seen shot on rainy city streets during the recent Winter Olympics.

Getting off the Air Canada 747 he was pleasantly surprised to find a modern, clean and reasonably efficient airport terminal. The customs agents, while obviously naive about the ways of the world, were at least polite, which was a step up from the uniformed gorillas he'd dealt with at Miami International.

He had purchased a Vancouver travel guide during the brief layover in Paris, and picked an appropriately lavish downtown Vancouver hotel in case his plan B required taking the elderly ladies out for tea. He booked a suite online using one of Euhler's credit cards, so when he picked up a taxi outside the arrivals terminal he simply told driver, "Hotel Vancouver."

As he left the airport it quickly became apparent that Vancouver was very much a city of water and bridges. The airport itself was on an island in a river delta, and on his left he could see the Pacific Ocean.

They traveled down Granville Street, a wide boulevard lined with pink-and-white blossoming cherry trees. There were mountains in the distance, cloaked in evergreens, and even more water as they passed over something called False Creek that seemed to be some sort of tourist shopping attraction.

Within fifteen minutes of leaving the airport the taxi arrived at the Hotel Vancouver. It was a city block–sized structure built like a French château, with a distinctive copper roof, long since gone green with age and the elements. He signed in using one of Euhler's credit cards again. Unlike most European hotels, there was no requirement to hand over or even show a passport, and no one seemed to care that a black man who spoke English with a decidedly French accent would have such an obviously Germanic name as Euhler. Saint-Sylvestre smiled.

Back in the Cold War days, and even now, Canadian passports were the document of choice among intelligence agencies, since they offered visa-free entry into 157 countries and visa on arrival for most others. In the sixties it was said that there were more spies entering the

United States on shuttle flights from Ottawa and Toronto than there were ordinary passengers, and even as late as 1997 the Mossad used Canadian passports in their botched assassination attempt on Khaled Mashal, the infamous Hamas leader. Very naive, these Canadians, Saint-Sylvestre thought for the second time that day.

An aging busboy took his suitcase up to the small suite he'd booked and he gave the man a five-dollar tip from the multicolored wad he'd changed his Swiss francs into before leaving the airport.

The suite was beige, conservative and came with all the bells and whistles, including big-screen TVs, Wi-Fi, a jet tub and bathrobes. Like advertisements in the Sunday *New York Times* for four-thousand-dollar A.P.O. Jeans and thirty-thousand-dollar purses from Marc Jacobs, this was the kind of luxury that provided the seeds of revolution to the masses, something that his esteemed superior, General Solomon Kolingba, with his bumblebee Range Rovers, his diamond-encrusted Rolex President and his three-thousand-dollar Dolce & Gabbana sunglasses, seemed to have forgotten.

And now, it seemed, his forgetfulness was catching up with him. Sadly, the fat, bullet-headed president of Kukuanaland was not the Robin Hood he'd pretended to be at first. The wealth he earned by the criminal enterprises he oversaw with Gash rarely went much farther than the garrison walls in Fourandao or beyond the front doors of the bank directly below Saint-Sylvestre's offices. Certainly none of it reached the impoverished people of the country.

Unlike the policeman, General Kolingba was not a reader of history, nor a reader of anything at all, for that matter, and was unaware of a truism that most high school history teachers and every overthrown dictator in the world could tell you: he who lived by the coup d'état had a very good chance of dying by it.

There were several restaurants within the hotel and an extensive room service menu, so, antirevolutionary or not, Saint-Sylvestre ordered himself a breakfast of freshly squeezed orange juice, cream cheese on a bagel with British Columbia smoked salmon, a breakfast steak frites with a perfectly fried egg on the top and a thermos of Viennese coffee. He had a quick shower, dressed himself in the fluffy white robe and was just settling in with a complimentary copy of the *Globe and Mail*, Canada's newspaper of record, when the food arrived. He ate heartily and plotted out the day ahead.

By eleven he was ready to begin. A quick check of the local telephone directory revealed that the Brocklebank sisters lived on a street simply called the Crescent in a district of Vancouver known as Shaughnessy. He spent twenty minutes in the hotel's business center Internet kiosk on the lower-lobby floor and discovered that the Brocklebanks were a respectable old Vancouver family with the requisite skeletons in the closet, including a huge silver mine that had gone bust in the 1920s after A. G. Brocklebank, the sisters' grandfather, had overleveraged himself, the bust virtually cleaning him out.

P. T. Brocklebank, A.G.'s son and the sisters' father, had married into a huge sugar fortune, but the marriage turned sour when his heiress wife discovered that he was not only having an affair with her sister's husband but had also embezzled millions from the family business to squander on the Standard Stock and Mining Exchange in Toronto.

The scandal in Vancouver was enormous, but womanizer, embezzler and poor businessman he may have been, he did love his daughters and had made them the beneficiaries of an extremely large life insurance policy well before he "accidentally" drove his wife's rather swank 1936 Packard V12 Convertible Coupe over the two-hundred-foot-high cliffs at what was now Wreck Beach near the Point Grey Campus of the University of British Columbia.

Since the insurance company could not prove suicide or inebriation, they had no choice but to pay off the claim, including the double-indemnity clause. The sisters, who were still living in the original Brocklebank mansion on the Crescent, were suddenly wealthy again.

Wisely consulting lawyers and bankers, the sisters had stayed wealthy ever since. Neither had married and there were no heirs or assigns. Upon their deaths the Brocklebank estate would become the property of the

University Women's Club of Vancouver, of which they had been active members after their graduation from McGill extension college in Victoria more than half a century ago.

Neither woman had ever worked, although both were longtime volunteers for various women's causes. For no good reason in particular, Betty was prochoice and Margie was antiabortion; Betty was a theoretical Marxist while Margie was an enthusiastic supporter of monopoly capitalism.

Saint-Sylvestre dialed the phone number he had found in the directory and after seven rings a small, slightly distressed-sounding woman's voice answered.

"Yes?"

The voice was thin, brittle and quavering: an elderly woman who received few calls and when she did get them they were usually bearing bad news. He could imagine a little old lady in a housedress, sitting in a hallway filled with dusty oil paintings of old family members and lit by low-wattage bulbs to save on the electricity bill.

"Miss Brocklebank?" Saint-Sylvestre replied, trying to keep his voice as unthreatening as possible.

"This is Betty Brocklebank; who is speaking, please?"

Saint-Sylvestre was ready for the question. "My name is Wolfgang Gesler, Miss Brocklebank. I represent the Gesler Bank of Aarau, Switzerland. I am here in your beautiful city on behalf of my father, Herr . . . Mr. Horst

Gesler, the president of the bank. This is concerning the disposition of your stock in the Silver Brand Mining Company, of which you and your sister are the majority shareholders."

"Now, isn't that strange," answered Betty Brockle-bank. "We had a telephone call from a representative of your bank only yesterday." Her voice brightened. "He's picking us up in a limousine and taking us to the Sylvia for tea this afternoon to discuss the situation."

Shit! Saint-Sylvestre thought. It hadn't occurred to him that Matheson's people would get to the sisters first.

"No, no, it's not strange at all, Miss Brocklebank," said Saint-Sylvestre, trying to put a laugh in his voice and only barely succeeding. "My father mentioned that the business of your shares was important enough to require two representatives from the bank. We seem to have gotten our wires crossed, yes?"

"Apparently," said Betty Brocklebank.

"I wonder if you could tell me which of our people he sent along to help me out?"

"A Mr. Euhler," said the Brocklebank sister. "If that's how you pronounce it."

"Your pronunciation is excellent, Miss Brocklebank," soothed Saint-Sylvestre. "And Leonhard was an excellent choice, a very good man. Did he leave a telephone number, by any chance? I'd feel a bit of a fool if I had to phone my father and ask."

"He's staying at the Hotel Georgia, room eleven twenty-four. I think they call it the Rosewood Georgia or the Georgia Rosewood now. Margie and I rarely get out these days, you see. Frankly she's gone a bit dotty, if you ask me. I'm afraid I spend most of my time picking up after her and reminding her that her precious Siamese cat died years ago . . . if you know what I mean. Margie can be something of a trial." She pronounced her sister's name oddly, with a hard *G* so that it came out *Mar-ghee*.

"How unfortunate," said Saint-Sylvestre. "Did Mr. Euhler say when he was coming for you?"

"Three," said Betty Brocklebank promptly. She suddenly made a startled little sound. "Good Lord, look at the time. I'll have to start getting us ready." There was a brief pause. "He *did* say a limousine," said the Brocklebank sister firmly.

"Of course," answered Saint-Sylvestre. "Not a problem at all, Miss Brocklebank. Until three, then."

"Until three," she answered. "Good-bye, Herr Gesler."

He hung up the phone and thought for a moment, then dialed the concierge desk in the main lobby.

"Two questions," he asked when the female concierge answered. "Can you tell me where the Rosewood Hotel Georgia is located, and where can I order a limousine on short notice?"

*   *   *

The Rosewood Hotel Georgia turned out to be within easy walking distance, only a few blocks away from his own hotel. After ordering a limousine from a local service, Saint-Sylvestre walked up Burrard Street and turned right onto Georgia Street. The sun was shining and to the north a wall of mountains stood crisply against a bright blue sky.

For the most part Vancouver seemed to be a very young city; none of the buildings the policeman saw were more than a hundred years old, and except for something that looked like a half-scale version of the British Museum that turned out to be the Vancouver Art Gallery, even though it was called the Courthouse, glass and steel seemed to be the order of the day.

The Rosewood Hotel Georgia was an older twelve-story building at the corner of Georgia and Howe streets, its bricks freshly acid-washed and a doorman under the canopy of the main entrance. The lobby, all reds and golds and deep browns, had that freshly renovated look that was a little at odds with the somewhat old-fashioned 1920s exterior. Saint-Sylvestre wasn't even slightly interested.

He rode the elevator alone up to the eleventh floor and found 1124. He reached into his jacket pocket, took out the same surgical gloves he'd used in Euhler's apartment and slipped them on. He knocked and then took half a step to the left. There was a moment of silence and then a muffled voice.

"Yes."

"Fax, Mr. Euhler." Room service could be denied and housekeeping refused, but a fax would almost certainly open the door.

Calling him Euhler was a risk, but a calculated one. Betty Brocklebank had given him the room number, but if she'd called back for some reason asking for a Mr. Euhler and the man wasn't registered at the hotel under that name, flags might go up.

Saint-Sylvestre heard the chain come off and the lock click. He let the steak knife from breakfast drop down into his right palm as the door opened, and moved forward, concentrating all his attention on the man's diaphragm.

There was no hesitation; with the knife's serrated edge turned upward, Saint-Sylvestre drove the steak knife into the man's body with all his strength, penetrating flesh just below the xiphoid process, where the ribs joined the sternum. The stainless-steel blade plunged into the right ventricle and straight up through the pulmonary artery and the aorta, virtually slicing the organ in half.

The policeman pushed forward into the short hallway, kicking the door shut behind him. Saint-Sylvestre saw the first blood begin to gush from the man's mouth and nose as five and a half liters of fluid began to flood into his chest cavity, and he pushed forward one last time before taking a step back and simultaneously releasing his grip on the knife.

The man fell backward and Saint-Silvestre moved away quickly, making sure the door was completely closed. He turned the lock and put on the chain before turning back to his victim. There hadn't been a sound except for the man hitting the beige broadloom carpeting when he dropped dead. A check in the hallway mirror confirmed that Saint-Sylvestre hadn't gotten a spot of blood on him except for the fingers of the right surgical glove.

He knelt on one knee, wiping the blood off on the carpet but leaving the glove on for the moment.

The body was lying at a slight angle, halfway into the room proper with its legs in the hallway. The man was tall, gray-haired and had what used to be called a military mustache. He was wearing a white shirt, the front of which was now covered in blood, pin-striped suit pants and highly polished, expensive-looking lace-up shoes. He wore a signet ring with a powder horn dangling from a rosette and encircled by the Latin motto *Celer et audax—The swift and the bold*. If memory served, once upon a time the man he'd just killed had been an officer in the King's Royal Rifle Corps.

There was nothing else of interest on the corpse and Saint-Sylvestre doubted the man was the type to keep his wallet in his rear pants pocket, so he didn't bother rolling him over. Instead he stepped over the dead man and entered the hotel room proper.

The room was much smaller than Saint-Sylvestre's

suite at the Hotel Vancouver but with the same beige-and-chocolate color scheme. There was a closed suitcase on a rack at the end of the bed, and an attaché sitting open on a small desk under the room's single window. The suit jacket matching the dead body's trousers was hanging over the back of the chair that stood in front of the desk.

He checked the inner pockets of the suit jacket. There was a Coach billfold in the left pocket and a BlackBerry Torch smartphone in the right. The wallet was full of British identification in the name of Allen Faulkener, including a driver's license, a firearms certificate from the Home Office allowing Faulkener to own and carry a Heckler & Koch P30 nine-millimeter/.40-caliber semiautomatic pistol, and a Matheson Resource Industries biometric key card.

He kept the wallet, sliding it into his own jacket pocket, and took the smartphone as well; there was no point in making it easier for the inevitable police detectives who would be called in to investigate this Faulkener man's murder to identify the body.

Saint-Sylvestre turned to the attaché case. A fat, blue-backed copy of the proxy agreements for the Brocklebank sisters' shares in Silver Brand Mining and a maroon European Union/United Kingdom passport for Allen Faulkener. Nothing else. The attaché case smelled brand-new. There was no ticket stub or boarding pass, which confirmed Saint-Sylvestre's assumption that

Faulkener had flown into Vancouver on a private jet. The Immigration Canada stamp in Faulkener's passport was dated yesterday. Somehow he'd found out about Euhler's death within hours.

It was enough to give the policeman pause. In Kukuanaland he could instill fear with a look and held almost as much sway with Kolingba as Oliver Gash, but this was Matheson's world, and it occurred to Saint-Sylvestre that perhaps he was biting off more than he could chew. By the same token, at least for the moment Matheson was unaware of his existence, and sometimes invisibility was the most powerful weapon of all.

Saint-Sylvestre dropped the wallet, smartphone and passport into the attaché case, then went to the end of the bed and gave the suitcase a quick once-over. There were two things of potential use: one was a silk green-red-and-black Rifles regimental tie and the other was the nine-millimeter H&K semiautomatic in a nice, molded leather Bianchi paddle holster. He took the weapon out of the suitcase, checked to see that the magazine was loaded, snapped the magazine back in place. It was certainly a step up from a steak knife, but dangerous if he was caught with it. Canadian gun laws were even tighter and more controlled than those of the Brits, and that was saying something. He went back to the attaché case, dumped the gun and the tie into it along with the rest of his booty, then closed it up without locking it by spinning the combination locks.

Taking the case, he went back to the body, knelt down and slipped the signet ring off the index finger of the right hand and then put it on his own finger; a little loose but it wouldn't fall off. He stood and looked around one last time. Nothing out of place except a body on the floor. He stepped over Allen Faulkener's corpse and went down the short hallway to the hotel room door.

Saint-Sylvestre set the lock, unhooked the Do Not Disturb sign from the knob, then opened the door and stepped into the main hall. It was empty. He closed the door, listening as the lock clicked, hung the sign and peeled off the surgical gloves, shoving them into the hip pocket of his trousers. Ninety seconds later he stepped into the empty elevator and rode down to the lobby. Thirty seconds after that he stepped through the main door of the hotel and back into the sunlight.

Invisible.

24

They had been marching through the jungle for most of the day, and now the sun was dropping low, the light filtering down on the broad trail going from dappled greens to copper and gold. The monkeys screeched their complaints and every now and again flights of angry egrets flew up squawking from patches of wetland as they passed by.

The trail moved almost due west, roughly following the line of the river, which they could sometimes catch glimpses of in the distance to the south. According to Limbani the trail was all that remained of an elephant walk, a migratory pathway that had not been used for decades or perhaps even longer.

They reached the head of a narrow valley between two low, jungle-shrouded hills and Limbani raised a hand and stopped. Holliday looked back over his shoulder and saw that all of the paler warriors had stopped on his signal as well. Directly behind him Peggy looked as though she were about to speak but Holliday shook his head. He heard a sharp whistle from somewhere well ahead and Limbani visibly relaxed.

"The point men will check out the way ahead," Limbani said.

Holliday smiled at the exotically dressed man using such a modern military term for his forward scouts. Limbani raised his fist into the air and Holliday watched as the pale warriors stood at ease along the trail behind them.

"We can rest here for a few moments," Limbani murmured quietly. He squatted down under a high-crowned tree covered with thin, waxy leaves and heavy with a blue, pear-shaped fruit.

"They look like Japanese eggplants," said Peggy, dropping onto the ground beneath the tree.

"Dacryodes edulis," said Limbani, smiling. "Sometimes called safou, African pear or the bush butter tree."

"Edible?" Rafi asked.

"Very. Pick one," said Limbani. "The bluish color means they're ripe. They taste like slightly acidic plums, if you're looking for a comparison." He shook his head. "Kolingba could have employed thousands of people to work plantations of these trees. The fruit is excellent both raw and cooked, the oil content of the fruit is higher than virtually any other organic species and if planted properly it could outdo sunflower oil as a crop. Even the wood is salable: an excellent substitute for mahogany and much more sustainable." Rafi stood, stretching his arms up to pluck the dangling fruit from the lowest branches.

Limbani suddenly winced and clutched his side as though he had a cramp. The spasm passed and the tension seemed to ease as his pain receded. It occurred to Holliday that Limbani must be in his late sixties by now and he'd been setting a much younger man's pace as they trekked through the jungle to their destination, wherever that was.

"Much farther?" Holliday asked.

"Another day." Limbani pointed at the hills ahead of them. "They are called the Crocodile's Eyes. We will camp on the right eye tonight," the older man said. Holliday let his own eyes go out of focus and he could see the similarity—two low humps rising above the surface of the river. Limbani spoke again. "As well as being a convenient place both to camp and to make an ambush, the Eyes mark the eastward limits of the territory of my people, the *Umufo omhloshana. Isikaya indawo.*"

Holliday glanced at Eddie and the Cuban gave him the translation.

"The home place," he said. "The place of our fathers, okay?"

Rafi had picked enough fruit for all of them and handed them around. Holliday took a bite. Limbani was right—it tasted like a combination of a plum and a pear.

Juicy, too. He took another bite, then wiped his sleeve across his mouth.

"You still haven't told me how you knew our names," said Holliday.

"You saw the mask," said Limbani with a wistful little smile. "Perhaps I am a griot—a witch doctor."

Peggy let out a dry laugh. "A witch doctor with a degree in tropical diseases from the Université de Paris. That's one well-educated witch doctor."

"So you know something about Amobe Limbani," said the black man, a glimmer of humor in his tired old eyes. "What do you think you know from what you have seen of him?"

"I think he's really good at changing the subject," said Rafi, biting into his fruit. "Why don't you answer Doc's question?"

"Doc?" Limbani said quizzically. "You are also a doctor, then? You move very much like a trained soldier."

"You're doing it again," said Holliday, laughing.

"Doing what?" Limbani said, eyes wide and innocent.

"Changing the subject," said Peggy.

"What was the question?"

"You know what the question was," said Holliday. "How did you know who we were?"

"*That* question? The answer to that question is very simple." Limbani shrugged. "I had a spy."

"Who?" Holliday asked.

"Think about it for a moment," said Limbani. "It will come to you."

It was a basic lesson he'd taught to his lieutenants in his days at West Point; sometimes you got so involved with the day-to-day, hour-to-hour, minute-to-minute tactics of a focused situation you lost sight of the overall strategy, the big picture that was going to win you the battle or even the war.

Ever since they'd landed at Umm Rawq the big picture had faded into the background as they dodged bullets and blowguns downriver. When he actually gave himself a moment to think about it, the identity of Limbani's spy was pretty obvious.

"Mutwakil Osman," said Holliday. "He's your spy."

"The floatplane guy?" Peggy said.

"The floatplane guy." Holliday nodded.

"Quite right," said Limbani. "He has been friend to the *Umufo omhloshana* since he first began flying upriver. A firm believer in leaving people alone, of letting them make their own destinies. He has brought medicine to us and some other necessities from time to time, but most important, he gives us an eye on what is going in the outside world that could impact us."

"Things like Archibald Ives."

"Precisely," said Limbani with a sigh. "A mineral engineer and prospector on this land could very well signal the end of these people, the end of everything here."

"That may have started already," said Holliday. "In

case you aren't already aware of it, Ives has been murdered and Sir James Matheson is interested in the land here. He owns one of the biggest resource development companies in the world."

"I know who he is," said Limbani.

"He's also interested in us," said Rafi. "He's become aware that we were interested in the area as well, but for different reasons."

"I know your reasons, too," said Limbani, sighing again and looking every inch the old man that he was. "King Solomon's Mines, the queen of Sheba, perhaps even Mansa Musa and Timbuktu. A great Technicolor fantasy of history that belongs with George Lucas and Indiana Jones. Cowboy science."

Holliday waited for Rafi's usual short-tempered answer to critics of his slightly more narrative and intuitive attitude toward archaeology but Rafi was remarkably polite.

"I assure you, Doctor, it's less about the mines and the legends than it is about the extraordinary people who followed those old stories. A tomb in Ethiopia led us here, not some 'Secrets of the Rosetta Stone' tract they give away for free on the Internet. The tomb was that of a Templar Knight named Julian de la Roche-Guillaume who searched for something that a Viking had searched for five hundred years before and which a Roman legionnaire had died for a thousand years before *that*. The stories and the legends get told and told again for a thousand years or two, but there's always a little truth left, just enough truth sometimes for the dreamers to believe in. Heinrich Schliemann read Homer, another dreamer, and found Troy." Rafi shook his head firmly. "I'm far more interested in the dreamers than the dream, Dr. Limbani."

Limbani gave him a slightly skeptical look, then shrugged. "A very nice little speech," said the older man. "How often have you recited it?"

"Once, to you."

Limbani scrutinized the young archaeologist for a long moment, then spoke. "If that is true, Dr. Wanounou, then you are in for a great surprise when we reach our destination, a very great surprise indeed."

The Brocklebank property was enormous, hidden behind a gated ten-foot-high stone wall and sitting on at least five acres of gardens. The house itself was a massive combination Tudor and Arts and Crafts–style brick-and-plank mansion with twelve thousand feet of living space, eleven bathrooms, three kitchens, sixteen bedrooms, eight of which had their own wood-burning fireplace, and one hundred and sixteen leaded-glass windows, some with colored panes and some without.

As the limousine drove through the gates and up the drive after being buzzed in, Saint-Sylvestre was astounded to see how well the gardens had been tended.

Either the Brocklebank ladies had an army of gardeners or they were obsessively compulsive about flowering plants.

The limousine went down the long drive and pulled up in front of the covered entranceway. Saint-Sylvestre leaned forward and spoke over the seat to the uniformed driver. "Wait here; I doubt if I'll be more than twenty minutes, tops."

"Whatever you say, sir," said the limo driver.

Saint-Sylvestre grabbed the attaché case, stepped out of the limo, went up the flagstone steps of the covered entranceway and rang the doorbell. Inside he could faintly hear the echoing sound of Big Ben. A full minute later he heard the clicking of heels and the door opened. The old woman who stood there looked shocked and surprised at seeing the color of Gesler's skin, but she recovered swiftly. A woman born in times when people of Saint-Silvestre's skin color came to the back door, not the front.

"Herr Gesler?" she asked. Her face was creased and pink with powder, her gray hair done up in a swirling bun that would have looked perfectly all right on a woman with a bustle dress and a big floppy hat. She was wearing half-heeled dark pumps and a perfectly tailored dark blue suit with white piping that had to be Chanel from the fifties. She had an enormous patent-leather purse over her arm. She bore a close resemblance to the late queen mother. No little old lady in a housedress here; this one was dressed to the nines.

"Miss Brocklebank?" Saint-Sylvestre responded, with a little bow. He thought about kissing her outstretched hand but decided it would be a little over the top, but not by much. He shook it instead.

"Indeed," she said. "My sister, Margaret, is in the library; shall I fetch her?"

"It occurred to me that we could finish up our business before we went to tea, Miss Brocklebank. We could make it a small celebration afterward, without any pressure."

"Well," said the old woman, "I wouldn't want us to be late. . . ." She didn't sound eager to be denied her pleasure; the Brocklebanks were obviously not used to being told no, even when it was going to put large sums of money into their pockets.

"Ten minutes is all it will require; I promise you," said Saint-Sylvestre firmly. "I only need to countersign the check and have you initial and sign the agreements again."

"I thought we'd already done that—the agreements, I mean."

"You have," said Saint-Sylvestre, purposely adopting the slightly condescending tone often used with the elderly and infirm. The old woman got the "a little forgetful, are we?" tenor of his voice immediately. She bristled but backed off.

"If you insist, Herr Gesler," she said, her voice brittle, then stepped aside.

"I'll make this as painless as possible, Miss Brockle-bank," he said, stepping into the house.

Betty Brocklebank led him across a short foyer and into the grand hall, all glowing inlaid wood and parquetry with a gigantic fieldstone fireplace beside the twisting stairway, the severed heads of a number of North American game animals hanging from the walls, glass eyes staring at nothing. The floor was covered by an enormous Persian carpet that was obviously the real thing.

They turned right into a large room, floor covered by smaller throw rugs, two walls covered by built-in oak bookcases, the third wall holding another big fireplace, this one gas, and the fourth wall taken up by a picture window of leaded panes that looked out onto the front gardens.

The outer row of windowpanes framed the view, with stained glass showing what had to be the Brocklebank coat of arms: a complicated device of swans, coronets and swords in blue, green, purple and gold.

The furniture was colonial India or Siam with huge wicker fan chairs and bamboo side tables. A second old woman sat on a curving rattan couch set under the window and upholstered in a dark blue fabric set with huge, colorful magnolia blossoms.

The old lady looked exactly like Betty except for her hair, which was permed into tight curls, the white shaded slightly blue, pink scalp showing underneath.

Her suit was the same as Betty Brocklebank's, the colors reversed, white with blue piping.

"Margie," said Betty Brocklebank, "this is Mr. Gesler from the bank in Switzerland. Mr. Gesler, my sister, Margaret Brocklebank."

"She was born three and a half minutes before me, which makes her the elder, so she thinks she's also the wiser, Mr. Gesler." Margie Brocklebank gave him a curious look. "I didn't know they had Negroes in Europe now. I don't remember seeing any there before the war."

"My mother was from Alexandria in Egypt. She met my father at the University of Zurich. He was taking mathematics; her degree was in physics," Saint-Sylvestre said blandly, pulling the lies out of the air like plucking cherries off a tree.

"I see," said Margie Brocklebank, obviously not seeing at all. A black man in her living room was difficult enough to fathom; a black woman taking a degree, let alone getting it, was too far out of the box for her to conceive. Saint-Sylvestre sat down in one of the fan-backed chairs opposite the couch, a bamboo-and-glass coffee table between them.

"I'll fetch the papers, then, shall I?" Betty Brocklebank said. She didn't wait for an answer and left the room, her footsteps clattering as they crossed the parquet between the carpets.

"I was valedictorian at Crofton House, you know,"

said Margie Brocklebank, whispering. "Betty was only salutatorian."

"Is that so?" Saint-Sylvestre said. He didn't have the slightest idea what she was talking about.

"Yes, it is," said Margie Brocklebank.

Betty Brocklebank came back into the room with an accordion file in her hands. She sat down on the couch beside her sister and put the file case on the coffee table. "Has she been telling you her 'I was the valedictorian' story, Mr. Gesler?"

Saint-Sylvestre said nothing. Margaret Brocklebank blushed. Her sister removed her hat, smiling triumphantly.

"Of course she was," said Betty Brocklebank. "It's her favorite except for the one about Mickey Hill standing me up at the Crofton House–St. George's Prom."

"Well, he *did* stand you up." The younger sister pouted.

"At least I was invited," said Betty Brocklebank sourly. She turned to Saint-Sylvestre. "Shall we get down to business, Mr. Gesler?"

"Of course," said Saint-Sylvestre. He lifted the attaché case onto the coffee table, unsnapped the locks and opened the case. He reached inside, took out the H&K P30 and shot both women twice in the chest. True to his word he'd made his business as painless as possible.

Never one for half measures, he stood up, went around the coffee table and shot the women again, one round to the head each. He wiped down the pistol carefully using the hem of Betty Brocklebank's skirt and laid it on the coffee table. When they ran the pistol's serial number it would slowly but inexorably lead back to Allen Faulkener, and from there to Matheson, hopefully putting the cat among the pigeons. That done, he emptied the contents of the accordion file into the attaché case, closed the case up and got down to work. The entire fate of Silver Brand Mining was now in his hands.

Fifteen minutes later Saint-Sylvestre stood on the covered porch of the Brocklebank house and breathed in a lungful of fresh air. In another fifteen minutes, with the gas jets wide-open and the pilot lights snuffed out in the kitchen and the fireplaces throughout the house, the simple cigarette-and-matchbox fuse he'd left behind would turn the entire downstairs of the old house into an inferno. It would take the local fire department another ten minutes to answer the call, and ten minutes after that for the news stations to receive the news.

This gave him a forty-minute window to take the limousine back to the Hotel Vancouver and get a taxicab to the airport. If everything went reasonably well the limousine driver wouldn't connect his last passenger to the fire on the Crescent for at least an hour or so, and by then the inimitable Leonhard Euhler would have been put to rest for good.

By the time Saint-Sylvestre reached the bottom of the steps the limousine driver was out of the car and standing beside the open rear door.

"Thank you," said Saint-Sylvestre.

The limo driver dipped into his pocket and handed the policeman what appeared to be a fairly clean, crumpled tissue.

"Got a spot of something on your tie," said the man.

"Thanks again," said Saint-Sylvestre. He dipped his head and sat down, the limo driver closing in behind him. Saint-Sylvestre lifted his tie and wiped the small gelatinous blob of Margie Brocklebank's brain tissue off the silk with the tissue. The limo driver climbed behind the wheel and they headed off.

25

They reached Kazaba Falls and the valley of the Pale Strangers at sunset the following day. They stood on the cliffs beside the smooth, hypnotic curve of the water as it raced over the precipice with a thunderous, all-consuming roar, a veil of mist rising like rainbow-tinted fog all around them, dampening the stone. The lowering sun had tinted all that it touched a shade of copper-gold.

"This is it!" Holliday said, raising his voice above the hammering bellow of the waterfall. "Your Templar Knight's vision of Eden."

It was the mural in the tomb on the island brought to life—the three separate cascades of the falls, each one flanked by a jutting prow of dark stone, the valley broken by the silver snake of the river far below and the three hills rising out of the jungle like the humped torsos of gigantic prehistoric beasts. It was the vindication of everything Rafi had speculated on since they'd left Jerusalem.

"The only things missing are those high-sided dugouts in the river and the miners with their baskets of ore winding down the middle hill." Rafi nodded.

"You sound as though you have been here before," said Limbani, who had been standing behind them, listening.

"A Templar Knight came here five hundred years ago," said Rafi. "He painted this place as a fresco on the walls of his tomb. His name was . . ."

"Julian de la Roche-Guillaume," said Limbani, nodding.

Rafi turned to him, startled. "Now, don't tell me you learned *that* from Osman, our Catalina flier, because I never mentioned it around him."

"I knew the name long before I ever met Osman," said Limbani with a wistful smile. "I knew it as a child when my father brought me here."

"Your father knew of this place?" Holliday said.

"And his father before him." Limbani nodded. "For more than a hundred years our family has been to the *Umufo omhloshana* what Mutwakil Osman, my spy, has been to me—their only connection with the present day and the outside world. It was because of that my father became governor of Vakaga province; this part of the country was prime to be developed: roads through the jungle, talk of damming the river and even using the Kazaba Falls for hydroelectric power.

"The *Umufo omhloshana* would have been discovered

and all their secrets and their legacy destroyed forever. A proud people turned to government handouts and squalor. When my father was murdered by the government I took his place. It is my sacred duty. To the people of this valley I am the *Umlondolozi*, the Protector."

"Conan Doyle's *Lost World*," said Rafi.

"More like *Turok, Son of Stone*," said Holliday.

"What on earth is that?" Peggy said.

"A comic book I used to read when I was a kid," answered Holliday. "Uncle Henry used to buy them for me when I visited during the summer. You're way too young."

"Come," said Limbani. "We must hurry now; the sun will set soon and the pathway down the cliffs is narrow and quite treacherous in the darkness."

They made their descent slowly, the path no more than eight or nine feet wide at best, some pounded earth but most of the way was wide stone steps worn smooth by uncounted centuries of travelers' feet.

"The steps were carved by the slaves of Dinga Cisse, first warrior king of Wagadou in the seventh century," said Limbani, reading Holliday's mind as he led the way downward. "Although the warrior kings, or 'ghanas,' had mined the hills in the valley for a thousand years before that."

"What about King Solomon?" asked Peggy, walking behind Holliday in the long file down the cliff.

"The ghanas of what became Mali were eventually

overthrown by the 'mansas,' or kings of that empire, one of whom was Sogolon Djata, or in English, King Solomon, and no relation at all to Solomon, king of the house of David. I am afraid that Christians, Jews and Muslims think history began with the Old Testament, but I can assure you, Africa's history is a great deal older than that."

They continued down the precarious cliff trail, which fortunately began to widen slightly. Staring down at the jungle far below them Holliday was suddenly aware that there were strange shapes in the landscape that didn't quite seem to make sense. He also realized that it was only the setting sun that was giving the secret away, throwing hard shadows where there shouldn't have been any. Going lower still, perhaps fifty feet from the jungle floor, he saw that it was. "That's incredible," he said admiringly. "You've got half the valley camouflaged! What are you hiding down here?"

"We adapt to the times," said Limbani. "My father got his first doctor of medicine degree at Cambridge University. He was a member of Jasper Maskelyne's magic circus during World War Two."

"The man who made the city of Alexandria in Egypt and the Suez Canal disappear," said Holliday. "He planted two thousand plywood tanks and painted entire fake armies on Salisbury Plain to throw off German reconnaisance flights just before D-day."

"That's right," said Limbani. "They knew that aerial

photography was an important part of protective coloration, and it's even more important now with three dozen satellites peering down on us at various times of the day and night."

"But why the camouflage?" Holliday asked. "What are you trying to cover up?"

"In the first place, the fact that the *Umufo omhloshana* exist at all. They are neither Baya, Banda nor even Kolingba's scourge, the Yakima. If he discovered them here it would be genocide. Like most African dictators, Solomon Kolingba is a racist, in his case a racist of insane proportions. In the second place . . . well, you'll see soon enough."

They reached the bottom of the cliff a quarter of an hour later, a steep path through scrub brush leading down to a wall of dense jungle foliage. Following the path, Holliday realized that what had appeared to be dense jungle in front of them was in fact a curtain of netting hung with strips of multicolored cloth and interwoven with twigs and branches. They pushed through a small gap in the netting and stepped into the forest beyond.

"Amazing," said Holliday, staring. "Absolutely amazing."

Oliver Gash sat alone at a table in the bar at the Hotel Trianon and slowly sipped his after-dinner café brûlot, enjoying the aroma of the cinnamon stick and the bitter orange tang of the Grand Marnier. Except for Marcel Boganda, the bartender, the room was almost empty. There were two Chinese trade officials in the corner getting drunk but that was all. Oliver Gash's appearance tended to clear most rooms he entered, but he was used to his effect on the local populace.

By now Kolingba was concentrating his attentions on the two prostitutes Gash had imported from Bangui who were willing to take their chances in bed with the three-hundred-pound dictator and his sometimes violent habits. Gash could relax for the evening, but somehow he didn't think relaxation was in the cards for him tonight. He'd fled from Rwanda the better part of twenty years ago and he hadn't survived that terrible place and the different jungle of Cherry Hill and the rest of south Baltimore by ignoring his intuitions and his hunches. Over the last ten days or two weeks those hunches and intuitions had set all his senses tingling and his alarm bells ringing, all banging out the same tune: *Get the hell out while you can.*

He slowly drank his coffee, trying to put things together in a logical progression, hoping to see something concrete take shape out of the kaleidescope of small impressions, rumors, facts and whispers that a man in his position came in contact with all the time.

It had started even before the arrival of the Canadian with the German accent; sightings of Limbani had increased and there was an air of expectation among the people, a desperate, uneven thing, the feeling you got when you saw someone die under the wheels of a bus. It didn't take jungle drums to tell you that the natives were restless and, more important, expectant. These people were perhaps two generations from being naked savages running after their prey. He had no doubt they'd be gnawing on the bones of any ruler who showed a single sign of weakness.

He hadn't heard from Saint-Sylvestre for more than a week now, which was worrying in itself, but he had done some investigation on his own. Archibald Ives had indeed been a mining engineer and it hadn't taken much to backtrack from the murder site on the Sudan highway to his boarding the *Pevensey*, which plied the course of the Kotto River from Umm Rawq to the first cataract, effectively the border between southern Sudan and Kukuanaland. From there he'd gone deeper into the bush by dugout. If Saint-Sylvestre was right, he'd found something with enough importance to get him killed. According to the police report he'd eventually bribed the Khartoum police, for the killing was no random highway banditry; Sudanese bandits used old Mannlicher-Carcano Italian infantry rifles from the Second World War. According to the police file, the weapon used to kill Ives was a South African .50-caliber sniper rifle. The men who shot those were neither cheap nor easy to find, let alone hire, so who had done so?

The .50-caliber weapon led somehow to the appearance of Lanz, who by any indication was no arms dealer. During his time in Kukuanaland he'd made only the barest attempts to do business, preferring instead to go for long walks around the town. In Saint-Sylvestre's opinion, Lanz was almost certainly plotting a takeover, and his own further investigations had seemed to bear that out.

On several trips to England made to open up lines of communication with large-scale drug operations there, he'd made a few private contacts who fed him regular tidbits of information about the men he was doing business with or might do business with in the future. Those contacts had only three days ago told him something of perhaps even greater importance: the appearance in London of none other than Francois Nagoupandé, dressed in a British Royal Army general's uniform. Nagoupandé had been the vice governor of Vakaga province and the man who betrayed Limbani. He was also a bee in Kolingba's bonnet. The fat dictator had a paranoid terror of Nagoupandé showing up with some phantom forces of arms raised God only knew where, even though Gash had men on a watching brief on the ex–vice governor, who rarely strayed out of his compound on a huge estate in Mali. Nagoupandé in a general's uniform; was it just wishful tailoring or was something in the works? The most forceful clue to come downriver was the sinking of the *Pevensey*, the riverboat freight carrier destroyed by something big, like a Cessna Caravan. A question arose: Who wanted to stop the freight carrier from brokering eggs to the villages on the river in return for animal skins, native meat, fish and vegetables and occasionally a bit of panned gold or a diamond in the rough? Unless *Pevensey*'s Cuban expatriate captain was up to no good and bringing more than goat meat upriver.

Unless that was the direction the coup was coming from. Gash thought for a moment about the fact that Kolingba didn't trust banks; the walls behind his third-floor private quarters were filled with billions in currency and bullion. Gash had checked the calendar today. In three days it would be the last phase of the moon. He had the feeling all the questions would be answered then. He finished his cup of café brûlot in a single swallow. No matter what he did or whose allegiance he honored he knew that Kukuanaland would be a very different place by the next time the full moon came around again. He got up from the table, only slightly pissed. He had a great deal to do and very little time to do it in.

He stood up and went to the bar to pay his account with Marcel the bartender. He paid the older, blank-faced black man thirty dollars in American bills, the generally accepted currency in Kukuanaland both because of its easy readibility and because it was the only currency in Africa that couldn't be forged with a box of crayons. Marcel gave him his change and a receipt and Gash handed him back the change as a tip. It wasn't until he got back to the compound and his quarters there that he unfolded the receipt.

Its message was simple and shocking: *Limbani seen alive and well in the company of a number of white men near the Kotto River at Kazaba Falls.*

He took out his old Baltimore Orioles Zippo and burned the piece of paper in the brass ashtray on his desk. He couldn't hear the banging, thumping and screeching from above him in Kolingba's quarters and decided that it would be more prudent to hold off on telling the general about it until tomorrow. Kolingba had an unpleasant habit of shooting the messenger, especially at times like this.

26

After standing at the foot of the cliff and then going through the foliage-threaded netting, Holliday could immediately see the genius of how the Pale Strangers had laid out their settlement. More than a settlement, actually—from what Holliday could see it looked very much like a small city.

At least half of the valley floor—well camouflaged by the high canopy of the trees and assemblages of woven mats of twigs and plants hung at varying levels in the trees—was made up of at minimum fifty kraals, circular enclosures made from bamboo rammed into high mud-and-earthen walls, topped by heavy bamboo palisades a dozen feet tall.

At the entrances to the enclosures there was a heavy ladder that could be drawn up the berm, making it impossible to get in. There appeared to be small holes higher up in the palisades, and Holliday had no doubt that there were battlements up there, ready for Limbani's warriors and their blowpipes.

Each of the enclosures had a central pole from which large triangles of fabric could unfold, covering the enclosure completely when it started to rain. Holliday recognized the design from the covering of the forum in Rome, and that stood to reason as well, since the lost legion was sure to have had engineers within the ranks.

"As I am sure you have already ascertained, the fabric roofs over each enclosure are of Roman origin," Limbani said in the lead.

"But not the compounds themselves," said Holliday.

"No, those are native, although the stone ones from Great Zimbabwe are roughly the same pattern."

"It's ingenious. Each compound is alone but at some point touches its neighbor. Any enemies have to fight down here on the low ground and what is, in fact, a garden maze. Easy to get lost, easy to bunch up if you were trying to take the place."

"Better yet, if one compound is breached the occupants simply flee into the next," Limbani said.

"The castle-within-a-castle design of a Templar fortress," murmured Holliday.

As they made their way through the extraordinary maze they even saw tall canopy trees growing up out of several of the circular compounds, and in other places on the pathway more trees had been left in place. With that kind of attention to detail and the hundreds of hanging latticework shields, the whole place would be invisible from only a few hundred feet. From a surveillance satellite, the compound wouldn't be seen at all.

"How many people live in each compound?" Holliday asked, following Limbani.

"It is difficult to say," explained the doctor, half turning as they made their way through the serpentine maze, "since many different things are done within them, weaving, tanning, making fishing line and nets for the birds. One is given over to keeping bees. There is a whole compound merely for the making of blowguns and their darts, and yet another for the various poisons that are used, both plant toxins and animal. The plant toxin we use most often is concentrated ricin from the coating of simple castor beans. The animal toxins are usually concentrated venom from the gaboon viper or the boomslang. Sometimes we use the fat-tailed scorpion, *Androctonus australis.*"

"Fatal?"

"Invariably." Limbani nodded. "My abilities in medicine have gone a long way toward improving the toxicity of their weaponry."

"But why so aggressive?" Holliday asked. "There can't be much in the way of real predators here."

"You're quite right," Dr. Limbani answered. "For thousands of years they have been left alone in the jungle, to live their lives as they please, to fulfill their destinies as their gods see fit. But that is changing now. Those days are swiftly coming to an end. Kolingba is the first of his kind; he will not be the last unless we do something about it. We must do it, Colonel, and that time is coming sooner than you think. It is only a matter of days now."

"How can you be so sure?"

"You think Mutwakil Osman is my only spy? There are a few others of my tribe who are friends to the *Umufo omhloshana*."

"What can you do about someone like Kolingba? If he decided to go after this place it would be all over within a day. He has helicopters, rocket launchers, machine guns. You wouldn't stand a chance. It would be suicide to fight those men."

"And it would be genocide not to," said Limbani calmly.

"You've got no defense against their kind of weapons," argued Holliday.

"Think of your history, Colonel."

"What kind of history?"

"Your specialty, as I understand it from Professor Wanounou. Military history."

"All right. It's simple: you're outnumbered, you're outgunned, and if laid siege to, you'd starve. It's no contest."

"Did you fight in Vietnam, Colonel?"

"Two tours when I was eighteen and nineteen. Exactly three hundred and sixty-five wet-behind-the-ears days, boots on the ground, and all three hundred and sixty-five have haunted me ever since. Not my favorite war, Doctor. Teenagers shouldn't be killing people. It does bad things to their brains; believe me."

"Then you know something about fighting in jungles."

"Some." Holliday nodded, a bitter, distant look in his eye.

"Helicopters are limited to some surveillance—the forest canopy sees to that," answered Limbani. "Rocket launchers and any other forms of artillery are useless in the jungle. Tanks and other armored vehicles are equally useless; wouldn't you agree?"

"For the most part."

"Even laser-guided and infrared sighting devices are useless, day or night. During the day there's too much interference and at night there's so much return of heat from the ground to the air a person wearing night-vision goggles would be blinded. The West has invariably used weapons ill suited for unfamiliar terrains—the Abrams tank was meant for traveling three abreast on a European autobahn, and so was the Soviet T-90. Air transport to places like Afghanistan or Bosnia is a waste of time, and sand gets in the bearings when they fight in the deserts of Iraq.

"In Afghanistan, Americans forgot everything they learned about guerrilla fighting in Vietnam, and the

Russians forgot the lessons they learned in their revolutions. Have you noticed that no foreign power has ever prosecuted a successful war on African soil against Africans—only against each other? Here warfare is reduced to its simplest and most terrible—two warriors, one against the other, where often it is the simplest weapon, least affected by terrain and the elements, that wins the day. With that kind of scenario, Colonel Holliday, we will not lose."

"A proud speech, Dr. Limbani," said Holliday. "But are you willing to bet your people's lives on rhetoric?"

"Life is a bet, Colonel Holliday, but sometimes the odds can be evened. Follow me."

He began to climb up one of the ladders laid down on the sloped berm around one of the palisades surrounding what appeared to be a larger-than-average compound close to the center of the maze. He reached the top of the mound of earth, bending over a little to catch his breath. Looking directly ahead, Holliday could see an indentation in the palisade: a doorway, perhaps.

"Skalle-odelle!" Limbani called out loudly.

"What language is that?" Holliday asked.

"They have sacred words; those are two of them. Their day-to-day language is an ancient Malinke dialect from Sogolon's time."

"It sounds Danish or Norwegian," said Peggy.

"Ragnar Skull Splitter," said Rafi softly. *"Skalle-odelle,* perhaps?" The archaeologist looked at Holliday.

"It would make sense if this is where Julian de la Roche-Guillaume wound up—and we've proved by now that it is. It would also explain the clothing worn by the Pale Strangers: a good imitation of what the average Egyptian workingman wore eight hundred years ago—a simple linen kilt. If Ragnar and his men actually came down the Nile it would have been reasonable for them to adopt a similar form of dress."

Limbani laughed. "You impress me, Wanounou; most archaeologists don't make interpretive leaps of thought like that."

"Rafi's not your ordinary archaeologist," said Peggy, smiling. "He's more the 'seek out new life and new civilizations, to boldly go where no man has gone before' type."

A few feet in front of them a seven-foot-wide section of the palisade lifted like an old-fashioned portcullis on a castle. Beyond the opening was an enclosed passage at least twelve feet high and made of solid planks on both sides and above. At regular intervals in the tunnel-like enclosure were small circular openings, each one a little larger than the diameter of the blowguns used by the Pale Strangers. The artificial tunnel was twenty feet long and ended in a second gate as solid as the walls and the roof.

"Ingenious!" Holliday said. "A barbican gatehouse, complete with *meurtrières*."

"Murder holes?" Limbani said as they made their

way along the enclosed corridor. "They had names for such things?"

"They've *always* had names for such things," said Holliday dryly. "That particular one is a French invention, if memory serves."

As the entrance behind them clattered shut, the gates in front of them swung open and they stepped out into the open compound within three palisades. A half dozen plank-cut Indian longhouse buildings were arranged in a semicircle at the outer edge of the compound, each one with a totemlike "figurehead" jutting out from the center beam of the sloping roof. One of them was identical to the rooster-shaped mask Holliday had seen Jerimiah Salamango, the "Christ's destroyer," wearing.

"Those are Viking longhouses!" Rafi whispered, his voice full of excitement. "This really is some kind of lost world."

Women and children were moving from longhouse to longhouse while very young children, naked except for loincloths, played in the dirt, chasing one another around amid the buildings. A dozen or so adolescents, male and female, were seated cross-legged in a line a hundred feet or so away from a series of narrow plank targets painted with rough bull's-eyes, the center marker white, the outer marker bright yellow.

Each of the young people had a blowgun in his or her lap and a woven, tubular quiver for darts slung bandolier-style across his or her chest. The boys were naked from the waist up while the girls wore simple cloth bands wound tightly over their breasts.

They were silent, their expressions serious, almost meditative. To Holliday it looked as though they were doing breathing exercises of some kind. An adult stood behind them, his long blowgun held like a stave. A broad *X* was drawn across his face in black. His eyes were an intense gemlike blue and, remarkably, his long, braided hair was as blond as corn silk.

"The yellow-haired one is called *umculisi*, a teacher. His students are *ibuso-sha*, young warriors. At the moment they are practicing the breathing of la Sarbacana."

"Doesn't sound very African to me," said Peggy.

"It's not," Limbani said quietly. "When Julian de la Roche-Guillaume left the Holy Land he traveled to the deeper East, perhaps even as far as Tibet, where he received the teachings of Drogön Chögyal Phagpa, the emperor who was also spiritual adviser to Kublai Khan.

"He returned to France briefly, establishing a small secret school for the study of what he referred to as Sarbacana, the joining of breath, mind and sight. It was apparently 'reinvented' by a French quasi-mystic guru in the nineteen seventies but it is clearly the same art."

"This is beginning to get very weird," muttered Peggy. "The Templar and his solid-gold tomb were strange enough, but now we're in Tibet with Kublai Khan. Next thing you know we'll have Olivia Newton-John singing 'Xanadu.'"

"We're talking martial art?" Holliday said, ignoring his cousin.

"Indeed," said Limbani.

"You really think this Sarbacana breathing can stand up to an AK-47?"

Limbani nodded to the blond man with the X across his face.

"Impumphuthe," said the blond man quietly. All of the young people reached into a small pocket sewn inside the waistband of their tunics and withdrew a strip of cloth, which they then handed to the person beside them. Each student in turn blindfolded his neighbor.

"Would you like to check the blindfolds?" Limbani said.

"I'll take your word for it," said Holliday. "This is no circus act."

Limbani nodded to the blond man again.

"Lungisela," said the blond man.

Each of the blindfolded students took a four-inch-long dart from his quiver and slid it into his blowgun. They then raised the blowguns to their lips.

"In battle, of course, the tip of each dart would be dipped in a fatal neurotoxin," Limbani explained. "Once upon a time the darts were made from iron, but we have found that aluminum nails ground to razor sharpness are a satisfactory and less labor-intensive substitute." He nodded to the blond man again.

"Dubulela," murmured the blond man.

There was a brief, rattling sigh, like raindrops on a metal roof, followed by a perfectly ordered series of thumps as the blowgun darts found their targets. Holliday stared, impressed. The students had fired in distinct, even sequence, blindfolded, and each of them had hit the stark white bull's-eye of his target dead center.

"Everyone, male or female, in this valley can do what you've just seen, some better and faster in the daylight or in the dark. There are four thousand people here, Colonel. They are the last of their kind and each one of them is willing to die for their freedom. How does that stand up to an AK-47?"

"I wouldn't like to give odds," said Holliday. "Too close to call."

"Will you stand with us, Colonel? We could use the help and advice of a real soldier."

Holliday didn't hesitate. It had been a long time since he'd had something worth fighting for.

"Yes," he said. "I'll stand with you. We all will."

27

Matheson chose room nine at the old Tate Gallery—Art and the Sublime—for his meeting with Lanz. The mercenary met him standing in front of John Martin's *The Great Day of His Wrath*, an immense apocalyptic painting of the end of the world, the artist's favorite subject matter.

"Do you know anything about John Martin?" Matheson asked.

"Never heard of him," said Lanz. For the mercenary, art was for chocolate boxes. He stared up at the six-by-ten-foot canvas. The horizon burned with orange hellfire, whole mountains slid into the abyss, while thousands of screaming, naked bodies came tumbling after. A single intense bolt of light ricocheted up the valley. Lanz supposed it was meant to illustrate the wages of sin, but it left him cold. He had as much use for religion as he did for art.

"He was quite mad, of course," murmured the industrialist. "Came from a mad family. Father was a fencing master. Martin was apprenticed to a painter of heraldic devices on coach doors. His older brother, also named John, was once known as England's greatest arsonist. Martin painted almost as a hobby—his real passion was designing a new sewer system for London. Quite mad."

"Your point being, Sir James?" Lanz asked.

"Sometimes great men are seen to be mad because so few people can appreciate the extent of their genius."

"Sir?"

"Am I mad, do you think, Lanz?"

"That's not for me to say." Lanz shrugged.

"Allen Faulkener is dead," said Matheson. "He was murdered in a hotel room in Vancouver, Canada. The same day the two little old ladies he was dealing with were killed in a fire. Although it later turned out they were actually killed by Faulkener's own weapon."

"Presumably this had something to do with the situation in Africa?" said Lanz.

"Yes."

"Do you wish to delay?" Lanz said.

"I haven't decided," answered Matheson. He moved along to the next painting on the wall of the gallery. This one was small in relation to the John Martin, not quite three feet on a side. *Death on a Pale Horse* by William Turner, a smoky, amorphous horror. The horse was barely visible; Death was an articulated, hungry skeleton, grinning maw spread wide. Matheson stood transfixed. He knew he was seeing the future, but whose?

"I've given guarantees," said Lanz. "Most of these men won't wait, and if we lose the dark of the moon we'll have to set back the clock by almost a month. It will be expensive."

"How expensive?"

"At least a million, maybe more. The men will all have to be paid for their wait time. If you want to be sure of your transportation, that will also be a premium."

The Brocklebank sisters were dead, their proxy held by someone as amorphous as Turner's figure of death. He already owned most of the outstanding shares, but if he risked using the shell company the mysterious forces responsible for the murders of Faulkener and the Brocklebanks would simply exercise the option and take over the huge find in the tiny African country.

If he simply ate the shares he'd purchased and did a separate deal with Nagoupandé, he could salvage the situation with a relatively small loss, but who knew how far Nagoupandé's bought-and-paid-for loyalty would last?

He didn't have any choice. What was that ridiculous motto Faulkener was always quoting—*Qui audet adipiscitur*? Who dares, wins. It hadn't done Faulkener much good. According to the Vancouver city coroner's office, the idiot had been killed by a common steak knife.

On the other hand, if there was ever a time for daring it was now. He'd tell Lanz to keep a gun to Nagoupandé's head until the mining concessions were turned over and loyalty ceased to be a factor. He turned away from the deathly vision on the wall. It had to be now.

"We continue as planned," he said. "No delays. At the dark of the moon."

Lanz nodded, his spine automatically straightening. "At the dark of the moon."

General Solomon Bokassa Sesesse Kolingba awoke abruptly and painfully, a blazing flare of sunlight spearing through a small space between the heavy velvet curtains that were usually drawn tightly together to avoid just such an event. He was not a man who met the day well, preferring instead to rise slowly, first slaking his thirst with several bottles of Mongozo banana beer and then spending at least half an hour in the bathroom voiding his bowels.

Following this he generally ate a breakfast of scrambled eggs, sausage, black pudding, bacon, mushrooms, baked beans, hash browns, grilled kidneys, a pair of Scotch kippers, three slices of fried bread and half a tomato for color, followed by several carafes of either hot chocolate or sweet black coffee, depending on his mood.

This meal was generally eaten in his living room

while sitting in his favorite reclining chair in front of an extremely large flat-screen TV while he watched CNN and the BBC on his satellite receiver. Sometimes if the news was boring he'd watch an old movie.

At eleven he would get dressed in a set of camo fatigues and shoot skeet on the roof for an hour before lunch. Any variation on this routine was fraught with danger, and interrupting it without an extremely good reason could prove seriously harmful.

On the twenty-sixth day of that month, two days before the dark of the moon, Oliver Gash entered General Kolingba's private quarters at four fifty-one a.m., one minute before official sunrise. He stayed in the shadows close to the door and well away from the big, curtained four-poster bed that stood in a far corner of the room. The worst of it was that Kolingba never snored; he slept almost silently, an immense, immobile pile in bright yellow silk pajamas and a black silk mask.

"General," said Gash quietly from the other side of the room. There was no response, but Gash heard a faint clicking sound from behind the curtains surrounding the bed. The sound of one of the silver-plated presentation Colt .45s being cocked. He squeezed his own hand a little harder around the butt of the cocked Glock 17P in the pocket of his jacket.

"General?"

There was a long pause.

"Have you come to murder me in my bed, Gash?"

"No, sir."

"I can see in the dark like a cat. I would kill you first."

"Yes, sir, I know that." From Rwanda to Banqui to Baltimore to here; it really was a long and winding road.

"I am *uSathane-umufo*, a devil man. I know your thoughts," said Kolingba out of the darkness.

"I know this, too, General, and I would never have disturbed your sleep without the most important of reasons."

The heavy curtains on the side of the bed facing Gash were thrust aside and Kolingba appeared out of the gloom, throwing back the black satin sheet that covered his huge body. He swung his legs over the bed, planting them wide apart like a Sumo wrestler. In his right hand the silver-plated pistol glinted. Kolingba lifted one giant buttock and broke wind explosively.

"Speak," said the dictator, yawning.

"There are several things, Your Highness. Together they point to a single conclusion."

"What things?"

"Saint-Sylvestre has disappeared."

"The policeman?"

"Yes."

"Why should I care about a policeman disappearing? This is not enough to wake me from my dreams, Gash. My dreams are prophecies. They guide me as I guide my country."

Oh, jeez.

"He disappeared while he was following a man he believed was a mercenary, Your Highness."

"What sort of mercenary?"

"He was traveling on a Canadian passport, but Saint-Sylvestre was sure he was German."

"Why would a mercenary come here?"

"Saint-Sylvestre thought there was a good chance that he was reconnoitering Fourandao."

"Reconnoitering? Why would anyone want to do that, Gash?"

"For a coup-d'état, Your Majesty." Gash waited for the reaction. There was none except for Kolingba's fingers tightening a little around the big automatic in his hand.

"That is impossible," said Kolingba. "My enemies are gone. My people love me."

"Perhaps, Your Majesty, but there have been reports of a mining engineer who showed an interest in the area around the Kazaba Falls."

"There is nothing there. Only swamp and jungle."

Gash summoned up his courage and spoke. "Limbani has been seen."

"Don't be foolish," scoffed Kolingba. "Limbani is *isipokwe*, a ghost."

"I'm afraid Limbani is no ghost, Your Highness. He has been seen at the first cataract talking to a group of white men. He is very much alive."

Kolingba bolted up out of the bed, eyes bulging in the semidarkness, a yellow mountain of flesh waving an automatic pistol, screaming. "Then find him! Find him! I will have him, Gash! Do you understand me!? You must kill him! I must kill him! He is a scourge! An infestation! Kill him!"

Then, just as suddenly as it had appeared, the anger vanished. Kolingba threw the pistol on his night table. "What are you going to do?" Kolingba asked.

"I thought we could take one of the helicopters and look for any signs of him upriver. It is clear that any attempt on Fourandao will come from the east—we would have heard about it long ago if it was coming from Banqui."

"My dreams tell me that the danger comes from the west. Perhaps from Banqui, or even farther."

"You could go yourself and see," replied Gash, knowing what the reply would be.

"You know I will not fly in one of those things, Gash," said the general petulantly. "Go for me."

"Of course, Your Majesty. I have your full authority in this, I presume?"

"Of course, of course!"

"In writing?" Gash asked. If there was to be a coup Gash would have to be the one who prepared against it.

"Yes! Yes!" Kolingba said, waving Gash from the room, his face twisted angrily. Gash had to stop himself from laughing as he suddenly understood Kolingba's urgency—he was desperate to get to the chamber pot beneath the bed.

Gash backed toward the door; the pistol was only a foot or two away from Kolingba's hand. "And have my breakfast sent here today, would you. I must think about all of this," the general added.

"Right away." Gash nodded. He found the door at his back and slipped quickly from the room. As he headed to the kitchens he found himself thinking about the cash hidden behind the wall in Kolingba's office and how it could be accessed quickly if it became necessary. As he made his way down the stairs he began to whistle the theme music from the old *A-Team* series, his favorite back in Baltimore. He smiled broadly as he reached the ground floor of the main compound building. He really did love it when a plan came together.

28

Sir James Matheson, Ninth Earl of Emsworth, maintained two official residences in England. One was Huntington Hall, the enormous seventeenth-century ancestral estate in Derbyshire. The other was a magnificent seven-bedroom apartment in Albert Hall Mansions located between Albert Hall and the Royal Geographical Society on Kensington Gore overlooking the Albert Memorial and Kensington Gardens.

The earl and his wife, the Countess Edwina, formerly Lady Edwina Talbot, had a long-standing marital agreement that neither party would arrive at the other's residence without an invitation and at least twenty-four hours' notice. The twins, Justin and Jonathan, had been packed away to Barlborough Hall School since their fifth birthday and still had another six years to go before being packed away once more to Oxford or Cambridge, and thus presented no particular problem to either parent.

Neither Sir James nor Countess Edwina professed the slightest interest in what the other was doing and each left the other alone, except for formal occasions such as Royal Garden Parties, the Grand National and Royal Ascot. For the most part, Huntington Hall was the countess's fiefdom and London belonged to Sir James.

Like most titled people in England with reputations to sustain, both the countess and Sir James had their various appropriate charities, and those charities required fund-raising. On the advice of his accountants, Sir James Matheson's cultural charity was the Royal College of Music—even though he was known to have a tin ear that had difficulty getting the tune for even "God Save the Queen" right. He sponsored several dinners, concerts and cocktail parties for the college each year to raise money.

Unfortunately the date for one of those parties fell just forty-eight hours before the dark of the moon in Fourandao, Kukuanaland, and the launch of Matheson's private invasion of that country. Even more unfortunate was the fact that these cocktail parties invariably took place at his apartment in Albert Hall Mansions.

Matheson's apartment was on the fourth floor of a five-and-a-half-story building, and dwarfed both the Royal Geographical Society and Albert Hall itself. Matheson's father, the eighth earl, either through great good fortune or liberal applications of money, had managed to purchase one of the center apartments, which had an arched, recessed balcony that stretched the width of the entire apartment and could be used in inclement weather.

A large black-and-white-tiled entrance hall led to a thirty-by-forty-foot reception room on the right. Kitchens, bedrooms, bathrooms and a sitting room were on the left. The first reception room led to a second reception room, which led out to the arched balcony; beside the reception room was a master bedroom that Matheson had renovated into a study-library, also leading out to the arched balcony. At the last tax evaluation, the apartment had been valued at eight million, two hundred thousand pounds.

At the present moment it was crammed with well over a hundred people grazing on several thousand pounds' worth of mini Parmesan baskets filled with cauliflower puree, wild-strawberry-and-cucumber jam on toast, wild mushroom palmiers with creamed goat cheese, dragachelio baby quail egg Florentine with pink pepper hollandaise and, last but not least, the eight-pounds-a-mouthful seared miso-infused tuna. On top of that were forty strategically placed crystal vases of cut flowers spread through the entrance hall, the two reception halls and the three bathrooms designated for guest use that evening, not to mention the endless spigot of expensive French, German and Italian wines and the full bar, all of it serviced by more than two dozen waitstaff, bartenders, presenters and a ten-person cleanup crew for after the party.

In the smaller of the two reception rooms a tuxedo-wearing deejay had hooked into Matheson's own apartment-wide Bose system, providing selections of classical music interspersed with jazz that nobody was paying the slightest attention to. There was a six-man armed security team, all dressed in tuxedos—provided by Kate Sinclair's Blackhawk Security—to make sure that no one stole the family silver or got into violent arguments about the respective merits of Alexander Konstantinovich Glazunov and Carl Heinrich Carsten Reinecke. All of it was giving Sir James Matheson a violent headache. He really did have much more important things on his mind.

By ten he was saying good-bye to his last few guests, all of whom promised to send large donations to the Royal Academy. By eleven thirty the caterers were on the way out the door, and by midnight the apartment was his own again. He unlocked the door to his study, which had been off-limits for the evening, and stepped inside.

The room was comfortingly dark, as it usually was, the only light coming from a small green lamp on the bar. He poured himself a glass of thirty-two-year-old Auchentoshan single-malt and went over to his desk to look for an old bottle of Rofecoxib. He flipped on the desk lamp and saw that there was already someone seated in his chair, blood leaking down the starched bib front of his evening clothes from the eight-inch gaping slash across his throat. The man's head was so thrown back by the wound that Matheson could see the cocaine frosted around his nostrils. There were several more lines of cocaine on the desk in front of the dead man, along with a rolled-up five-pound note. Matheson put down the heavy glass of whiskey. He recognized the slaughtered body: it was Simon Wells, a puff-piece writer who made the circuit putting society names into his column in boldface. A completely harmless individual with a not-uncommon taste for drugs. For a moment Matheson thought about doing the dead man's lines on the desk to calm his nerves a little, but thought better of it.

A pole light came on in the far corner of the room. It illuminated a tall, thin black man holding an automatic pistol loosely in his hand. The man was dressed in an expensive-looking set of evening clothes and there was a glass of something that looked like gin and lemon on the table beside him. He reached for it with his free hand and took a moderate sip, the ice cubes tinkling pleasantly against the expensive Czech crystal.

"My name is Captain Jean-Luc Saint-Sylvestre of DGASEK, the Direction Générale d Action et de la Sécurité Extérieure de Kukuanaland, or to put it more simply, the secret police of that country."

Matheson was smart enough and sober enough not

to try to bluff and bluster. If the man in the chair had wanted to kill him he would be dead by now; if Saint-Sylvestre was from Kukuanaland he knew about the huge neodymium and tantalum strikes discovered by Ives, a discovery of rare earths in such concentrations that he could single-handedly break China's monopoly overnight.

"May I ask why you killed poor Simon here?"

"Sadly for him he was in here doing his drugs when I came into the room. His death was necessary to keep my presence secret."

"The door was locked," said Matheson, trying to think as he kept up the stream of macabre chatter.

"The French doors on the balcony weren't," said the black man. "They were either open or your dead *toxico* behind the desk there slipped them open with a credit card."

"May I sit down?" Matheson asked.

"No," said the black man. "Remain where you are."

"How did you get into the apartment? The party was by invitation only."

"I pickpocketed Elton John coming up in the elevator, or at least it looked like Elton John. Nobody gave me a second look. I could just as easily have come in with the caterers and gone around poisoning all your guests."

"What do you want?"

"A great deal of money and a share in whatever it

was Archibald Ives found below Kazaba Falls. Say one million pounds in cash and one full percent of any mineral concessions granted to Matheson Resource Industries, payable in preferred shares of MRI, since you can no longer use Silver Brand Mining as your shell company."

"One percent isn't very much," said Matheson. How the hell did he know about Silver Brand but not what Ives had discovered? Was there any value in that? Matheson's brain tried to cut through the patchy fog of his headache and alcohol. Was there an advantage?

"I'm not a greedy man," said Saint-Sylvestre. "One percent and a million pounds isn't enough for you to risk my divulging what I know before the fact, and after the fact I'll be able to hold it over your head for the rest of your life. You know as well as I do that this is the sort of thing that brings down governments, let alone industrial concerns like yours."

"I deal in minerals, Mr. . . . ."

"Captain," said Saint-Sylvestre. "And you're about to deal in potential genocide."

"What is it you think you know that I would value so much?" Matheson asked.

"In thirty-six hours you intend to launch a coup d'état against Solomon Kolingba that will promote Francois Nagoupandé as his successor. The coup is to be led by a mercenary named Konrad Lanz who has been recruiting officers and noncoms from the Ali Pasha Hotel on Clapham Street. The private soldiers will be hired by agents in Sierra Leone, ex-members of the Revolutionary Front Army of Liberia and butchers each and every one.

"If you win the coup and install Nagoupandé he will immediately set about to kill as many Baya as he can—Kolingba's people. When he's done that, he'll murder the Yakima. You think Kolingba is dangerous because he is mad, but your good friend Nagoupandé in the silly uniform you bought him is even more dangerous simply because he is sane. He is a pragmatist, Lord Emsworth. A new broom sweeping clean, and in Africa that means killing your enemies. You are about to turn Kukuanaland into a killing field."

"You think you know a great deal," said Matheson.

"I'm not one for verbal jousting, Lord Emsworth," Saint-Sylvestre said quietly. "I killed your banker, Leonhard Euhler from the Gesler Bank in Aarau. I killed the Brocklebank sisters in Vancouver, negating the value of your Silver Brand short-sell plan, and I killed Allen Faulkener because he got in my way. You will pay me what I ask because you *are* greedy, and because you know that I can and will murder without compunction.

"I will murder your wife in her bed at Huntington Hall, which would not unduly concern you, but I shall murder her in your bed along with Jeremy Congreve, the twenty-year-old son of your estate manager, Tom

Congreve, which you would find mortifyingly embarrassing, since there already are rumors extant of your impotence. I would kill your twin sons, Justin and Jonathan, at Barlborough Hall School, gutting them like fish and leaving them floating in Butchertown Pond in the copse behind the main building. And if that didn't convince you I'd kill your eighty-three-year-old mother at her assisted-living apartment in Oxfordshire. I'd take my time with her, Lord Emsworth; I can guarantee you that."

"Why are you doing this?" Matheson asked. His legs felt rubbery and acid was creeping up his throat.

"The same reason you are," said Saint-Sylvestre. "Money. And you'd better make it quick; you're running out of time."

29

Konrad Lanz stood in the baking heat of Mopti Airport in northeastern Mali and watched as a dozen workers crawled like busy ants over the rickety wooden scaffolding surrounding the old Vanguard cargo aircraft. They were painting over the green cedar on the tail, as well as the striping that was the usual livery of Lebanon Air Transport, covering it with a flat black spray paint that would render the place virtually invisible from the ground at night.

Reflective chrome strips were being painted over around the windscreen, and the windscreen itself was being covered on the inside with polarizing film. Even the wheels on the landing gear, the bare aluminum tips of the propellers and the open engine nacelles were being given the flat black paint job. Not that stealth was a real concern for Lanz.

Mali had few jet fighters, Nigeria had only fifteen Chinese fighters with five pilots fully trained on them and Cameroon had four light attack aircraft, three of which were out of service and the fourth having been grounded since the death of the Cameroon Air Force's only instructor the year previous.

It was doubtful that they would have any trouble in the air from any military source. Nigeria had twenty ancient Russian antiaircraft guns, most of them placed around the capital city, Mali had no air defense system at all and Cameroon had twelve of the same antiaircraft guns as the Nigerians, also placed around their capital. With no moon Lanz considered it very unlikely that there would be anything else in the sky when the time came.

He watched the men working for a few moments more, satisfied that they'd make their deadline of ten p.m. tomorrow. As well as the painting, the Vanguard had to be fitted with extra webbing for cargo, and jump seats for the two-hundred-man companies. The end-user certificates for the small arms they'd purchased in Belgium, Spain and the Croatian port of Rijeka had passed inspection in Beirut and were supposed to be delivered to Mopti today.

The small tent city at the end of the airport's single runway and the two hundred men occupying it had also been ignored, as had the strange paint scheme of the old prop-jet cargo planes. Enough palms had been greased to keep officials at bay for the next thirty-six hours, but Lanz knew perfectly well that rumors were flying about their presence in the town of more than a hundred thousand only a few miles away on the river.

Lanz turned away from the Vanguards and crunched across the hard-packed sand to the oversized marquee tent they were using as base headquarters. He nodded to the guards on each side of the opening. They were well kitted out in worn lowland leaf–pattern camo fatigues from the Vietnam era, and instead of berets they wore the much more useful boonie hats. Officers wore camo baseball caps, which were the only indicators of rank.

He stepped inside the tent. There were three large models laid out on tables in the center of the tent. All were to scale. The one on the left showed the airport, the one in the middle showed the compound and the surrounding square and the one on the right showed the dock area.

Captain Pierre Laframboise, leader of Vanguard One, was studying both the airport and the compound models carefully. Lanz had worked with Laframboise on several different projects over the years and the two men both liked and respected each other. Laframboise was a big man with a big beard and a big belly. He liked to eat almost as much as he liked to fight.

"Having second thoughts, Pierre?"

"I *always* have second thoughts, *mon vieux*," said the big man.

"About what?"

"About news getting back to this *bizarrerie de nature* Kolingba so that he's ready and waiting when we come. About the distance we have to march from the airport to the palace or fort or whatever it is."

"It's barely a mile," said Lanz. "Fifteen minutes at a trot."

"And all jungle. He could have a battalion waiting for us in ambush."

"He doesn't have a battalion—we're going in at two-to-one odds." Lanz smiled, listening to Laframboise clucking away like a worried hen. It was almost a ritual, this fretting of his. But it was fretting that had saved both their lives on more than one occasion. "But I see your point. Why don't we stagger the companies—five minutes between Vanguard One and Vanguard Two down the airport road."

"Better." Laframboise nodded. "Not perfect, but a little better."

"Anything else?"

"This Limbani character. It would be *un catastrophe* if he showed up. We can't fight on two fronts any better than Hitler or Napoleon did, *mon brave*."

"Limbani's a myth, a pipe dream. It's been almost seven years since Kolingba took over. If Limbani were alive he'd have made a move by now."

"Your bones are getting brittle with age, *mon ami*; you speak in absolutes and you know that in this business there is no such thing."

"He's paying us well, Pierre, enough to retire maybe, to open that restaurant of yours in Tours, for me to see my daughter a little more, to be an ordinary citizen."

The big man smiled sadly. "They always pay us well, Colonel, as well they should—we are supposed to die for their money if necessary. And we are not ordinary citizens; we are what we are because of you, and so we have bad blood with our families, and the restaurants in Tours are always somewhere in the future. We're going to die in a place like this someday, Konrad, and you know it."

Lanz turned away and stepped out of the tent into the sunlight again. He climbed up into the cab of the postwar Bedford S Type canvas van that stood beside the marquee and headed into Mopti and the waterfront, where the two big pinasse cargo vessels were bringing up the arms from Bamako.

He swung the heavy old army truck down the track that ran between the lines of tents farther along the runway. Most of the men were outside, sitting on camp stools or old lawn furniture they'd found somewhere.

They were stripped to the waist in the heat, playing cards or board games and drinking Castel beer that Lanz had figured into the budget. Some of them were doing small bits of housekeeping: shining boots, replacing laces, even pipe-claying belts.

Most of them were young, not much more than twenty-five, and of those almost all were black—

discards, deserters or just plain fed up from armies of other African nations that barely fed them and rarely paid them. With the money each one of them hoped to make in the next few days they could keep their families for months and sometimes years. To these it was worth the risk.

Almost all of the boys, black or white, young or old, were laughing and smiling and telling jokes together, but as he drove by he caught the occasional long look into nowhere, usually from the scarred, sunburned older ones, his best men from the Belgian days and some from even further back. Addicted to it, just like him, throwing the dice with the devil one more time, trying to beat the odds once again.

He reached the end of the hardened track in the sand and turned onto the highway leading into Mopti. As he drove toward the town and the teeming port on the banks of the wide, sluggish river he thought about his conversation with Laframboise, one of the old guard and, like most of them, Lanz included, inclined to be superstitious.

He'd told Pierre that Limbani was a myth and for the most part he believed it, but myths and superstitions sometimes had some basis in fact. What was the old adage? "Where there's smoke, there's fire"? Limbani had been out of the picture for almost ten years now; was slight hope keeping a faint trail of smoke rising, or was it something more substantial? He stepped on the gas, pushing the lurching old truck a little harder. He put any thoughts of Limbani out of his mind. What was substantial was the crates of AK-47s still wrapped in their paper, and wooden boxes of ammo sitting on the docks, waiting for him.

The Kamov Ka-52 "Alligator" attack helicopter lifted nose-down to the hardstand, its counter-rotating rotors sounding like a pair of hammering commercial washing machines. The sudden furious noise and lurching take-off brought Oliver Gash's lunch abruptly into his throat. The takeoff was completed with an equally sudden lift of the nose, the small yellow stucco buildings of Kukua-naland International rotating in front of him like a yo-yo until all he could see was a patch of sunlit blue sky and all he could feel was his gut falling along with his lunch, his bowels simultaneously demanding to be opened.

Gash gritted his teeth but that only made it even worse. He told himself that the pilot was risking his own life as well, but the broad, gum-chewing face of Flying Officer Emmanuel Osita Ozegbe, eyes hidden behind his mirrored sunglasses, didn't give him the security he needed. Ozegbe looked about sixteen years old and about sixty pounds overweight, like someone who smoked too much weed, watched too much TV and ate too many Doritos. He'd met lots just like him back in Baltimore. Welfare weenies who'd never get off it until

Medicare cut off their legs from diabetes and they went on disability benefits instead.

"Where you want to go today, boss?" Ozegbe said, speaking the standard Sango patois. He spun the helicopter slowly around on its axis. It was only through an incredible application of willpower that Gash didn't simultaneously soil his pants and puke all over his lap.

"Upriver," Gash managed, using the same language. "Kazaba Falls." This was where the rumors consistently placed Limbani.

"No problem," said Ozegbe. He swung the helicopter around until he had the appropriate compass heading, put the stick and the helicopter into a nose-down attitude and gunned the throttles. Gash was jerked back in his seat and suddenly they were in rapid motion, tearing through the sky a hundred feet above the ground, the great sound of the big Klimov turbo shafts blotting out everything. Except the sound of his own ragged breathing and his companion's gum snapping.

The helicopter flew like a video game, everything controlled from one complex stick with thumb buttons, finger-grip controls and toggle switches like a Christmas tree. Ozegbe threw it around the sky like a farm boy driving a tractor—there was no finesse or subtlety or sense that the young man was managing a stupendously complicated piece of machinery.

With the stick and the heads-up weapons panels and the virtual dials and controls displayed on little screens here and there in front of him it really was no more than a video game; he was flying some exotic version of Microsoft Flight Simulator and was barely aware that he was actually flying a weapons platform that would have taken out all the pilot's competition in south Baltimore in a single twenty-minute session with a stop at the nearest New York Fried Chicken to top things off.

"How long you been flying this?" Gash yelled into his microphone. The kid's eyes stayed glued to the controls.

"Two hundred hours on a flight simulator and another two hundred hours on the full-sized simulator at the Ukhtomsky factory outside Moscow."

"How much time actually flying?"

"Thirty hours with the instructor. Fifteen hours here. I do a two-hour patrol of the western border once a week. That's all we have gas for."

"What about weapons?"

"The missiles are dummies, but the Shipunovs are real." Ozegbe squeezed one of the buttons on the control stick and the helicopter seemed to shudder as the twin cannons pulsed. From his seat Gash could see the rounds impacting the left-hand bank of the river, sending up huge gouts of mud and water.

A pair of rounds caught a dozing alligator and tore it to shreds before it had time to move. In front of them the Kazaba Falls rose like a wall split by the three tumbling, mist-shrouded cascades of water.

Gash gripped the edges of his seat but the young pilot just twitched the control handle, the nose came up and they rode above the falls to find themselves hurtling along barely twenty feet over the water.

"I've seen enough," said Gash. "Take me back."

"No problem," said Ozegbe. He twitched the control handle to the left and they went into a long swinging turn over the jungle. For a split second Gash thought he saw something out of place, a shape that wasn't quite right among the canopy trees, but he wasn't about to ask his teenage pilot to go back for a look.

"How often do you patrol this sector?" Gash asked instead.

"Only once in a while. Everybody thinks that Banqui's eventually going to try to take us out from the west but I don't think so."

They headed back downriver, leaving the falls behind them.

"Did he see us?" breathed Holliday, drenched by the spray coming up from the base of the waterfall closest to the village side of the river. Limbani crossed the slippery slabs of slick black slate ahead of him while Eddie came behind.

"The spray hid us, I think," said Limbani, raising his voice above the pounding of the falls. Directly beside them the sheer cliff rose a good two hundred feet straight up with only a ten- or fifteen-foot path between the edge of the cliff and the roiling whirlpooling water at the foot of the falls.

"Do they patrol often?" Eddie called out.

"Almost never," yelled Limbani. "That is why I am worried. That and the new moon. They're getting ready for something."

"Does that have anything to do with us getting soaked?" Holliday asked.

Limbani didn't answer. He turned slightly, took a step or two and simply vanished.

"What the hell?" Holliday said.

"Poof," said Eddie, just behind him. "This guy is a magician, yes?"

"Apparently," said Holliday. He was glad Rafi and Peggy were back at the main camp taking pictures and taking their first steps at understanding a new civilization. If there was one thing Peggy hated it was small, dark tunnels. He took another two steps, stumbled in sudden darkness and then took a third step. Everything had become silent; the sound of the waterfall had become nothing more than a dull throbbing. "You with me, Eddie?"

"Right behind you, *compañero*," said the Cuban. "This is the way to *el infierno*, I think."

"Pretty damp for hell," answered Holliday.

"Maybe *el diablo* has a sense of humor," Eddie said.

"Gets you wet and cold before he roasts you for eternity."

There was a scratching sound on rough metal and the flame of an old glass chimney oil lamp blossomed. The lamp was being held by Limbani only a few feet ahead of them. Behind the doctor was a large rusted metal hatchway studded with rivets.

"So where exactly are we, Doctor?" Holliday asked.

"The doorway to the past." The older man smiled. He spun the wheel on the hatchway and pushed it open, stepping aside to let Holliday and Eddie go through first.

"Mierda!" Eddie whispered, stunned.

"No way." Holliday grinned, suddenly finding himself laughing. He'd never seen anything like it in his life. "You really are full of surprises, Limbani."

They were standing in an immense cavern behind the waterfall, the sides of the cave a football field or more apart, the stalactite-studded rock more than a hundred feet overhead. The rock was streaked with thick, threading seams of what could only be gold, those veins in turn surrounded by even thicker strands of what appeared to be quartz but which Holliday knew were not.

"Gold?" Holliday asked.

"In quartz and diamond matrices. The caves are the far end of the mother lode back at the three hills. King Solomon's Mines, a greedy man's Shangri-la."

Dozens of torches illuminated the sight as at least a hundred of the Pale Strangers worked on the giant object resting in its cofferdam, cradled by more than a score of heavy tree trunks on each side.

"Unbelievable," said Holliday. "It's a Viking *snekkja*. What the British called a dragon ship. What the hell are you up to, Limbani?"

The boat behind the cofferdam was sixty or seventy feet long, clinker built from fresh planks, the planks overlapped, sewn, riveted and the spaces stuffed tightly with moss. The workers were almost finished now, thirty rowing benches installed between the gunwales and a raised platform for the helmsman at the rowing oar. The gunwales seemed higher than ones Holliday had seen on replica ships but it didn't take long to see why. Between the rowing benches were firing positions for rows of ballista, outsized crossbows used in medieval siege warfare, capable of piercing stone walls, killing dozens at a time and even casting enormous fireballs.

"Roche-Guillaume's idea?" Holliday said.

"Presumably." Limbani nodded. "The ship itself goes back to Ragnar Skull Splitter, who remained here until his death. According to Roche-Guillaume's manuscripts the local people had already intermarried with the Romans who came here first. It is as though each explorer who came this way left something of his culture behind. Ragnar's own vessel was used to bury him when he died of fever, but the design for the pirogues my people used for travel and fishing were of much the same design. This ship, which is called *Havdragoon* in the old language—*Sea Dragon*—was nothing more than those small piroques scaled upward."

"But why have you built her?" Holliday asked. "Why now?"

"Because war is coming."

"You can't be certain of that."

"As a matter of fact I can. I've told you that I had my own spies and the battle is to be very soon. It doesn't matter who the winner is between Kolingba and his enemies. Either way we will be sought out and slaughtered. We have hidden long enough. With the dark of the moon we strike." He waved toward the ship. A group of kilted workers were fitting a bloodred curling snake figurehead on the high, delicate stem of the ship.

"This cavern stretches the length of all three sections of the falls. When the cofferdam is opened the cavern floor will fill and the ship will be thrust out into the stream with sixty men at her oars. And sixty more at the crossbows. A hundred pirogues will join us on the downriver journey, each paddler armed with a blowgun and a hundred killing darts."

"You're mad!" Holliday burst out. "You're leading your people to suicide!"

"We never asked for war. We never wanted war. But we will not run from war. I know Kolingba and his mind. Just as I know the kind of men who will be fighting him. It may well be suicide to fight, but is it better to wait like sheep for genocide instead?"

"*Tiene razón, mi amigo,*" murmured Eddie. "Better to die fighting than praying."

"Is that a quote?"

"*Sí*. Fidel, I'm afraid."

"Well, I guess this time I agree with him." Holliday turned back to Limbani. "We'll fight with you, Doctor, but I want Peggy and Rafi kept safe from harm."

"I think I can manage that."

"When is the new moon exactly?"

"Tonight."

30

Time is a fickle concept during battle. Ask most survivors of D-day and they will tell you that it seemed to take forever for the combined American, British and Canadian forces to establish a beachhead, when in fact it took slightly less than three hours, from six twenty-nine a.m., the official start time, to nine seventeen a.m., roughly the time it takes the average office worker to rise and shine and get to work. In that same period of time on D-day there were approximately twenty thousand casualties incurred by both German and Allied personnel, which was almost two every second. So battle time is relative—it seems to take forever to survive and only a split second to die.

Peggy's photograph of *Havdragoon*, the *Sea Dragon*, bursting through the curtain of water at Kazaba Falls, big square sail set and stitched with its indisputably Templar cross, all sixty of her long oars out and her bloodred dragon figurehead glaring ahead, eventually appeared on the front page of every newspaper in the world and on the cover of every magazine. It made Peggy a wealthy woman in her own right, got her unbelievable assignments and introduced a whole new civilization to the world. But all that was in the future.

Both Holliday and Eddie were on the steering platform as the brand-new ship with its thousand-year-old design hurtled through the cave mouth and dropped down into the foaming, churning maelstrom below. As well as Holliday and Eddie, two of the Pale Strangers, Baltazar and Kaleb, manned the heavy steering oar with them, hanging on for dear life as the *Sea Dragon* hurtled down into the water, then rose again like its namesake, the great red dragon figurehead streaming water, its golden teeth seething with froth and a sudden wind from behind them bellying the sails as the sixty oars dug into the deep black river water and drove them forward.

"My God!" Holliday breathed, soaked to the skin but feeling an exhilaration deep in his soul he thought was long forgotten.

"*¡Increíble, mi hermano!*" Eddie roared ecstatically.

"*Krigsanggen!*" screeched Baltazar and Kaleb beside them, and in that moment they knew they all spoke the same language, whether they understood one another or not. Something had risen from the deep past and propelled them forward and there was no way back.

Sea Dragon steered easily out of the whirlpools at the

foot of the falls and slid effortlessly toward the near bank of the river, the land-side oars rising at a single command from the ship's undisputed captain, Loki, a dark-skinned, dark-eyed, bearded fury who stood in the bow of the ship, his strong right arm hooked around the red dragon's neck like a lover. He carried not one but two blowpipes across his back and, according to Limbani, could use them both at once and so quickly that the motions were only a blur.

A gangplank was thrown aboard and Limbani crossed into the ship with Peggy and Rafi on his heels. Ahead of them on the river the sun was setting quickly.

"It will be dark soon," said Limbani. "We need to load the rest of the warriors and their supplies on board. Even with this wind Loki says it will take almost until dawn to get us downriver to Fourandao."

"That should be just about right." Holliday nodded. He paused and gave Peggy a short look. "Did you bring our weapons?"

She nodded. "Stripped from Jerimiah Salamango's imps."

Three men came across the gangplank carrying a sagging litter loaded down with AK-47s, ammunition belts, two RPGs with a half dozen rounds each and a pair of brutal-looking Saiga automatic shotguns with nine or ten eight-round magazines each.

"Bueno," said Eddie, "my favorite, *un acelerador de cabeza."* He grinned, looping the sling crosswise over

his shoulder and pushing a half dozen magazines into his belt. "In the army we called them *Fidelitos*—small but with a big mouth."

Holliday turned and looked directly at Peggy. "Now, look—" he began.

"Don't even start, Doc. I'm a big girl; I've taken photographs in a dozen war zones. I'm not your responsibility. We're coming, and that, cousin o' mine, is that."

"You don't have anything to say about this?" Holliday said, turning to Rafi.

"I've spent the last hour arguing with her. I lost. We're coming, because if she goes then I'm damn well going with her."

"You're both crazy," said Holliday.

"No, *mis amigos*," said Eddie with a grin, "we're *all* crazy."

Konrad Lanz had been sitting in the navigator's jump seat of the old Vickers Vanguard for three and a half hours and his legs were beginning to cramp. Looking between the pilot and copilot's seats there was nothing to see but the velvet black of the night and the green and yellow glow of the instruments. For the past hour or so they had been flying at under five thousand feet, and so far they hadn't heard a single query on the radio.

"How much longer?" he asked the pilot, another one of the old guard named Janni Doke, a South African in his late fifties who could fly anything from a Piper Cub to a jumbo jet.

"Twenty minutes, maybe twenty-five."

"I'd better get the boys ready, then," said Lanz.

"You do what you want, baas; just make sure you leave me a couple of roughies to top up the tanks. We're on fumes as it is," responded the gruff old Afrikaner.

"Will do," said Lanz.

"You're sure about the landing lights?"

"Positive. The approach lights are on all night. They get some late cargo going in and out." He paused. "There's only one runway, eight thousand feet, just like I told you in the briefing. The runway lines up with the tower. You can't miss."

"The helicopters? Even on the ground they could blow us all to Hades."

"Three RPGs. One each for the Kamovs, one for the tower. There's an old armored personnel carrier but there's no one manning it at night. The wheels are flat. It's just for show."

"All right." The Afrikaner half turned and looked at Lanz in the darkness. "Radio checks every ten minutes, okay, baas. No radio check and I'm gone with the wind. No screaming savages putting this old cheeky prawn in the pot for his dinner, understand?"

"Every ten minutes." Lanz turned and went back

through to the aircraft cabin. The original twenty-eight-row, triple-double seat configuration had been removed and replaced with twenty-five double rows of quad buckets from a few old C-47s they'd raided in Europe and North Africa.

Since the Vanguard's folding air stairs fore and aft would be far too slow for egress, they'd been removed, and Janni Doke and a few others at Mopti had cobbled together emergency slides from several old parachutes that would let everyone off quickly, gear and all.

Most of the boys were sleeping or pretending to as Lanz made his way down the narrow aisle between the two cramped rows, shaking shoulders and giving out the five-minute warning. With that done he stood by the rear exit door with the three RPG teams and waited.

The PA system clicked on. "Three minutes. Approach lights in sight," Janni Doke said crisply. The old aircraft seemed to sag in the air, yawing a little to the left and sending Lanz lurching against the bulkheads.

"Final approach two minutes. Interior lights off." The airplane went dark.

Now was the time for the Kamovs to come off their hardstands and flank them all the way down the runway, tearing them up with cannon fire.

"Approach. Landing, one minute. Clear!" No Kamovs, at least for the moment. Thirty seconds from now and it might be a different story.

Lanz could feel everyone tense. This was the worst, the final few seconds of stillness.

"Contact!"

The wheels shrieked as they touched the runway and skewed a little as they hit. Janni straightened the plane out and kept both feet on the brakes. The big props howled as they ran down. . . . Lanz counted backward from ten. At zero he gave the order.

"Doors open!" He and one of the men from an RPG team worked the wheel until there was a quick hiss of air. Lanz pushed the heavy door outward and to the left against the fuselage. The first RPG team dropped the homemade inflatable slide out the doorway and Lanz pulled the lanyard that activated the big CO_2 cartridge. The ramp bellied out perfectly.

"Go, go go!" The three-man teams hit the ramp first and deployed twenty feet beyond the wingtip of the aircraft, giving them a clear shot. The Russian-made rocket-propelled grenades went off almost simultaneously, leaving a long, twisting trail of smoke that vanished into the darkness.

Three explosions lit up the night as the first projectiles hit. The teams had already reloaded and a second volley went screaming through the air. Only one of the Kamovs had been fueled and armed, and it detonated spectacularly, a black-and-yellow gobbet of greasy, fiery smoke bubbling up into the air. The first strike on the tower had hit just below it, smashing into the air traffic controllers' chamber. The second volley hit the tower directly and the lights went out.

The Battle of Kukuanaland Airport had begun.

On the presumption that the coup attempt would be made on this night, Oliver Gash had seen to it that General Kolingba's last three Bacardi and Cokes that evening were laced with two milligrams each of the drug known as Rohypnol, or roofies. The general got only halfway through the second drink before he passed out in front of his enormous wide-screen TV watching *Operation Petticoat*, his favorite Cary Grant movie.

Kolingba would ideally be out of it until somebody came along and put a bullet through his head, but Gash wasn't taking any chances. As soon as the first snores started erupting from the immense body, Gash made his way down to Kolingba's office, let himself in with a key he'd made for himself long ago and began cutting a picture window–sized hole in the floral wallpaper–covered drywall.

It took fifteen minutes to cut the hole, revealing several thousand tightly wrapped, pressure-sealed bricks of American hundred-dollar bills. As he recalled, each of the bricks was made up of one hundred bills, or ten thousand dollars. One million dollars, or one hundred of the bricks, filled up roughly half of an ordinary Samsonite hard-shell suitcase, and twice that load weighed roughly forty-four pounds. It took Gash four hours to fill twelve of the suitcases, for a total weight of 528 pounds.

Twenty-four million dollars was certainly nowhere near enough for the humiliation and idiocy he'd had to put up with over the years with Kolingba, but it gave him more than enough liquidity to get to the lion's share of the money he'd hidden away in a variety of banks from Cyprus to San Remo and beyond to even more obscure bits of geography that specialized in hiding other people's money.

When he was finished he lined up all the suitcases outside the door to Kolingba's office, gave two guards a hundred-dollar bill apiece to carry them down to one of the bumblebee Rovers, explaining to them that he was running a late-night errand to the airport for the general. It was a common enough occurrence and neither one of the soldiers questioned the order.

Gash went back upstairs for one last look at the monster and then, whether out of spite or simply for fun, he slipped the diamond-encrusted Rolex off Kolingba's pudgy wrist. On the television Cary Grant and Tony Curtis were discussing various methods of getting five navy nurses off their submarine, which had now been painted bright pink.

Gash watched for a moment, marveling at the Americans' ability to make war funny. He briefly thought once more of killing the general with his own silver automatic, but instead simply took the automatic and slipped it into his waistband. He checked the Rolex. Four fifteen in the morning, time to go unless he wanted to get caught in the cross fire. He zipped up his Windbreaker to cover the silver-plated pistol, went out into the compound and climbed into the Rover and flashed his lights at the gate guards. They jumped to it, throwing open the gates, and Gash drove out onto the square.

He turned left toward the waterfront rather than right toward the airport, but nobody seemed to notice or care. He was halfway to the docks when every light in Fourandao went off and an explosive echo came rolling down from the airport. He'd made it in the nick of time. Or maybe not. He put on a little more speed, his mind working as he drove. He'd expected the coup to be centered on the airport and all the communications hubs located in and around it. What if it was a two-pronged attack, coming up from the water as well, catching anyone fleeing in a pincer movement?

"Shit!" He pulled out his cell phone and tried it. No signal. They'd already hit the microwave towers. "Shit!" he said again. He reached the docks and the turn onto the road to Banqui. The drive would take him four hours; if they were coming up the river road he'd be squeezed and caught. There was no use turning left, because the road ran out half a mile or so upriver, turning into nothing more than a native track. "Shit, shit, shit."

There were more explosions coming from the direction of the airport. He rolled down the window and craned his neck, looking back the way he'd come. The sky was on fire.

With the window still open he paused and cocked an ear. He knew the sound. Outboard engines, lots of them.

"Goddamn!" he whispered. They were coming up the river! He stared out through the windshield. Directly in front of him was the entire Kukuanaland navy, the single rigid inflatable defended by an old Russian machine gun. He barely paused to think about what he was doing. He drove the last few yards down to the docks and began humping the suitcases out of the back of the Rover and into the patrol boat, keeping an ear out for the approaching outboards coming from the other direction.

By the eighth suitcase he was sweating and the engine noise was too close for comfort. He abandoned the rest of the cases, untied the boat from the old wooden bollard and hit the ignition button on the engine. It coughed, coughed again and died. The engines from downriver were getting closer.

"Go, you bitch!" he hissed. He hit the button again, there was another greasy cough and then the engine caught. Grinning through the sweat pouring from his brow, he gunned the engine, turned the wheel hard and hauled the boat upriver. There was nothing in that direction but bush and jungle. He'd hide there for a night or two, then slip down the river to freedom. He eased the throttle forward and turned the boat through a large curve in the night-black river.

And saw a nightmare. If front of him, no more than a hundred yards away, there was a monstrous dragon-headed ship coming right at him, oars like the huge legs of some unearthly water bug rising and falling in perfect cadence with a giant cross-scribed sail billowing over everything.

"No," he said, wide-eyed. How could a Viking ship, of all things, be here, on this river, now? It was impossible. And in that instant he knew he wasn't getting out of this one alive.

The white-feathered dart caught him at the base of the throat. The neurotoxin hit his brain within two seconds. He had just enough time to raise the Rolex to his face before he died.

Gash didn't see the *Sea Dragon* as it swept around the bend in the river; nor did he see Edimburgo Vladimir Cabrera Alfonso standing at the bow with his *Fidelito* unlimbered in his arms, singing quietly to himself.

Beside him Holliday waited. They made the turn and kept on sweeping downriver, all sixty oars lifted from the water now, carried only by the current. With the first pink light of dawn at their backs they saw the oncoming Zodiacs, twenty of them, spread in an arrogant line across the river almost from bank to bank. In the stern of the *Sea Dragon*, Loki, standing at the steering oar, gave a single, loudly shouted order.

"Strybord!" Thirty starboard oars hit the water as one and held there, the men on their benches straining at the current as the *Sea Dragon* turned her broadside to the looming inflatables, each filled with well-armed men.

Holliday and Eddie began to fire, the AK making its distinctive death rattle and the *Fidelito* sounding like fifty noisy doors slamming.

"Brand ambroster!" Loki yelled. At fifty yards each of the huge ballistas found its mark, ripping into the Zodiacs and their occupants, sinking thirty-five of the rubber boats. The heavy packs worn by most of the men dragged them under the black water to drown. Crocodiles slid silently from their perches on the riverbanks to slaughter the rest. The few Zodiacs managing to escape the initial barrage were slammed into by the *Sea Dragon* and crushed under her hull. A very few soldiers still in the water were finished off by dozens of blowguns on board.

"Adios, pioneers," Eddie whispered, jacking the empty magazine out of the shotgun.

Loki called out the order, the oars dipped and *Sea Dragon* turned in toward shore.

*   *   *

At first it seemed like a rout. There hadn't been a single survivor at the airport and Lanz hadn't lost a man, but he was worried. According to Zodiacs A and B, the two inflatables waiting with the amphibians, everything had proceeded on schedule right up to the time the other half of Lanz's force was supposed to land and make its way inland to the compound. There had been a few garbled messages, some scattered gunfire and then a single transmission about a Viking dragon that no one understood.

By the time Lanz and his men reached the compound it was clear that all hell was breaking loose. A few crazed townspeople were talking about ghosts and silent death, and instead of having to break through the compound with mortar fire, as they'd expected, the entire compound simply threw open the gates and asked to be taken prisoner, something Lanz hadn't been prepared for.

He discovered Kolingba asleep in his bed, obviously drugged, and without any orders from Matheson he simply handcuffed the snoring dictator to his bedpost.

He tried to radio Nagoupandé's party, which was being helicoptered in from Maiduguri in northeastern Nigeria, but so far he hadn't been able to raise them. In the end he simply let the garrison go, collecting all their weapons first, then posted pickets and sat back and waited for Matheson and the new dictator of Kukuanaland to arrive.

By five a.m. there was still no sign of the two hundred men coming in from the river, and their mysterious absence was starting to make his own men nervous. They were beginning to talk about pulling back to the airport, which was not a good sign.

Half an hour later the first reports of mysterious deaths began to reach Lanz in the compound, where he was busily digging the rest of the cash out of Kolingba's office wall and stashing it in his senior officers' packs as a bonus. Pickets and guards around the square were turning up dead, unwounded except for something that looked like an oversized blowgun dart. At first Lanz didn't believe it, but one of the few men left outside the compound brought one to him.

"What do you think, Pierre?" Lanz asked, turning to his old friend and colleague Laframboise.

"My honest opinion, Konrad?"

"As always."

"This is your ghost, Limbani. I sent a patrol down to the river, six men. Two came back—one babbling and feverish from some kind of blowgun dart that had grazed his leg through his trousers, the other one talking about a dragon boat like the Vikings once used."

"That's insane," said Lanz.

"They say there's a Viking ship on the river and our Zodiac teams have vanished. They say there are ghost walkers, griots and sorcerers in masks, killing our men with darts, and there you are." He pointed to the dart on what had once been Kolingba's desk.

"What do you suggest?"

"How much money did you find in that wall? Twenty, thirty million?"

"Something like that."

"Then we get out while we can, what's left of us. We make a flag of truce and march out of this compound and hope we aren't murdered as we go."

"Matheson? Nagoupandé?"

"It's their bed; let them lie in it."

When the Sikorsky UH-60 Black Hawk helicopter made a pinpoint landing in the center of what had been the Fourandao garrison compound at six thirty a.m., there wasn't a soul in sight. Brigadier General Francois Nagoupandé, dressed in full uniform, and Sir James Matheson climbed out of the helicopter accompanied by eight heavily armed members of Blackhawk Security as bodyguards.

Papers fluttered in the wind, including several dozen American hundred-dollar bills. Several dead bodies littered the ground, but there wasn't a living human being anywhere.

"Find out what the bloody hell is going on!" Matheson snarled at the Blackhawk Security force. The men ran off in various directions to search the buildings. A moment later one returned.

"Yes?" Matheson snapped.

"There's a big fat guy in there asleep, or maybe drugged. He's handcuffed to his bed."

"Ah," said Nagoupandé. "Show me," he said to the man. They went back into the main building. A moment later there was a single shot.

Nagoupandé reappeared, slipping his Colt .45 back into its holster on his web belt. He had blood spray across the lower part of his face and across the front of his jacket. "The king is dead."

"Long live the king," said a voice from the blasted front gates of the compound. Limbani appeared with Holliday on one side and Eddie on the other. Behind them were Jean-Luc Saint-Sylvestre and a half dozen uniformed members of the Kukuanaland secret police. Seeing Limbani, Nagoupandé struggled to drag his gun from its holster. Saint-Sylvestre beat him to it.

"Do something!" Nagoupandé screamed at Matheson.

"I only deal with winners, I'm afraid," said Matheson smoothly. "Who that is remains to be seen."

Limbani stepped forward, looking up at the infuriated man in the brigadier general's uniform. "You look very foolish, Francois. The English have a word for it—popinjay, isn't that correct, Sir James?"

"You know who I am?" Matheson said, impressed.

"Of course." Limbani nodded, resting his hand on Saint-Sylvestre's shoulder. "My nephew has told me a great deal about you and what you wish to do to my country."

"Your nephew?" Matheson said, dazed. Horribly a

number of things clicked into place and the man visibly sagged.

"On his mother's side."

Nagoupandé began to scream, his fists clenched like a child having a tantrum. "It's not your country, Limbani; it's my country! I am the president of Kukuanaland!"

"No, you're not," said Saint-Sylvestre, putting the muzzle of his Glock against Nagoupandé's forehead. He pulled the trigger, and Nagoupandé slid to the ground like a deflating balloon.

"So," said Matheson, trying to put some heartiness back into his voice. "Presumably it will be you I'll be dealing with, Dr. Limbani."

"No," said Limbani, "you'll be dealing with my minister of resources, who is also my foreign minister and who is, by chance, my nephew.

"The first thing you're going to do," Limbani continued, "is get back in your helicopter, taking your nasty little friends with you. The next thing you will do after arriving back in England is establish something called the Kukuanaland National Trust, a nongovernmental organization headed up by my friend Colonel Holliday here, as well as his cousin Miss Peggy Blackstock and her husband, Dr. Rafi Wanounou.

"The purpose of the trust is to develop ideas for utilizing the three-hundred-million-pound endowment you will give the trust for the betterment of the people of Kukuanaland, especially where it regards such things as infrastructure and education. Should you prefer not to establish the trust my nephew can take all of the concrete antitrust and war-crimes information he has on you personally as well as a number of your employees and disperse it throughout the world press as he sees fit. Then perhaps we shall discuss your rare earths; agreed?"

"I'll be in touch," said Matheson coldly, his face an angry mask. Without another word he waved the bodyguards back onto the helicopter, followed them aboard and slammed the door shut. The group in the compound stepped back as the rotors began to whir, and a moment later the Black Hawk lifted off the ground, tilted away and disappeared into the morning sky.

"His nephew?" Holliday said to Saint-Sylvestre.

"A spy in the house of love, I believe it's called." The secret policeman shrugged his shoulders. "He needed someone on his side to even the odds a little."

Holliday toed the rumpled body of Nagoupandé, sprawled on the ground and bleeding into the hard-packed earth. "We should get this cleaned up."

"And after we do," said Peggy, "I do believe it's going to be a very nice day."

"Always the optimist," said Rafi, smiling fondly at his wife.

Peggy stared at the body on the ground. She shrugged. "Beats the alternative."

EPILOGUE

Eddie and Holliday stayed with Peggy and Rafi for almost three months. It was fall by the time they left Kukuanaland, flown out to Khartoum by the inimitable Mutwakil "Donny" Osman on his rattletrap Catalina. Neither man knew where they were going or what the future held, but the few hours as warriors for a cause again had shaken both men deeply, arousing some strange wanderlust that they both thought it was unlikely they'd be able to satisfy. One thing was sure enough: Holliday wanted to go back to the States for a while, maybe consider teaching again, and even though Eddie could probably get refugee status, especially with Holliday's sanction, the Cuban was still Cuban enough not to want to give up his passport. He told Holliday what he'd been saying for years, even though he knew it was a lie—"Maybe when Fidel is gone, maybe then it will be better."

They sat in the very new glass-and-white-marble departure lounge at Khartoum International Airport drinking complimentary coffee and waiting for their flights, Holliday's to New York via Paris and Eddie's to the Amazon via a half dozen stops along the way.

"You really think you'll find work there?" Holliday asked.

"It's a river, and I'm a river pilot, *mi amigo*. It's what I do."

"I'm wondering now if we should have stayed a little while longer with Limbani and his people. You've got to admit, it was fascinating."

"But not for us, Doc," said Eddie. "It is Peggy and Rafi's passion, not ours. There's enough to keep them there for years, maybe for the rest of their lives."

"Maybe we're getting too old for passion," said Holliday.

"Saying that is the *beso de la muerte*," said Eddie. "The kiss of death."

"These old bones are starting to ache." Holliday shrugged. "Maybe I should just retire."

"Pah!" Eddie snorted. "You are only as old as you think."

"And I think I'm pretty damn old!" Holliday laughed.

A tall, very distinguished-looking man had been hovering close to their seats in the lounge for the last few minutes and Holliday was wondering when he'd make his move for a few coins or bills. From the neck up he looked like a university professor, right down to the wire glasses and the badly knotted tie. The rest of him was on the slide, a cheap blue suit half a century out of style, frayed at the pockets lap and cuffs. The shoes might have been made of cardboard.

Finally he stepped forward. "Excuse me," he said, speaking to Eddie in heavily accented English. "I think you are Cuban?"

"*Sí.*" Eddie nodded.

"I speak very little Spanish. Do you perhaps speak Russian?"

"*Da.*" The Cuban nodded.

"*Otlichno!*" The man beamed happily. Holliday presumed it meant *good*, or *excellent*. The man began to babble away at breakneck speed, plucking at Eddie's sleeve and finally drawing him a few feet away and muttering softly into his ear, then gave him a small slip of paper, folding it into Eddie's hand. At first Eddie seemed confused but eventually he shrugged, patted the man on the shoulder and went back to sit beside Holliday. The Russian-speaking gentleman peered at them anxiously.

"Now, what was that all about?"

"I didn't get all of it. He says his name is Victor Ostrovsky and he's a curator at the Hermitage. Something about the Romanov jewels and the Fabergé royal eggs. He says that something terrible has happened and he insists that you and I go with him immediately."

"You and I?"

"You don't speak Russian. According to him I am to be your translator. He asked if I trusted you. I said yes. He asked if I trusted you with my life. I said yes."

"That's all very nice," said Holliday, "but just where is it he wants us to go?"

"A church," said Eddie. "In Constantinople."

"Istanbul?" Holliday said. "That's just plain nuts. For one thing they don't speak Russian in Istanbul."

"He told me you'd say that." Eddie nodded. "He asked me to give you this." Eddie handed the slip of paper to Holliday. He stared down at the spidery, old-man's handwriting.

Helder Rodrigues

He remembered it all in an instant. The dying man's blood on his hands, the tiny island in the Azores, the notebook with a thousand years of secrets on its blood-stained pages. What had Rodrigues said, dying in his arms? *Iacta alea est. Vale, amici. The torch is passed; goodbye, my friend.* And then with his last breath before life fled him in the middle of that terrible storm, those awful, awful words: "Too many secrets . . . too many secrets."

"He said there was a flight in twenty minutes." Eddie raised an eyebrow. "He said something else. I think it is Latin. *'Ferrum Polaris.'*"

Dear God. Ferrum Polaris. The Sword of the North.

Holliday crumpled the little scrap of paper in his hand and stood up.

"We might just make it if we run."

Read on for a special preview
of Paul Christopher's next thriller,

RED TEMPLAR

Coming from Signet in 2012

The bearded man stumbled out of the kitchen entrance of the enormous house, blood and vomit streaming from his open, gasping mouth. The snow was blinding and he beat at it furiously, desperately trying to see where he was going. The pain in his upper back was excruciating and his right ear had been torn to shreds by Felix's second shot. The bearded man brushed a bloody hand across his face. His eyes were almost swollen shut from the beating he'd taken but if he could only make it home, home to his little girl, Maria, he would be all right.

He heard muffled footsteps in the snow behind him, the footsteps of a running man. It had to be Rayner, Felix's sodomite friend from Oxford. Despite the awful pain welling up in his stomach and the blood draining from the stab wounds in his back, the bearded man increased his pace, his heaving lungs on fire, his bleary eyes searching for the steps that led down to the frozen canal. If he could cross to the other side he could disappear into the maze of streets and alleys and, if he was very lucky, reach safety.

He gritted his broken teeth and forced himself onward through the blizzard, silently cursing the cowards who would so savagely attack a man of God. He had never wanted anything more than to bring his knowledge and his powers to the world but to them he was a danger: light to their darkness, good to their whispered evil, his courage to their cowardice.

Somehow he managed to find the steps and staggered downward, his left hand gripping the cold metal railing. He risked a quick look back over his shoulder. There was no sign of Felix or his foppish, smooth-faced friend. His heart beat faster. There was hope! Of course there was hope, for wasn't he one of the chosen of God, with nothing less than the healing faith of the Xristos coursing through his hands? He had brought a sick and dying prince back to his mother's arms; there must be hope for him as well; certainly Saint Seraphim would not abandon him now.

The bearded man reached the ice of the canal, then slipped and slid toward the bridge two hundred yards away, where he knew there was another set of steps. There would be lamplight on the bridge and perhaps even a policeman. Here and there the ice was black and thin, cracking beneath his feet. He skirted those areas, his eyes on the snow-shrouded span of the bridge.

The bearded man reached into the pocket of his dark, heavy coat and felt the heavy oval object deep in the fleece lining. . . . This at least he could keep from them, their foul crucible, their blasphemous secret. Such things were monumentally dangerous and could change the world if revealed by those without the understanding to deal with them. The proverb learned by the bearded man from his friend Spiridon Ivanovich still held true—"For upright men there are no laws"—and if he was nothing else in this frozen hell of a city on the edge of the world, he was an upright man.

The terrible pain deep within his chest caught him by surprise. He stopped dead in his tracks and stared downward. There had already been bloodstains on his white cotton shirt from the beating and the stabbing, but this was something else. This was blood from a spigot splattering out in thick, gouting splashes, deep red, heart's blood.

The bearded man looked up. Across a narrow patch of dark, thin ice he could see a figure with a large pistol in his hand. The man was slender, with a tweed overcoat over his uniform. Oswald Rayner, George Buchanan's man from the old Saltykov Mansion on the Neva.

"*Вы убили меня!* You've killed me!" said the bearded man, his accent that of a peasant. He fell to his knees, his hands cupping the blood still streaming from his chest.

"*Еще я не имею,*" said Rayner. "Not yet I haven't."

He raised the big Webley again, aimed it at the bearded man's face and pulled the trigger. A large circular hole was punched in the man's forehead, and the back of his head turned into a fountain of blood, bone and brains spraying back for several yards along the ice-covered canal. "*Now* I've killed you," said the young lieutenant. He stuffed the Webley back into the pocket of his overcoat. The body of the bearded man sagged forward and then struck the ice. The ice cracked and then broke under the weight of the body. The remains of the bearded man slid instantly into the black, freezing water. The Mad Monk was gone at last.

Grigori Rasputin was dead, taking his secrets with him.

New York Times bestselling author

Paul Christopher

THE TEMPLAR CONSPIRACY

In Rome, the assassination of the Pope on Christmas Day sets off a massive investigation that stretches across the globe. But behind the veil of Rex Deus—the Templar cabal that silently wields power in the twenty-first century—the plot has only just begun.

When retired Army Ranger Lt. Col. John Holliday uncovers the true motive behind the pontiff's murder, he must unravel a deadly design to extend the Templar influence to the highest levels of power.

Available wherever books are sold or at penguin.com

S0186

New York Times bestselling author

Paul Christopher

THE TEMPLAR THRONE

In the 14th century, Templar knight Jean de St. Clair was tasked with piloting the order's treasure-laden fleets off the coast of France. To this end, he used the Jacob's Staff—a nautical instrument supposedly developed in his own time. But retired Army Ranger Lt. Col. John Holliday possesses a Staff he found in the hands of a 4,000 year-old Egyptian mummy. Holliday suspects that St. Clair may hold the key to unlocking the mystery of the ruthless, enigmatic Templars.

But there are those who believe that some questions should remain unanswered. And that the answers Holliday seeks should go with him to the grave...

Available wherever books are sold or at penguin.com

The *New York Times* bestseller

THE TEMPLAR CROSS

Paul Christopher

Retired Army Ranger Lt. Col. John Holliday has reluctantly settled into his teaching position at West Point when young Israeli archaeologist Rafi Wanounou comes to him with desperate news.

Holliday's niece—and Rafi's fiancé—Peggy has been kidnapped. Holliday sets out with Rafi to find the only family he has left. But their search for Peggy will lead them to a trail of clues that spans across the globe, and into the heart of a conspiracy involving an ancient Egyptian legend and the darkest secrets of the Order of Templar Knights.

Secrets that, once known, cannot be survived...

Available wherever books are sold or at penguin.com

New York Times bestselling author
Paul Christopher

THE SWORD OF
THE TEMPLARS

A mystery that spans the past.
A conspiracy that lives on in the heart of
an ancient order.

Army Ranger Lt. Col. John Holliday had resigned
himself to ending his career teaching at West Point.
When his uncle passes away, Holliday discovers a
medieval sword—wrapped in Adolf Hitler's personal
battle standard. But when someone burns down his
uncle's house in an attempt to retrieve the sword,
Holliday realizes that he's being drawn into a war that
has been fought for centuries—a war in which he
may be the next casualty.

Available wherever books are sold or at
penguin.com

S0010